Books by C. A. Newsome

SNEAK THIEF
MAXIMUM SECURITY
DROOL BABY
A SHOT IN THE BARK

DROOL BABY

A Dog Park Mystery

C. A. Newsome

TWO PUP PRESS

This is a work of fiction. All of the characters, places and events portrayed in this book are either products of the author's imagination or are used fictitiously.

DROOL BABY

Kita by Carol Ann Newsome
Cover design by Elizabeth Mackey
Copyright © 2012 by Carol Ann Newsome

ISBN-13: 978-0-9963742-2-4

Published by Two Pup Press
1836 Bruce Avenue
Cincinnati, Ohio 45223-2060

For Anna, Pat, Angie and Rudy.
Without you I would be in sorry shape.

Acknowledgments

I'd like to thank Cincinnati firefighters Randell Lindsey and Joe Rosemeyer for their invaluable information about natural gas. Thanks to my beta readers for their unvarnished opinions, and to the other writers on the KDP forum for their advice and support. A big thank you to my dog park buddies for allowing me to continue to fictionalize them in these pages. Thanks also to Lisa Story and to cat-lover John Morgan for the same.

Prologue

I saw Catherine again last night. It was after midnight, with the moonlight spilling down onto her garden labyrinth. I followed her up the twisting path, stepping carefully on the mosaic pavers, avoiding the gravel packed around them. Catherine was absorbed in her thoughts and did not realize I was there.

Anticipation pounded through my blood, delicious anticipation fueled by my hatred of this vain and vapid woman. It was hard to remember to creep along as adrenaline rose up in me. Years of restraint and self discipline served in those moments of ecstatic tension as I followed, silent, silent, until she neared the pond at the center of the maze. I picked up a decorative rock and hefted it, much like a pitcher with a softball. I gently bounced it in my hand and felt its weight, its irregular shape. It was about the size of a grapefruit with a rough texture that bit into my skin.

Catherine paused at the edge of the pond before the stepping stones that would take her to a miniature island. I stood behind her, almost close enough to touch, and still she did not sense me. When was this woman ever anything but oblivious? I took a deep breath, then stepped deliberately onto the gravel, the crunching sound overloud in the silence of the night. She stiffened and turned, starting when she saw how close I was. Good. I wanted Catherine to know me, and to know what was happening.

"I thought you left," she said, taken aback. "I thought everyone was gone."

"It's so wonderfully peaceful here, don't you think?"

"Yes," she smiled thinly, "that is rather the point. But what are you still doing here? The party is over." Her eyes narrowed as she tried to figure out how to get rid of me.

I kept my face placid, fighting the glee bouncing inside of me like an eager child. She had yet to notice the rock, veiled in darkness as we were. Seconds stretched to eternities as I considered my moment.

I took two steps towards her, bringing myself within striking distance. "I thought we should talk."

Catherine glanced at her little island with its lovely bench inside a mosquito netting tent full of sleeping butterflies, a party extravagance. She wanted to be on her island, not talking to me. "It's awfully late."

"Do you think?" I smiled then, mocking.

She looked puzzled. Then, through some intuition, she realized that I did not mean her well. Her eyes widened in alarm as I brought the rock up in a two fisted roundhouse. I allowed my hatred to surge up. Ecstasy flashed through me as I swung the heavy weight and felt the impact as it smashed into her temple. She fell face-up into the pond. Her diaphanous silk caftan fluttered, softly settled on the surface, then sank. She lay still on the bottom, half in, half out of the water. The single blow seemed to have done its work. How many times had I practiced swinging a rock in anticipation of that one shattering moment?

I was not finished, though. I pulled a battered cellphone out of my pocket. I reached into the water for her caftan, then felt through the dripping folds for her pocket. Once I placed the phone in the pocket of Catherine's caftan, I picked up her hand. Treading carefully on the stepping stones, I pulled her arm to drag her further into the water. I dropped the stone into the pond, and waited while the life bubbled out of her. I smoothed the mulch at the edge of the pond and then I left as soundlessly as I had come. My heart was still pounding, pounding, pounding out my exultation as water dripped from my *hand, forming a faint trail in the gravel as I retreated up the mosaic path. A trail that evaporated as if I had never been there.*

My heart was still thudding when I woke up. I have had this dream a dozen times, and my heart always feels like it will burst when I wake. I lay back and felt it slowly subside.

I never knew it could be like this. I have never felt so alive as I did when I spun with that rock and felt it connect with Catherine's skull. I have killed before, but I always used means that distanced me from the person I killed. Poisons that took effect when I was not there, accidents staged to happen when I was safely alibied, a bullet delivered with no preamble and designed to look like suicide. Clean, neat deaths masquerading as something else.

This was the first time I faced someone, saw that glimpse of mortality in her eyes and truly felt myself the direct instrument of her death. The first time I felt the power ringing through my body. My sly satisfactions of the past were nothing compared to the primal joy of killing with my bare hands.

And I can't wait to do it again.

Chapter 1

Thursday, August 16

Anxiety gripped Lia as she felt the muzzle of the derringer press into her temple, a circle of terror that bore into her brain, leaving her unable to think. Bailey's voice echoed in her head. *Think loving thoughts, Lia.* Tears fell as she clutched Honey's silky fur reflexively.

"Remember your exercises. If you can't breathe in, breathe out and you'll automatically breathe in. Deep breaths, take your time. The gun doesn't exist, it's just a memory. Open your eyes and look around you. It's just you and me and the dogs. Feel the bark of the log you're sitting on. Feel Honey's fur. Watch the light through the trees. It's a beautiful morning and you're safe here today."

Lia dutifully pushed her breath out, then inhaled deeply. Slowly her muscles relaxed and the clenching fear abated. When she was calm, she looked at Asia, sitting next to her. Asia was an anomaly with intricately coifed hair, gold jewelry and a sapphire pantsuit that vibrated against her mocha skin. Lia's own paint-smeared shorts and faded tee were more the norm for the park, but she still felt like a bag lady next to Asia. "Wow, that was intense," Lia said.

Asia smiled. "You're learning. You came through this much more quickly than last time."

"I'll admit, I didn't want to do this, but I think it's helping."

"Acute stress disorder is tough to handle. Nobody likes reliving those memories. But you will have the memories, whether you treat it or not. We can take the teeth out of them so they won't continue to incapacitate you. We don't want this to turn into PTSD."

Lia looked around the clearing with the creek bubbling through it. "This used to be my favorite spot. I walked Honey and Chewy down that creek practically every day. Then I'd sit here and listen to the birds and think. Do you suppose I'll ever get to where I can enjoy it again?"

"It takes time, and every case is different. But, yes, I think it's possible. Exposure Treatment has proven very effective in cases like this.

"We've done enough for one day. I know this log is a particularly charged spot for you, since Bailey tried to shoot you here. Why don't we stroll around a bit and get out of the 'hot seat' so to speak?"

Lia stood up, stretched, then bent over to ruffle the ears of her patient Golden Retriever. Honey looked at her with chocolatey eyes and lolled her tongue. Lia laughed. Chewy had been reconnoitering; he returned now to head-butt her leg, looking for attention. "Hey, Little Man, I didn't forget you." She took his face in both hands and vibrated them the way he liked.

Asia picked up the towel she'd been sitting on and folded it over her arm. "I can tell they're a comfort to you. You're lucky to have them."

"Yes, I am."

Lia Anderson was a pretty, slender woman of about thirty with streaky chestnut hair below her shoulders and jade eyes framed by exotic cheekbones. She was of medium height and had a light, uneven tan from the mornings she spent at the Mount Airy Dog Park and hiking the surrounding forest.

They climbed up the incline, watching as Chewy pawed and snorted through last year's leaves. "Don't you worry about what he's getting into?" Asia asked.

"I don't worry until one of them lays their neck on the ground and starts rubbing."

"Why is that?"

"They're either rolling in poop or something dead."

"Eww." Asia cringed and fanned her long ruby nails, then took a moment to regain her professional demeanor. "We have a few minutes before our session is up," she said. "Is there anything else you'd like to talk about?"

"I'm probably going to sound stupid."

"Try me."

"I'm seeing this great guy, and part of me is waiting for the shoe to drop."

"Tell me about the shoe. When you're waiting for a shoe to drop, it means you've already heard one fall. So what was the first shoe?"

Lia pondered. "I guess it was Luthor. Not what happened to him, though that was bad enough. More about me choosing Luthor in the first place. I started dating him, letting myself get sucked in and it turns out he's not only spoiled and demanding, he was also cheating on me and lying to me.

"So here's Peter, and I think he's really great, but can I trust myself? My judgement is obviously whacked. And then there was the investigation and he knew things about Luthor that he didn't tell me. So I freaked, like he was lying the way Luthor lied. But it wasn't the same thing at all because this was about being a cop, not about pulling one over on me. And then I think, at one time I thought Luthor was great, too, so what does that say about me? Am I making any sense?"

Asia laughed. "That's a lot to process in ten minutes, but let's do what we can. Think back to when you first met Luthor. What was your first impression, and be honest. Did you think he was great as in good, kind and honest, or was it something else?"

Lia took a moment to consider. "He was interesting and funny. And hot looking."

"If someone told you he was running for president, would you have voted for him?"

"Luthor? . . . Geezelpete, now I really feel stupid."

"Why is that?"

"I never really thought about it, but Luthor wasn't the kind of guy you rely on for something important."

"Do you truly feel the same way with Peter as you did with Luthor?"

" . . . No-o-o," she breathed out slowly.

"How is it different?"

"Peter's so easy. He's not 'on' all the time. And he does what he says he's going to do."

"Do you feel energized or drained when you've been with Peter?"

"I'm pretty up."

"And Luthor?"

"Luthor could be tiring."

"I think your judgment is fine. I think the problem is in the female notion that all relationships are supposed to lead to the same place. Let me ask you this. How do you feel about getting married?"

Lia sputtered, "What?"

"Thought so."

"Huh?"

"You want me to spell it out for you?"

"Please do."

"You're not afraid of repeating your relationship with Luthor. You're afraid of not repeating it. Peter scares you because he represents that white picket fence you don't want."

"Wait a minute."

Asia looked at her with eyebrows raised, a teasing salute that dared Lia to protest. "Yes?"

"Are you telling me you think I'm afraid of marriage?"

"I think you're afraid of your own expectations about marriage, and it has been safer for you to choose men who weren't marriage material."

"Peter and I haven't said a thing about marriage. It's much too soon," she defended.

"Peter has nothing to do with your expectations, but your expectations have everything to do with your feelings about the men in your life. I believe we're back at the parking lot and our time is up. Same time next week?"

"You dump that on me and then leave?" Lia accused.

"It'll give you something to think about until we meet again."

"Thanks a lot." Lia bent down and leashed Honey and Chewy.

Asia's little Kia drove out of the lot. A blue Blazer pulled in. She watched as a tall, lean man got out with a medium sized black dog. He had dark brown hair that flopped on his forehead, overdue for a haircut. It framed a face with nice bones and a touch of boyishness. She couldn't see his eyes, but she knew they were a deep blue and drooped a little on the outer corners. Sweet, with a whisper of sadness. She appreciated his legs as he approached. His elegantly curved mouth quirked up on one side when he saw her.

"Hey, Babe," Peter said, handing her a cup of coffee. He leaned over to kiss her.

"Babe is a pig."

"That makes us a pair, then," he said agreeably.

She sniffed the coffee. "Mmm. Hazelnut. You're learning Kentucky Boy."

"I is a smart lad."

They turned to walk up the curving drive to the dog park. "What brings a smart Kentucky lad up here today?"

"I thought you might like someone to hold your hand after your session."

"Damn. And here I am with full hands." She gestured with leashes in one hand and coffee in the other.

"I can wait. How did your session go?"

"A bit nerve wracking, but good. I don't like the Exposure Therapy, but I think it's going to help get rid of my dreams."

"Good." They passed through the picnic pavilion that separated the two halves of the dog park. Peter opened the gate to the entry corral and held it while Lia walked Honey and Chewy in. He closed the gate and unclipped the leads from all three dogs while a pair of Beagles set up a hullabaloo on the other side of the inner gate. "Luke, Henry, hush up," Lia said. She opened the inner gate and Honey, Chewy and Viola shot past the Beagles. They capered around the nearest tree with their noses up in the air and their tails wagging.

"Squirrel," Lia said.

"Must be," Peter agreed.

He took her hand. She liked that simple act of affection. She liked being able to be with someone without saying much at all. She liked it and yet she was just a little nervous. They were so different, and she was still getting to know him. He liked country music, she liked New Age world rhythms. He grew up in the Kentucky hills and she was a city girl. He was a cop and she was an artist. He was a man of few words and she was used to intellectual, verbal types. *Get out of your own way,* she told herself. *You're holding hands with a nice, considerate, hot guy who happens to like you. Just enjoy.*

They found a picnic table and climbed up on the top. They sat, watching the dogs harass the squirrel, who was running around the tree trunk just out of reach. Or maybe it was the squirrel taunting the dogs. Lia didn't know.

"How did you know I needed coffee?" she asked.

"Wasn't hard." He shrugged. "You said you and Asia were going down in the gully first thing this morning. I didn't think you'd want to be carrying coffee down that path."

"What about you?"

"I drank a Coke on the way over."

"That stuff is bad for you."

"So you keep saying. Tell you what. You quit nagging me about my Cokes, and I'll try some of those gummy things that look like rubber bands."

"I don't nag."

"Sure you do," he said pleasantly.

"Sorry. I'll stop. I won't push you to try anything weird anymore, either."

"Oh, I don't know, that's kind of an adventure. What do you call those gummy things, anyway?"

"Kelp noodles. You really want to try them?"

"I live for danger," he intoned with a straight face.

She nudged him with her elbow.

"Children, children," a heavy-set woman of medium height admonished.

"Hey, Anna," Lia said.

Anna Lawrence was a middle age woman with a square face and thin lips. She had intense, intelligent eyes. Dark eyebrows contrasted with hair that had paled to gold with age and waved around her no-nonsense face. She was accompanied by a black and tan Tibetan Mastiff named

CarGo. CarGo looked at the trio harassing the squirrel and whuffed softly but stayed at her side.

"Is this a private conversation, or can anyone join in?"

Peter turned to Lia. "What do you think? Should we let her in?"

Lia eyed Anna. "I dunno . . ."

"I've got to get to work, anyway," Peter said. "Why don't you ladies hang out." The two women watched Peter as he went to collect Viola.

"That man is very smitten with you," Anna commented. "How are you getting along?"

"We're still trying to figure each other out. He's very different from anyone else I've dated. So, what's new with you?"

"The foundation I work for is buying a building in Northside. They're going to turn it into an education center. I've got to meet some of the bosses over there this morning. They want me to coordinate with the architect and the contractors."

"Sounds like a fun project. Maybe you'll get your very own hard-hat."

"Maybe," Anna laughed. "Did you hear? Nadine is throwing a birthday party for Rufus next Monday. Cupcakes for the grown ups and home made dog biscuits for the furry ones."

Lia rolled her eyes. "Some people have too much time on their hands. I suppose it's okay, as long as she keeps everything out in the picnic shelter. The dogs always go crazy when there's food inside the fence."

"I won't be able to make it, anyway. I have that girl who helps me around the house on Mondays. I need to be at home when she comes."

The two women began strolling. Honey and Chewy abandoned the squirrel to join them. They said hello to regulars as they made their way to the back of the park.

A slight, grizzled figure sat on a bench with a Border Collie and a gangly Bloodhound by his side. A small, Asian woman sat next to him with her chin tilted at a rebellious angle. Dark bangs with electric blue highlights hung in her eyes. A beefy gentleman wearing a camouflage concealed-carry vest stood, waving his arms. Underneath a nearby picnic table, a skinny hound excavated while a small Golden Retriever mix supervised.

The beefy gentleman bore a striking resemblance to Teddy Roosevelt. He wore a walking cast on one leg. As they neared, he turned to the hound. "Jackson! No dig!" Jackson and Napa took off, spied Honey and Chewy, and started racing in circles.

Terry Dunn, the Roosevelt look-alike, turned back to Marie Woo. "Anyone who votes Democratic has their head up their ass. There's a reason the party mascot is a donkey."

"Anyone who still believes in trickle down economics thinks denial is a river in Egypt. The only way money trickles in this country is up, and . . ."

Jim, the man on the bench, kept silent, but his lips were flattened into a thin line.

Lia leaned over to Anna. "Looks like diversionary tactics are in order."

Marie flipped her bangs and overrode Terry's protestations. "Every time someone asks a Republican what they're going to do about the economy, they respond by diverting attention to gay marriage and abortion. And at least Democrats tax before they spend. George Dubya Bush cut taxes and then spent fifteen trillion dollars more than was coming in. That's how we got into this mess."

Anna reached into her tote bag and pulled out the Living section of the paper and a pen. She climbed up on the picnic table and began scanning the page. Lia climbed up beside her as the pair argued on. Anna waited for a lull in the hostilities, then called, "Oh, Terry?"

He turned. "Yes?"

"What's the name of the political party whose name means "renaissance" in Arabic?"

He frowned for a minute, then smiled. "Baath. Like bath, with two a's." He wandered over to the picnic table. "What else have you got?" He tried to peek at the paper, but Anna held it up to her chest.

"Hold on a minute. Let me see what else. . . 'Four time Indy 500 winner,' four letters."

"That's easy. Foyt. F, o, y, t."

"Thanks." Anna continued scanning the clues for obscure trivia questions.

Lia looked over at Jim. He no longer looked like he was about to explode. Marie winked at her.

"So, Lia, was that Detective Hottie you were talking to earlier?" Marie asked.

"He'd be so embarrassed to hear you call him that. He brought me coffee this morning."

"That was very chivel. . . chiver . . ." Jim said.

"Chivalrous." Lia completed automatically.

"That was very chivalrous of him," Jim said.

"He's a chivalrous kinda guy," Lia said.

"Lucky you," Marie said. "Last officer of the law I met looked like a bulldog and had onion breath. And he gave me a speeding ticket."

"And I bet you were doing fifty going down that hill on Montana," Lia said.

"Hey, if I stuck to the speed limit, somebody would run me off the road."

"Tell you what," Lia offered. "I'll have Peter ask them to post only pretty girl traffic cops in that speed trap. Maybe the next time you get a ticket, it'll be worth it."

"If only," Marie said. "Any way he can request pretty, gay, girl cops?"

"I can always ask."

Jim stood up and picked up his walking stick. "Fleece and Kita and I have to go."

"I'll walk out with you," Lia said. She held up a hand to the group in an abbreviated wave. "See you tomorrow." Honey and Chewy saw her walking away and stopped playing. They ran to catch up.

Chapter 2

Saturday, August 18

"Gina left me again," Roger announced to the early morning crowd at the Mount Airy Dog Park. "I want to kill myself." He was a tall, gaunt man, with a reddish beard that had a stripe of white down the middle. The hair peeking out from under his ball cap was gray. He was nearing sixty, and he had the rode-hard look of a wind-burned cowboy.

Lia looked out over the dog park, a ridge of land abutted on three sides by more than a thousand acres of forest. She lifted her face and felt the breeze that often blew over the ridge. She'd been running her two dogs at the park for four years. Now she was beginning to dread the mornings when Roger showed up because he could always be counted on to share his latest domestic drama. But Honey and Chewy had to run and mornings were best, Roger or no Roger. The lithe artist sat on top of a picnic table and concentrated on her coffee, inhaling the hazelnut scent. She'd let the others handle Roger for now.

Jose was a prematurely bald man of Italian descent with the build of a ball player and a Fu Manchu mustache. He heaved a big sigh. "Roger, you know we talked about this. You been drinking beer and staring at your gun again, haven't you?"

"Yeah," Roger admitted. "I wanna shoot myself, but I can't do it."

"Oh! Don't do that!" Marie exclaimed from her perch beside Lia. "The mess will cost a fortune to clean up and make it impossible to sell the house in this market. Hanging's better, but be sure to go to the bathroom first, maybe take an enema."

"Marie!" Anna admonished from Lia's other side.

"Just trying to help." Marie shrugged her dainty Asian shoulders and flipped her zebra striped bangs. "If he's going to do it, he should do it properly. Right, Roger? You could gas yourself, but that might blow up the house. An overdose of sleeping pills will leave nasty blue blotches all over your body. Then there's always the risk someone would find you and pump your stomach. There's carbon monoxide poisoning, but you'd have to clean out the garage first. I think you should commit Hari-kari on Gina's doorstep."

"You want me to stick myself with a knife? How do you expect me to gut myself if I can't pull the trigger?" Roger turned to Jose, "You do it. I'll give you my gun."

Jose rolled his eyes, "No, Roger, I'm not going to shoot you."

"Surely Gina isn't worth dying for," Anna said.

"She's not," Jose answered. "She takes his money and lives off him and runs around and never gives anything back." He turned to Roger. "Why do you let her treat you like that?"

"I love her," Roger insisted. "I can't stand to be alone. I'm not like you."

Lia had been content to let this conversation proceed without her input up to now. "Roger, would therapy be so bad? I'm finding it really helpful."

"The only thing that will help me is Gina coming back."

"Don't worry about that," Jose reassured. "She'll be back as soon as she needs some money."

"Too bad Bailey's in the nut house. She'd shoot me. Oops! Sorry, Lia, I didn't mean to bring that up."

"It's okay, Roger," she said, though it really wasn't. She didn't need reminding that her partner and friend had held a gun to her head six weeks before, and was now confined to a psych ward. Lia had a lot to say about how it felt to face your mortality, but talking to Roger always went nowhere.

Roger had been talking about suicide since he first showed up at the dog park following his wife's death a few years earlier. He often came at 4:00 a.m. and usually left before anyone showed up. Jose was his best friend. It was Jose who checked in on him when he was depressed. When Roger lost his job, it was Jose who found him a new job doing custodial work at the apartment complex where he supervised maintenance. It was Jose with the patience of Job who listened to Roger's stories of the many ways his girlfriend Gina abused him and his frequent announcements of suicidal intent.

"C'mon, Roger," Jose urged. "We need to get going or we'll be late for work. Don't matter that it's Saturday. Her Bitch-ness will read us the riot act." Jose called his gentle mastiff, Sophie, while Roger gathered up a pair of mixed breeds named Maddie and Lacy.

As she watched their retreating backs, Lia commented, "Suicide before breakfast. Just what I need."

Anna turned to face Marie and tsked. "He had no business bringing up Bailey. And what did you think you were doing egging him on, Miss Marie Woo?"

Marie gave Anna her inscrutable Chinese look from under those shocking zebra bangs. "Jose being his friend doesn't help. Lia telling him to get therapy doesn't help. Maybe telling him to do it will help. Too bad Terry's not here, he could have given him directions on how to properly commit Hari-kari and what kind of knife to use."

Anna shook her head, setting her shoulder length mane of pale gold hair bobbing. "It's in entirely poor taste."

"Poor taste is what Roger said about Bailey," Marie said. "What's happening with Bailey, Lia? Has Peter said anything?"

Lia looked out across the park from her perch atop her favorite picnic table. Her Golden Retriever, Honey was playing tug-of-war over a stick with Marie's champion Schnauzer, Nita. Lia's Miniature Schnauzer, Chewy, yipped encouragement from the sidelines. Anna's Tibetan Mastiff, CarGo, lolled at her side, aloof from the skirmish. The dogs, at least, understood how one should spend one's time at the park. In the distance, she spotted a pair of dogs, one a large hound, all flopping ears and graceless lope, and the other a compact Border Collie with a tidy trot. Behind them Jim stumped along with a walking stick.

"She's still in the psych unit. Last I heard, she hadn't said a word for more than a month. She'll eat if someone puts food in front of her, but that's about it. She's not fit for a trial. The case is on hold as long as she's catatonic."

"Do you have any idea why she snapped like that?" Marie asked. "You're the one who knew her best."

Lia chewed her bottom lip. The topic was uncomfortable, but talking about it helped. "I can't say. She seemed fine until we were in the middle of building Catherine's labyrinth. Then she got moody and edgy. I just chalked it up to working for Catherine."

Marie made a face. "Catherine was enough to make anyone edgy."

"She was reading some wacko book about reincarnation and karma. Stuff about using evil to promote the highest good. It was way out there. I don't know where she got it."

"Weird." Marie rolled her eyes.

"It's complicated. No one's really sure what happened."

"What happened is she held a gun to your head!" Anna interjected. "There can't be any question about that."

"Not that," Lia explained. "All the other stuff. They still haven't been able to connect Bailey to Catherine and Luthor, but the DA figures it's a moot point until she gets well enough to stand trial."

"Confusing," Marie agreed.

Just then, the large hound jumped up on the table behind Lia and lavished her cheek with a wide, rough tongue. She left behind a long, sticky streamer of dog drool. Lia swiped her face with the back of her hand and wiped it off on sweat shorts covered with colorful smears of oil paint.

"Ugh." Anna made a face and scooted away.

"Sorry about that," Jim said as he trotted up. "Kita, down!"

Lia put a protective arm around the hound. "She can stay. You're a good girl, aren't you Kita?" she said to the soulful brown-eyed Bloodhound as she stroked the dangling ears. She turned to Jim, "How's she doing? Has she adjusted yet? Any luck finding someone to take her permanently?"

"Fleece doesn't like her, but they've struck a truce. I thought it would be easier to find her a home. She mopes a lot. I don't know if she's missing Bailey or if that's just how she actu."

"You're a saint for taking her in," Anna said.

Jim gave a noncommittal shrug.

"Roger's going to shoot himself," Marie offered cheerfully.

"Again? Still?"

"Who knows?" Marie continued. "I think he just likes the attention. I don't think he'll ever do it. For all we know, he said the same things to his wife for twenty years before she died."

Anna looked thoughtful. "Maybe we should find out. He'd tell Jose, wouldn't he?"

"Probably," Lia said. "He tells Jose everything."

"Why is he so hung up on this Gina, anyway?" Marie asked.

"He says he can't live without a woman's touch," Jim said. "Not that I can see anything womanly about the way she treats him."

"I asked my therapist about him last week," Lia said. "She says there's not much you can do with someone who won't accept help, especially if they drink a lot. But we should pay attention if he suddenly gets in a good mood and starts giving away his possessions, or if he stops going to work. If he starts giving away his possessions, it could mean he's committed to a plan and is settling his affairs. The real kicker would be if he found a new home for Maddie and Lacy."

"I think you're right," Anna commented. "I don't think we need to get too concerned until that happens."

"So what's this I hear about a new project?" Marie asked Lia in a change of subject.

"I got a call from Renee, one of Catherine's friends from the solstice party. She wants a solar marker for her garden, something fanciful, with lots of mosaics."

"What's a solar marker?" Jim asked.

"You know, like Stonehenge and all those other places that were built to mark the calendar. Only smaller. You have a tall object of some kind, like a megalith, and the shadow it casts on dawn of the equinox lines up with a marker. You add other markers for the solstices."

"How will you know where to place the markers?" Anna asked. "That would be awfully difficult to figure out, wouldn't it?"

Lia smiled. "I'll cheat. I'll build the megalith, and when the equinox and solstices come, I'll see where the shadow falls and install the markers."

"Brilliant," Marie commented.

"Hail, good people! Talking about me again?"

Everyone turned to see Terry approaching, followed by Jackson and Napa. He was joined by a trim, sporty grandmother with a snub nose, white, boy-cut hair and a Basset Hound at her heels.

Kita and Honey jumped off the table and chased Jackson off towards the rear of the park. Napa, the Golden Retriever, and Rufus, the Bassett, trotted after.

"And there they go," Marie announced. "We could have used you earlier, Terry. Hey, Nadine."

"Do tell," Terry said.

"Roger's committing suicide again," Marie said. "You could have given the historical perspective on Hari-kari."

"Ah. Hari-kari, also known as Seppuku, which translates as 'stomach cutting', the traditional Japanese ritual of suicide by disembowelment performed in front of an audience by plunging a knife into one's belly and moving it from left to right. Committed by a Samurai to avoid falling into the hands of the enemy or because one has brought shame onto one's self. So who is to be the lucky spectator?"

"Marie thought Gina should have the honor," Anna commented dryly.

"Sacrilege!" Terry cried. "No self-respecting Samurai would fall on his sword over a woman."

Chapter 3

Saturday, August 18

It is delicious to sit in the park and listen as my friends talk about the deaths that happened earlier this summer. I am responsible, and they are oblivious. The echos of my actions are like ripples in a pond from a dropped stone, washing against my skin. So cool and delightful. It is marvelous to contemplate murder, each memory a sweet frisson of pleasure.

I know who I would remove next, if I could. Roger begs for death but is too cowardly to pull the trigger. I would do it for him, if I had not indulged myself with Luthor and Catherine. It would be so easy. Too easy, I tell myself. Not worthy of me.

It is much too soon. I have killed twice since May, when I rarely allow myself more than one a year. I need to be careful about removing someone connected to the park. Repetition forms patterns and patterns draw attention. I must be cautious if I do not want everything to get out of control.

Until recently, I had rules, and the rules kept me safe. Removing people was such a simple solution for impossible situations. Each removal was a rational decision backed up by meticulous planning. Each provided the satisfaction of a job well done.

Then Catherine changed everything. I broke my rules, and the risk was exhilarating. Almost as exhilarating as killing Catherine. This is perhaps why people dive off cliffs and rob banks. Why some people court danger. It is a secret I never knew, that you could feel such intoxication.

Still, my recent acts received attention and I have always avoided attention. It has been a long time since the police were involved in one of my little adventures. The first time, I feared discovery. This time, outwitting them became part of the pleasure. But it was still more risk than I liked. I want the thrill, but I want protections as well. Murder should be like bungee jumping, where one can enjoy the dive but stop short of the rocks.

For now, all is well with Bailey safely away and all but convicted. To kill Roger might be a risk without reward. He is a pathetic man whose miserable life has little impact on my own. I do not need him gone. Removing him might draw that attention again. Still, if the opportunity presents itself, I may not be able to resist. The important question being, would I get the same satisfaction if I see relief instead of fear in his eyes?

Chapter 4

Thursday, August 23

Lia was still unsettled from her session with Asia when she heard the arguing. She spotted Jim and Anna at a table, talking to Roger while he threw a disc for Maddie. From the sound of his voice, Roger was getting angry.

"That don't mean anything. Ask her the questions!" Roger pointed at Lia as she walked up with Chewy and Honey.

"What questions?" Lia asked.

"Jim thinks I'm a alcoholic and he says this test shows it."

"I only pointed out that he said yes to the first four questions," Jim shrugged. "You asked me to bring the quiz. You didn't have to answer the questions."

"I answered them. Somebody else can answer them too." He turned to Lia. "You do it."

Lia shook her head and sighed. "Sure, why not. What's the first one."

"Here, let me have the list. I want to pick the questions," Roger demanded.

Jim surrendered the AA quiz to Roger. Roger scanned the page. "This one. 'Do you ever lose time from work due to drinking?'"

"No."

"You don't have a work schedule. You work when you want to. That one shouldn't count. Try this one. 'Do you want a drink the next morning?'"

"No."

"Humph. This one. 'Have you ever had a complete loss of memory as a result of drinking?'"

"Nope."

"What about this? 'Do you drink to escape from worries or trouble?'"

"No."

"You're lying. Everybody does that. 'Do you crave a drink at a particular time of day?'"

Lia shook her head. "Uh-uh."

"Aw, c'mon. Everyone wants a drink at five o'clock. That's why they invented happy hour."

"Not me," offered Jim.

"You don't count. You don't ever drink. You're not normal."

"Okay," Roger turned back to Lia and scanned the list. "One more. 'Do you drink alone?'"

"Sure."

"See, I'm not the only one."

"Water, juice, tea, coffee. Mostly water."

"That's not what I meant, you know what I meant. I was talking about liquor and beer, stuff like that."

"I don't keep booze around. The beer's for guests. So I guess not."

"You're a girl. It's different for girls." He glared at Jim. It still don't mean anything." He shoved the list back at Jim. "Here, take this."

"Jose says you were sitting at your kitchen table, staring at your gun and drinking. Do you think that might mean something?" Jim asked.

"I was just having some beer. It didn't have anything to do with that, and what's Jose doing talking about me anyway?"

"Roger," Lia asked gently, "How do you know it doesn't have anything to do with the beer?"

"I just do. Look, if I was a alcoholic, I wouldn't be able to work, would I? I work every damn day."

"Didn't you lose your last job because you were late and hung-over?" Jim asked.

"I lost my last job because the foreman had it in for me. He was just using that as an excuse. I always did my work. I don't need no AA."

"I'm sure you're right," Lia said, "but I bet Terry could use a ride to some meetings. He still can't drive because of the cast on his leg. I've been helping some, but I'm starting to get busy and I don't have the time anymore."

"What do you go to them meetings for? You ain't a alcoholic."

"They're pretty interesting. The people are nice. I enjoy them."

"I'd take him," Anna offered, "but my ceramics class is starting up, and it's going to take up most of my evenings."

"I don't want anyone getting after me," Roger warned.

"They don't do that. They just talk about how drinking affected them and how they got better. You don't have to say anything if you don't want to. And you'll get coffee and cookies."

"I don't want to hang around a bunch of old fart losers."

"Please, Roger? I need someone to take Terry tomorrow night. Donna can't because she's going to be out of town and I can't because it's Peter's only night off this week."

"Oh, all right," Roger grumbled. "I'll take him to his meeting. But I ain't saying nothin'."

"Roger," Lia squeezed his arm, "you are such a peach."

"Whatever. I gotta go. I gotta doctor appointment. Maddie, Lacy, c'mon."

Lia and Jim watched Roger's lanky form shamble across the park. "I didn't know you were giving Terry rides to AA." Jim said.

"I'm not. And I'd better call Terry before he runs into Roger. Anna, since when do you do ceramics?"

"Since never. It was the first thing I thought of. You won't rat me out will you?"

"Do you think manipulating him into going to a meeting is going to help?" Jim asked. "He's not ready to stop drinking."

"No, he's not. But he's a lonely man. I think he'll enjoy the company. Maybe the group will have a better idea what to do with him. They've been dealing with this type of problem for decades."

"You know what they say," Anna added.

"What's that?" Jim asked.

"Whatever works."

Lia turned back to Jim. "Where'd you get that quiz, anyway?"

"This internet friend sent it to me."

"Internet friend, huh? Is this a girl internet friend or a boy internet friend?"

"None of your business!"

"Girl, then."

Anna changed the subject. "Who was that woman I saw you with in the parking lot earlier? She looked like she was dressed for church."

"That was Asia, my therapist."

"What brought her to the dog park? That's unusual, isn't it?"

"I've been having these flashbacks from that business with Bailey. I haven't been able to go in the woods, so we're doing therapy where it happened."

"I'm so sorry, I didn't know."

"I haven't told anyone before."

"I hope it's helping."

"Too soon to tell, but I think so."

Kita had been lounging on the table beside Lia. At the mention of Bailey's name, she lifted her head and looked around. Now she sat up on her haunches and looked Lia in the eye. Lia stroked the doleful bloodhound's head while she talked. "I really miss Bailey, the Bailey that was my friend. She was so funny, she always kept me going. I can't reconcile her with the crazed lunatic who attacked me. It's like they're two different people in my head. I told Peter I missed Bailey. You know what he said?"

"What?" Anna asked.

"He said he once interviewed a woman whose boyfriend stabbed her seventeen times with a screwdriver. And she told him, 'Besides that, he's a really great guy.'"

"Peter has a point," Jim said.

Chapter 5

Friday, August 24

I love hiking Red River Gorge in the fall. In the fall you can start to see natural rock formations hidden by all that summer green. The best view of the natural arches is in winter, but then it is too cold to hike for long, and ice often makes the trails dangerous. If I had a choice, I would take the fall, when the trails are covered with dying leaves in lovely shades of brown, tan ovals larger than my feet, rusty pine needles, and a variety of smaller leaves in various shapes in a kaleidoscope that Lia will paint for me when she gets around to it.

Lia has been promising the painting since last year, but the increasing popularity of her paintings, and now her mosaics, make it hard to find time to paint a picture at the "buddy" discount. I want the painting. It would allow me to return here to the trails anytime I wanted, in the season I like best.

Today was not fall, and the summer green closed in around me like a cocoon. I found it sometimes comforting, other times it suffocated. It was cool enough at 9:00 a.m. I suspected it would be blistering before I left. Thank heavens for layers I could peel off, and the bottles of water in my pack.

There had been no rain for weeks on Swift Creek Trail. The ground was baked hard. My beautiful dog strolled by my side.

I'd hoped coming here for the day would give me an opportunity to arrive at some decisions, see things from a different light. But the first thing I needed to do was simply enjoy the day. And who better to enjoy that day with me than my baby, the most beautiful dog in the world?

I stopped for a moment, leaned on my new walking staff and stroked my darling's head. Baby rarely barked, never chewed, and wasn't fond of digging. My dog was always solid, always there, always perfect. As my dog should be.

I'd missed the dog park this morning, opting instead for a drive down into Kentucky. I rarely did anything spontaneously. But my usually ordered mind had been awash with thought that required solitude and a different environment to settle. I thought a chance encounter with a stranger along the path might be pleasant, or even illuminating.

I'd been walking for more than an hour. To get to Swift Creek Camp Trail, you first have to take the Rock Bridge trail loop. This is paved with asphalt and runs in a scenic loop beside Swift Creek with a lovely low waterfall and a natural bridge of moss covered rock that is especially pretty. This short trail is always populated, too populated for my needs.

Halfway around the loop, I branched off to Swift Creek Camp Trail. This trail was narrower and started to climb. I normally would have stopped by the waterfall for a short break, but I wanted to reach my spot in time for lunch. I'd discovered this place on a previous trek. It was an overlook with a lovely, long view of the gorge, a widening of the trail with a natural rock outcropping that stood a good hundred feet above the creek. I arrived shortly before noon and sat on a large rock, just the right size and shape for a good rest.

I took off my day-pack and pulled out a container of cottage cheese mixed with canned peaches along with a plastic spoon and a bottle of water. Baby whuffed for attention, smelling food. I extended my hand out, palm down, and lowered it in the 'down' signal. Baby plopped on the ground and smiled, using charm to beguile me. I pulled out a pig's ear and Baby started salivating. They were disgusting things. I never let them inside my home, but my darling loved them and today was special.

As I ate, I closed my eyes, breathing deeply and enjoying the clean air, the rustle of wind in the pines and the birdsong emerging from the woods around me.

"Mind if I join you?"

I started, then opened my eyes to see a gentleman about my age standing in front of me. He said his name was Bill. He was of average height and build, with a tanned complexion and pleasant smile. He admired Baby properly, then pulled his own lunch out of a hip pack. He began to eat, punctuating his meal with observations that ran from the weather to politics and the ongoing conflict in the Middle East.

". . . now, if those marines had wrapped the dead bodies in an American flag before they urinated on them, the Liberals would have been fine with it. Hell, the NEA would have given them a grant for performance art. Crying shame one of those boys had to put the video on YouTube."

Inwardly, I shook my head. I'd driven over a hundred miles and hiked more than three hours, and who do I find? A Terry clone. Must be fate.

I changed the subject. "Have you ever looked over the side here? There's some kind of structure at the bottom of the gorge. I can't make it out, but it looks like it might be a ruined cabin."

"Really? How interesting!" He walked confidently onto the outcropping and looked down. "I don't see anything."

"Look over on the left. You might have to move a little closer to the edge. It's right up against the side of the cliff."

"You don't say." He placed his hands on his knees and peered more closely. "I still don't see it."

"Hold on, I'll show you."

I am always nervous around heights. I stood behind him, cautiously picking my way across the rocks, carefully placing my feet. I lifted my hiking staff, gripping it firmly in anticipation of my next step. I set the staff solidly on the rock, then leaned on it as I raised my foot. Bill turned his head and gave me a perplexed look as he eyed my posture. His mouth widened in awareness. I planted my foot in his rear and gave a tremendous shove. Bill gave a surprised "Oof!" He flailed his arms helplessly while teetering on the edge in slow motion, then pitched over the side with a strangled gasp. He disappeared from sight, but I heard him crashing through the pine trees and rhododendron thickets until he landed with a faint thud at the bottom.

I leaned against my stick and waited for a moment, listening. I watched as Baby continued to gnaw the pig's ear, untroubled by Bill's fall. There was no sound but the sighing of wind in the trees. The birds were momentarily silent, having been startled by the noise of his fall. I scanned the area for any telltale remains of my lunch, then picked up my daypack and stick. I called to Baby and we headed up the trail. In a few moments Bill would just be another careless hiker, a statistic.

Well, that settled that. The physical act of kicking Bill over the ledge was gratifying in the way most of my removals had been gratifying. I'd eliminated another obnoxious person. There was the mild thrill of a brief period of anticipation, and the rush of exerting myself during the push, as well as a sense of danger. He was not a small man. There had been some risk that I might not have had the strength to push him over, or that he might turn and grab my stick, grab me. But I'd not felt that surge of passion, that frisson of ecstasy I'd been hoping for.

The mere act of killing someone in a physically present way was not enough to satisfy me. If this had worked, I could have limited myself to spontaneous kills with random strangers, but that would obviously not do. Shame, that. It was so hard for the police to make any headway with stranger killings. I would have to spend more time looking for answers.

I wished there were leaves on the ground. Lovely, lovely layers of leaves that would take no impressions, leave no footprints. Yes, I really want that painting from Lia, then I could come back here in my mind as frequently as I liked.

I continued on the trail, scuffing when I came to a place where the bare ground was soft from a tiny tributary. I could not afford to leave any footprints. Baby padded quietly at my side. I suppose I should have been concerned about paw-prints, but I do not think police science is to the point of looking at dog prints as evidence, not yet.

Soon after, there was a little known branch in the trail that took me back to the road, not far from the parking lot where I'd left my car. Once I was back on I-75, I would take off my ridiculous wig and tacky sunglasses. I would just have to put up with the itching a little while longer.

Chapter 6

Sunday, August 26

A handsome, white haired man with a mustache waved at Lia as she and Peter herded their dogs through the corral. "Burn any flags lately?" he called. Jose, standing next to him, snorted.

"I was going to, but my matches are wet. Can I borrow your lighter?"

"Sure thing, Lia." Charlie clamped his cigarette between his teeth, then fished in his pocket and held the Bic out for her. Viola trotted up to him and sniffed inquiringly.

"Gee, thanks, but, you know, I think I'll get my own," Lia said.

Charlie leaned over and scratched Viola behind the ears. Oggie, his jealous lab, nosed in.

"I'll keep the lighter handy, just in case," Charlie called as Peter and Lia headed towards the back of the park.

"What was that?" Peter asked.

"I'm a Liberal, so I must burn flags in my spare time. He's mostly teasing."

"Mostly?"

"Mostly."

They joined Nadine, Marie and Anna at their usual spot.

"Hey, Lia, Peter. You won't believe this." Marie was staring at her iPhone.

"What won't we believe?" Lia asked.

"I was looking online for a new headset, and I came across this thing called a Kavorker."

"What, in heaven's name," Nadine asked, "is a Kavorker?"

"Remember Doctor Kevorkian? It's a suicide machine. Only they spelled it wrong."

"You're kidding," Lia said.

"And how much are suicide machines going for these days?" Anna asked.

"It's five hundred dollars. You can't buy them, you can only rent them," Marie said. "Apparently this is because you only need to use it once."

Peter shook his head. "The things you folks find to talk about first thing in the morning."

Lia scoffed.

"This is too much," Marie continued. "They're talking about 'death with dignity' here. Take a look at this thing." Marie turned her iPhone towards the rest of the group, displaying a picture of a blue tube.

"What is that thing?" Lia asked.

"It's a toilet. The 'death with dignity' machine is shipped to you disguised as a porta potty, complete with toilet seat, so the guy who delivers it won't be arrested for assisting with a suicide."

"Oh, you can't be serious," Anna said.

Marie resumed reading the catalog entry. "It's totally serious. They aren't disguised as toilets in Russia because assisted suicide is legal there, according to this web site. Selling this can't be legal. Is this legal, Peter?"

Peter scratched his temple. "Hell if I know."

Nadine frowned.

35

"How does it work?" Lia asked.

Marie scrolled through the page. "Well, you have to plug it in, and you plug in a phone line. Um . . . you go inside the porta-potty and sit down. See here, it says 'press green button to exit.' Then in 'ten painless seconds' you're dead. Um . . . then the porta-potty senses your lack of vital signs and dials 911 and tells them to come pick you up. They don't say exactly what it does. They just say they've never had a repeat customer."

"And do they have any customer testimonials?" Anna asked.

"How on earth is someone supposed to have death with dignity in a portable toilet?" Nadine demanded.

"You got me," Marie said. "Oh, and the return shipping is pre-paid. Think we should chip in and rent one for Roger?"

"Marie!" Nadine scolded.

Terry stumped up in his walking cast. "Is Marie acting badly again? What is this? More sick jokes about Republican Bar-B-Qs?"

"Worse," Anna said. "She wants us to pool our money and rent a suicide machine for Roger."

"You can rent suicide machines?"

"Apparently," Lia said dryly, "you're only ten painless seconds away from heaven."

"Sounds like a carbon dioxide generator," Terry said. "Is it in an enclosed space?"

"It's a porta-potty," Marie stated.

"Marie," Nadine said seriously, "I hope you aren't going to show that to Roger. That would be cruel. He's not here, is he?"

"Nadine, you're a spoilsport. Oh, all right, if you insist."

"I do insist," Nadine said firmly.

"Nadine," Lia said. "Marie's pulling your leg. She would never show that to Roger, would you, Marie?"

"Nah, I guess not. Officer Friendly here might arrest me for assisting a suicide."

"Marie, dear, your sense of humor is sometimes a bit much," Nadine said delicately. "I can't tell when you're joking and when you're not."

"Hey, I didn't invent the machine. It was some other twisted puppy who did that. I was minding my own business, looking for a head-set. Don't worry. I promise I won't show Roger."

"Thank you," Nadine responded.

"Speaking of Roger, how did it go?" Lia asked Terry.

"How did what go?"

"The meeting? Roger? Spill!"

"Yes, Terry, do tell," Anna asked.

"I can't believe you two conned Roger into giving me a ride to AA."

"Really?" Anna asked. "You can't believe we did it or that he fell for it?"

"Neither. Well, he grumbled all the way there, and he said he was just giving me a ride and it didn't mean anything. Then he stared up at the ceiling all during the lead. Then afterwards all my female friends came up and wanted to know who he was. He was chum on the water."

"Seriously?"

"He's decided he can give me a few more rides, but he still said he was going to crack a forty-ouncer when he got home."

"It's a start," Anna said.

"Indeed it is. Brilliant of you to come up with the scheme."

"That was Lia, I just helped. It was really kind of you, Lia. Peter, you should have seen her. Butter wouldn't melt in her mouth." Anna said.

"That's my girl," Peter said.

"It was nothing," Lia said. "Terry was the one who had to listen to him grumble."

"He was humming on the ride home. And that was one Friday night he didn't spend wondering where Gina was, at least for part of the evening."

Chapter 7

Wednesday, August 29

Lia and Nadine were helping Anna with her crossword. Marie was scanning the park. She spied a pair of familiar figures crossing the acreage, dodging a mosh-pit of beagles near the corral. "Oh, here comes the walking I-wish-I-were-dead," She announced.

"Marie!" Anna and Nadine scolded simultaneously.

"Be nice. You promised," Nadine said.

Terry clomped up in his walking cast, Roger with him. "Hail to the Fearsome Foursome," he said.

"Hey, Terry, how are you doing, getting around in that thing?" Lia asked.

"Greetings, all. It comes off in a few more weeks. I, like Lazarus, will not be kept down."

"Lazarus?" Anna asked sweetly. "I'm thinking more like a bad burrito."

"Direct hit!" Terry clutched at his chest dramatically. "What did I do to deserve such cruelty?"

"So how are the AA meetings?" Lia asked Roger.

"Oh, they're okay."

"Ha!" said Terry. "Our Roger has captured the attention of several members of the usually, and present company excepted, gentle sex. They crowd around him like moths to a flame."

"Oh, really?" Anna said.

"It's the haunted cowboy expression," Terry said. "They can't get enough."

"Is this true, Roger?" Lia asked.

"I guess so," Roger shrugged.

"Tell us all about your new girlfriends," Anna said.

"New girlfriends, Roger?" Nadine inquired.

"We must know all," Marie added.

"They're just a couple of women, they talk to me at the meetings."

"Are they pretty?" Nadine asked.

"They're okay," Roger said. "They're younger'n me," he added, as if this were inconceivable. "One of 'em's under forty, even."

"So what does Gina think about all this?" Anna asked.

"Gina? She don't know because she ain't been around. I oughtta tell her to pucker up an' kiss my ass."

"Better take back that car you bought for her first," said Terry.

"Aw, that was a gift. I can't take back a gift."

"My friend, you also can't continue to drive that bucket of bolts you call an automobile."

"I'll do something but I'm not taking back a gift. I love Gina, even if she treats me bad."

"But Roger," Marie asked, "how will you explain to your new girlfriend that you can't buy her a car because you're too broke paying off the one you bought for your old girlfriend?"

"I ain't got a new girlfriend. They probably don't like me that way, anyway. Besides, I couldn't live without Gina."

"Roger," Anna said, "You are living without Gina. You just said she's not around."

"I don't wanna talk about it anymore. I'm takin' Maddie an' Lacy for a walk."

Marie watched him go and said, "What's the verdict? Do I need to send my black suit to the cleaners?"

"He hasn't said anything lately about killing himself, if that's what you mean," Terry said. "He's still drinking, but I think the meetings are doing him some good."

"Too bad you can't keep your cast on for a few extra months until it has a chance to sink in," Lia said.

"I'm hoping he'll keep coming back for the women," Terry said.

"He's a nice man," Nadine said. "He had a hard time of it when his wife died. It would be nice to see him with someone who really appreciates him."

Well," said Marie, "That won't happen until he stops chasing someone who doesn't."

"Alas," said Terry, "true insanity is doing the same thing over and over again, and expecting different results."

"I'll keep the black suit handy, just in case," Marie said.

Chapter 8

Friday, August 31

Jim looked up from his solitary pursuit of Sudoku to see a slightly built black man in a navy t-shirt and shorts approaching his picnic table. It was midmorning on a Friday and the park was otherwise empty. Kita lifted her head, watching the stranger, eyes focused and alert while the rest of her sprawled on top of the table. Fleece lay under the table, unconcerned.

"You're right, Kita. He doesn't have a dog. That's very suspicious." Jim watched as the man crossed the acreage, not fast, not slow, and heading straight for Jim as if he knew him.

When he was ten feet away, Kita sat up on her haunches. The stranger stopped. "I'm Frank. You must be Jim."

"I'm Jim," Jim agreed. "How do you know me?"

"We have a friend in common. She told me I could find you here. Can we talk?"

Jim gestured to the other end of his bench. "Have a seat. Who's your friend?"

"Her name is Bailey, and if I'm not mistaken, this is Kita, her dog." Kita tilted her head at her name. Frank held out his hand to her. Kita sniffed it, considered, and relaxed. Frank ran his hand along her head. "She sure misses you. Calls you her

Drool Baby. Now why would she give you a silly name like that?"

"Frank," Jim interrupted, "Bailey and I aren't exactly friends."

"She could sure use one right now."

"I took in her dog, but I don't want to get mixed up with her problems. It's up to the court to sort that out. How do you know her?"

"I'm an orderly at the psych unit where she's undergoing treatment."

"Then you know she's crazy."

"I know she's been very ill. There seems to be more going on than just Bailey's bi-polar condition. Is it true you've had two deaths and an accident with other dog park patrons?"

"Is that what she told you? I didn't know she was talking to anyone. I thought she was cata-something."

"Catatonic. She's come out of it. She told me that, and that some people believe she's responsible. What do you think?"

"I know she held a gun to Lia's head. Did she tell you that? Why did you come to me?"

"Bailey says she was stable on her medication for eight years before this happened, and she never stopped taking her meds. She thinks someone tampered with her pills and it sent her into a schizophrenic episode. She thinks, and I agree, that the police are likely to sweep this under the rug and ignore it. Her doctor is a real twit. So she's hiding the fact that she's doing better. I'm the only one who knows. "

"So you want me to believe that someone made Bailey pull a gun on Lia? How would they know she'd do that?"

"She said someone was coaching her in a metaphysical forum, got her thinking all twisted around while she was in a vulnerable state and convinced her that it would be a loving act to send someone on to the next life. She said they didn't name anyone specifically. I checked the forum. Bailey's posts are still there, but the other posts have been pulled."

Jim's wheels were turning. Last summer, Peter Dourson had been convinced there was someone stalking dog park patrons. Is it possible it wasn't Bailey? "What do you think I can do? Why come to me?"

"Bailey says you're the most trustworthy of her dog park friends. Not out of loyalty to her, you understand, just that you're a principled man. Her first choice would be Lia, but of course, that's impossible."

Jim's mouth twitched in embarrassment at the compliment. "That was nice of her to say. But I still don't see how I can help you."

"We were thinking, the first thing that needs to happen is to get her Depakote to a lab and see if someone tampered with it. Then we could go from there."

Jim nodded, acknowledging the sense of this. "There's a problem. We need a police presence to verify the chain of custody. Who's to say we didn't tamper with the pills?"

"I see what you mean. Who would take this seriously?"

"Peter would take this seriously. But he's off the case."

"Peter? Would that be Detective Dourson? The officer who arrested Bailey? Why would he be off the case?"

"He's dating Lia. Conflict of interest."

"Then how can he help?"

"Peter will take this seriously, and he'll know what to do and where to go."

Chapter 9

Friday, August 31

Peter opened the door of Sitwell's Coffee House and cautiously entered. He hesitated just inside the door. The dark, funky restaurant was full of old, mismatched tables and chairs. The walls were covered with a showing by a local artist, of the kind of art Peter would never understand. There were laptops open on almost every table, taking advantage of the free wifi. One wall was painted with the slogan, "Friends don't let friends go to Starbucks."

A woman at the large, round table in front stood up. She was medium height, with short, wavy blond hair. Her hair was not styled, and her face was clean of make up. Still, to Peter, she should have been wearing her hair in a bob dating back to the Forties. She should be wearing bold, stop-sign red lipstick. Her squarish black glasses should have cat's-eye frames. She felt very retro, in contrast with the hip clientele. She gave him an appreciative up-and-down look and smiled. "Hey, there, you look lost." Her voice was husky, friendly, and confident. It spoke of speakeasies and smokey rooms.

"I am, a bit," Peter said.

"I'm Lisa, this is my place. What can I help you with?"

"I'm looking for someone. He's about your height and bearded, an older gentleman."

"Oh, you mean Treebeard."

"Treebeard?"

"You know, the ent in *Lord of the Rings*."

Peter smiled at the comparison. "That would be him."

"He's in the back, in the only booth. He's the guy without a laptop."

Peter worked his way through the tightly packed tables. Lisa returned to her companions. He heard her laugh at something one of them said. It was a Betty Davis laugh.

Peter spotted Jim immediately and slipped into the empty side of the booth. "I never would have guessed this was your kind of place."

"It's not," Jim said. "I didn't want to run into anyone we know."

"Lia comes here sometimes. She likes the salads," Peter pointed out.

"Does she? Then maybe we should leave."

"It's okay, she's seeing a client today."

They were interrupted by a waitress with a crew cut, a pierced nose, and colorful tattoos on each arm. A tattoo of a Japanese-style goldfish wrapped around her neck. Peter ordered a cup of coffee. When she was gone, he asked, "Okay, what's all the secrecy about?"

"I don't know how you're gonna feel about this," Jim started.

"Neither do I. I won't know until you tell me."

Jim pointed his chin at the waitress returning with Peter's coffee and remained silent. When she left, Peter asked, "What is this, *Mission: Impossible*?"

Jim nodded to himself, affirming his decision to talk to Peter. He placed both palms flat on the table and leaned across so he could speak quietly. "Remember that conversation we had a couple months ago? About a serial killer?"

"What about it?" Peter frowned.

"I had a visit from this fellow earlier today. He works at the hospital where Bailey is. He says she thinks someone messed with her medication and that made her go crazy."

Peter snorted in disbelief as he rolled his eyes. "Seriously?"

Jim sighed, "I was afraid you'd take it that way."

Peter was angry. "How am I supposed to take it? She attacked Lia. You were there! I can't believe you'd buy into this. And if Bailey's responsive, I need to report that so she can be brought to court."

"It's not that simple. Hear me out. He also said she was being manip . . . manipliate . . ."

"Manipulated?"

"Manipulated by someone online, and they pulled their posts later. I went online and saw Bailey's posts. There may be something to this. I don't know if I believe it. But what if it's true? Too many things happened this summer. Were you ever able to connect Bailey to Luthor or Catherine's death in any way?"

"No, I wasn't," Peter admitted. "Officially, we left it that Catherine murdered Luthor and drowned accidentally."

Jim shook his head. "You know how I feel about that. Catherine couldn't have staged a convincing suicide, even if she could bring herself to pull the trigger. You can't tell me you were happy with that decision."

Peter rubbed his temple and made a face. He took a sip of his coffee to give himself time to think. "No," he finally admitted. "I wasn't happy. I always thought there was another person out there responsible for Luthor and Catherine. Bailey never felt like a good fit, but I found it hard to believe there might be two killers running around. I guess it might be possible that some other person targeted Bailey, too."

"Don't forget Terry's fall."

"Heaven forbid." Peter leaned back and considered. "I guess I can give her a little time and look into this."

Jim took this as a promising sign and moved forward. "Frank gave me this list of people. Bailey wrote down everyone who knew where she kept the spare key to her back door. She figures it has to be someone connected to the park, so those names are underlined."

"She thinks it was someone she knew?"

"Frank says she never saw signs of a break-in. Your guys never noticed anything like that, did they?"

"No, we never did. Not that we were looking."

"So, if this happened, they probably used a key."

Peter noted the underlined names. There were several in common with a list Lia created last summer, of people who could have stolen her cell phone. He'd deduced back then that whomever killed Luthor, had also stolen Lia's cell. "What are Jose and Charlie doing on the list?"

"Frank says Bailey thinks they're both mechanically inclined enough to break into her house without leaving any evidence."

"Maybe so, but they're both going to the bottom of the list."

"Why is that?"

"Whoever did this is sneaky and vicious. We don't know any sneaky, vicious people at the park. So that means they have to be able to hide that part of themselves."

"Oh. I hadn't thought of that. You're right. Jose can't keep a secret to save his life and Charlie isn't one to hide his feelings. But that would mean a woman did this. You think a woman could pull all this off?"

"We thought it was Catherine, then we thought it was Bailey. Why wouldn't it be a woman?"

"I guess you're right. I guess I'm too old fashioned to think a woman would be a murderer."

"I'm not convinced it was anybody, and I don't care to do Bailey any favors. I'm willing to consider the possibility, because, if someone framed Catherine and messed with Bailey's head, Lia could be a target. I either want to rule that out or do what I need to do to keep her safe."

"So what do we do?"

Peter frowned. "The first thing is to tell Lia."

"Do you think that's a good idea?"

"I'm not looking forward to it. But I learned the hard way not to keep secrets from her. I won't go through that again."

"And after that?"

"We check out Bailey's meds. I don't recall them being on the inventory sheet for the items we took from her house. Likely they're still there. If they are, then anyone could have got at them at any time. That means Bailey could have sent her friend Frank to doctor them before he came to you with this story. Do you understand?"

"You mean Frank and Bailey could be pulling a con job on us?"

"Exactly."

"So why bother to test her medicine?"

"You never know what we'll find out. Maybe something conclusive. Maybe a fingerprint."

"So how do we start?"

"Look, all of this has to be kept off the clock. I can't bring it into the department or Roller will blow a gasket. After that, he's going to pull Bailey out of the psych ward and put her in jail so she can go to court. He is not going to want to reopen a case that's resolved as far as he's concerned, not on a flimsy theory by a mentally ill perp. He'll say it's up to her defense to

49

investigate that. I doubt Bailey can afford a lawyer who would invest that much in her case.

"I can help you, but I can't act as a police officer or use department resources. I might be able to pull in a favor with the fingerprint tech, but that's about it.

"If lab results suggest we investigate further, we need to narrow down the list and do deep background checks on the most likely suspects. Deeper than I could do last summer. We'll have to find people who knew them years ago."

"Lotta work."

"Yes."

"And we say nothing to anyone except Lia?"

"Exactly. I'll call you after I talk to Lia, and we'll figure out how to get started. I've got to think about this."

~ ~ ~

Friday, August 31

Renee is too outrageous, Lia decided as she studied the drawing she was making for the ebullient socialite. Lia was sitting on the wood floor of her living room with her back against the mission style couch. She had a drawing pad braced against her knees. Chewy and Honey snoozed comfortably on the sofa.

She'd met with the petite brunette at her East Walnut Hills home overlooking the Ohio River. Renee's house was placed outermost on a curve in the river, giving her a clear view of both the eastern and western horizons. The view from the flagstone patio was a breathtaking panorama of the sinuous river and the hills of Kentucky on the other side. Below she could see the B & B Riverboat paddling along on a lunchtime cruise. Off on the right was the Big Mac Bridge, a pair of elegant yellow arches reminiscent of the first McDonald's restaurants. Past that was the Roebling Suspension Bridge, a prototype for the Brooklyn Bridge that caused Lia to occasionally mistake New York for Cincinnati in a certain television commercial. Renee's collie, Dakini, lay in the middle of the yard, queen of all she surveyed.

Lia looked over the piece of land Renee had set aside for her solar marker. "You've picked your spot well," she'd told the fun-loving woman. "First thing I think we should do is plant a ten foot PVC pipe where you want the pillar. The equinox is coming up, and this is something I can do in a hurry. With the pole up, we can figure out where the markers should go for the equinox. That will give us an idea how we're going to lay out the whole piece."

"How exciting! We should have a sunrise party, and breakfast afterwards."

"A party?" Lia nearly stammered at the thought.

Renee's eyes danced. "No need to get nervous. Just you and me and some pre-dawn lattes. Harry will join us for breakfast, I'm sure. Company for breakfast will give Esmerelda an excuse to show off her eggs Benedict. She makes it with smoked salmon. It's to die for."

"That would be lovely. Now tell me what you had in mind for the design."

"You mustn't tell anyone."

"It'll be our little secret."

"The standing stones I saw in Carnac looked like so many erect penises," Renee began.

Lia sputtered. "Really? How evocative."

"Precisely. I'm imagining this enormous phallic shadow reaching across the lawn, all dressed up, so to speak, and the poor thing has nowhere to go. So I remembered how the

Hindu have their lingam stones, and how they pair them with a yoni stone. Are you familiar with that?"

"No, afraid not."

"I have a set inside. I can show you. Anyway, it's a pairing of male and female. I'd like this to also be a pairing of male and female, but abstract, of course. Sheriff Si Leis is retiring. We wouldn't want him coming back to ban us. The poor man's wasted enough of his life fighting pornography and adult entertainment. We absolutely must leave him in peace."

Lia couldn't help laughing. She, too, had found the sheriff's moralizing tedious.

"I'd like this to be subtle, so it can be my private bit of symbolism. Is that enough to get you started?"

"Sure, I'll put some drawings together."

"Excellent. Come inside and I'll show you my lingam stone. Oh, and I mustn't forget to pay you. Is two thousand enough to get you started?"

Lia smiled at the memory. This project was going to be fun. *Too bad Bailey's not here, she would enjoy Renee,* she mused. The lapse shocked her out of her reverie. What was she thinking? What was she doing missing someone who tried to kill her? Peter was right. Once somebody hurt you that badly, you had to cut them off.

She scowled, angry at herself. She got up from the floor, stretched, and went to the kitchen for a glass of water. She sat down on the sofa. Honey put her head in Lia's lap and Chewy snuggled up against her on the other side. She pet each in turn. "You would never try to shoot me, would you?" she asked them.

"Of course not," she answered herself. "You couldn't get your paws through the trigger guard. Okay, I need a change of scenery. Who wants a walk?"

An hour later, Lia was at her drawing table, reviewing her sketches. The brisk walk had cleared her mind and returned her to good spirits. She'd sketched out a variety of ideas for the markers that would indicate the equinox and solstice. She'd started with the obvious, then simplifying to create the abstraction. The first one was a "Venus of Willendorf" type fertility figure, an enormous belly overlapped by two ponderous breasts. No . . . It wouldn't do. It looked too much like Mickey Mouse ears.

Next was a chalice and blade, symbols mentioned in *The Da Vinci Code*. These were signified by overlapping reversed triangles. This formed a Star of David. While Renee was Jewish, she didn't think Renee would go for this bit of misdirection, so she removed the baselines of the triangles to form interlocking, reversed V's. Then she removed the upward pointing triangle and just left a "V" shape. Perhaps if she pointed the top of the pillar, and everything lined up just right, the shadow would create the 'blade' and interlock with the 'chalice.' She'd show it to Renee, though she thought it too stark for the lusty woman lurking beneath the society wife veneer.

She'd done another sketch of a pair of spread legs. Very obvious. She'd played with it for a while, but found no way to abstract it. It just looked dumb. None of this was earthy enough, pagan enough, subtle enough.

Suddenly, she flashed back to her college days, when everything she painted reminded some professor of a vagina. That was the problem with flowers. Everyone compared her to Georgia O'Keefe, and talked about how sensual her flowers were. And she'd constantly said, "Georgia O'Keefe found such comparisons boring, and so do I."

A flower wouldn't be quite right. But hadn't that one adjunct teacher compared her bay leaves to vulvas? A nice, big leaf split by a vein, symbolizing the earth and fertility. And the pillar representing the sun, which is necessary to make things grow. The sun which is the male principle. She could wrap the pillar in flames, hot yellows, oranges, reds, against cool greens. There would be six large leaves to represent each of the sunrise and sunset points, placed in a circle made of pavers in a repeating motif of some kind.

She could include copper verdigris in the design somehow, or should she make the leaves out of copper? Copper is the metal of Venus, symbolizing beauty and the female principle. What metal was associated with the sun? Gold, she'd use gold metallic tiles as part of her flame design. And while she was at it, she should include the Golden Mean in the proportions of the piece, as much as she could. She'd get out her old copy of The Da Vinci Code and read the pages where he explains the ancient symbolism. Renee would love this.

She sat back satisfied, and relaxed. She jumped at a touch on her shoulder. The large hand settled in, warm and familiar and began kneading the back of her neck.

"Mmmm. Since when do housebreakers have such strong, talented hands?"

Peter leaned over and whispered in Lia's ear, "Your door was open and the screen door was unlatched. Pretty girls shouldn't be so careless. They could get into trouble."

"Doesn't sound so bad. How much trouble?"

"A whole lotta trouble." He bit her earlobe.

She yelped, then whirled around, glaring. "That wasn't nice."

Peter grinned. "But it was fun."

"Just wait, Kentucky Boy, I'll get you back. You won't know what hit you."

"Viola will protect me."

"I've known her longer. Where is she, anyway?" She glanced over and found the bundle of black fur curled up on the couch with Honey and Chewy. "How long have you been here?"

"A while. I like watching you think."

"You like scaring me to death, more likely."

"Poor baby. You in the mood for sushi? My treat."

Lia perked up. "Can we go to The Painted Fish and get one of those wooden boats?"

"For you, Darlin', the sea's the limit."

Lia was gazing fondly at the wreckage she and Peter had made of the sushi boat. She enjoyed the kitschy vessel and refused to let the server take it away from the table. She took a bite of tempura ice cream and sat back in her wide rattan chair.

"That was excellent. You can always count on Nick," she said, referring to the chef. She noticed a worried look on Peter's face. "What's wrong? You look like you're not feeling well."

Peter heaved a sigh. "We need to talk. It's serious, Lia."

Lia looked at him quizzically. "This isn't one of those staged break-up scenes, is it? You know, doing it in a nice restaurant so I won't go berserk because we're in public?"

"No, nothing like that." He smiled but it didn't reach his eyes. "But I was trying to butter you up." He nervously tapped his fingers on the black linen tablecloth.

"Oh, really? And why is that?" She cocked her head.

"I talked with Jim today. He had a visit from a guy named Frank. Frank works at the psych unit where Bailey is staying."

"This has something to do with Bailey?" Lia tensed.

"Yes. I hate worrying you, but I promised I wouldn't keep secrets from you. I haven't made my mind up what to think, but I have to look into it."

"Look into what?" Peter's dithering made her nervous.

"Bailey's come out of her catatonic state. She thinks someone tampered with her medication to send her into some sort of schizophrenic episode, and that's why she attacked you."

"Seriously?" Lia scoffed. She sat back and folded her arms mutinously.

"I'm not crazy about this, but I feel like I have to check it out."

"Why?" The one-word question came out harshly, an accusation.

"I know she assaulted you, and nothing changes that. But if someone tampered with her medication, then maybe it's not over. Maybe someone is still out there, picking off people you know, one by one. And if that's true, you could be next."

"Oh." The sound was breathy and small.

"Yeah, 'oh.' I hate what Bailey did to you, but I'm not going to ignore this. You're too important to me, okay?"

"I don't know what to say," Lia said, stunned. "I thought once you arrested Bailey, that was it."

"That's what I was hoping. Promise me you'll start locking your screen door?"

"Uh, yeah, sure. No problem. Peter, I think I'm getting scared."

"Me, too. That's why I want to check this out as soon as possible."

"What does Roller think about it?"

"He doesn't know, and he's not going to."

"Why not?"

"All we've got is a woman in a psych ward claiming someone else made her do it. It's not enough. And if I tell Roller she's talking, she'll be back in jail in a heartbeat. I want to take a minute to find out what's going on first."

Lia dreamed of the gun that night. Bailey was wearing a straight jacket. The dogs sat in a row and howled. Peter was running towards her, but he kept getting smaller and smaller, as if he was running backwards and getting further and further away. Someone she couldn't see held the gun against her head. The gun was still pressing into her temple when it went off.

Lia woke up with her heart pounding, the fear strangling her. She remembered what Asia said, to breathe out so she could breathe in. She sat up and looked out the window at the moon, reminding herself where and when she was. She focussed on the sensation of sitting on the bed, grounding herself in the here and now. The pounding slowed as she continued to breathe smoothly and rhythmically. Inhale, two, three, four. Pause. Exhale, two three, four. When she was calm, she turned and saw Peter's back rising out of the top sheet. His breathing was deep and even. She thought about waking him up, then decided against it. It was enough that he was there. She laid back down, spooning her body behind his.

Chapter 10

Saturday, September 1

Peter and Jim got out of their cars in front of Bailey's house. The neat little red brick bungalow was out of keeping with the tall, weedy grass and neglected flowerbeds. The mailbox was stuffed to overflowing and ad circulars littered the walkway and porch.

"Hoo Boy," Jim said, shaking his head. "She's lucky if no one has broken in to steal the copper yet. She must not have anyone looking after the place." He took the pile of mail out of the box. "I'll take the mail if you'll grab those papers."

They found a trash can around the side and Peter dumped his load of weekly circulars. "I suspect she has other things on her mind right now besides home maintenance," he said.

They proceeded to the back yard. Pots of dead geraniums and other, unidentifiable flowers lined the porch. The yard had been well maintained until Bailey's arrest. It was obvious nobody had attended to it since.

"Where's the key?" Peter asked.

Jim pointed to a stone planter beside a pergola. He handed the mail to Peter. "Second row from the bottom, fourth stone from the right is loose. It should be behind there." He counted, then leaned over and tugged on the rock. It stuck for a moment, then came free. He reached inside and felt around until he found a baggie wedged in the back of the cavity. He stood with his prize and held it up so Peter could see. A brass key with a pentagonal head was inside.

"As a hiding place, it's a lot better than the ledge over the door," Peter said.

Jim unlocked the back door and they entered the kitchen. Peter dumped the mail on the dusty counter and looked around. The place should have been cosy. The air of abandonment lay like a miasma over the lovingly refurbished vintage furniture. There were a few plates in the sink, and a dirty glass on the counter. A faceted crystal hung in the living room window. It cast rainbows over the opposite wall, a counterpoint to the sad air of the place. The dining room was lined with book cases topped with clusters of natural crystals and several large stone orbs on decorative stands.

Peter bent down to read the titles. "*Crystal Healing, Making Friends with your Medicine Animal, Astral Projection for Dummies, Dream Interpretation and Prophesy, Your Spirit Guides, How to Read Auras.* Looks like a New Age bookstore. But I don't see *Reincarnation and Soul Contracts.* That's the book that Lia told us about, the one that Bailey was reading earlier this summer. Too bad it's not here, I'd like a look at it."

Jim, a devout Catholic, merely grunted. "I think the bathroom is this way." He pointed to a small hall off the living room.

The bathroom floor was a checkerboard of pink and seafoam green tiles in a classic pattern from the thirties. The wainscoting consisted of bands of green and pink tile, punctuated in several places by hand-painted tiles of day lilies. The shower curtain was covered with peonies. There was an old, wood medicine cabinet over the sink with a glass knob on the door.

Peter moved into the small space while donning a pair of latex gloves he pulled from his pocket. He opened the cabinet and scanned the shelves. "Depakote. This must be it." He picked up the bottle and showed it to Jim.

Jim eyed the bottle in Peter's hand as if it would leap up and bite. "What now?"

"I take this to a friend who will examine the bottle and capsules for finger prints, then it goes to a private lab. But first I want to check something out." He carefully opened the bottle and poured some of the capsules into his hand. He eyed them for a minute. "Shit." He ground the word out on a massive, resigned sigh.

"What?" Jim asked, looking and seeing nothing.

"Look at the lettering." Peter pointed his chin at the turquoise and white capsules.

"What about it?"

"When they come out of the factory, the print on the two halves of a capsule will line up exactly. Someone tried to line these up, but it's a little off. There are slight variations. See?"

Jim looked more closely. The differences were minute, just a hair, but they were there. "You think someone's been into these."

"I know someone's been into these. What I don't know is if it was Frank, creating a defense for Bailey, or if some nut job did this to her, and sent her off the rails. I wish we'd found this when we first arrested her." He looked at Jim. "You don't know how badly I was hoping to find nothing."

Jim gave him a wry expression. "I guess that means we give Bailey the benefit of the doubt for now. Suppose I'll come over and mow her lawn. If someone put her in a psych unit, I'd hate to see her house get vandalized while she's stuck there."

Peter poured the caps back in the bottle. He pulled a zip-lock baggie from his hip pocket and sealed the bottle inside. "I'm trying to look at all sides of this. No matter what we find, this could open a whole can of worms. If we find something, it's fuel for Bailey's defense, even if we can't prove who doctored the meds or when it happened. I guess there's some chance Catherine did it before she drowned in her pond, but I think we agree she wasn't meticulous enough to pull off any kind of crime without leaving evidence. And she wasn't on Bailey's list. If it wasn't Frank, it's likely there's somebody out there laughing at all of us."

Before they left, Peter examined the doors and windows for signs of forced entry. He found nothing.

Chapter 11

Saturday, September 1

I've been considering my options, how best to recreate the sensations I experienced with Catherine. It occurs to me that these sensations were not a result of killing her with my hands. I believe my disappointing experiment at Red River Gorge proved that.

I am thinking the thrill resulted from the way I engaged directly with her before I killed her. I let her see me, know me and my intent. I unleashed a part of myself, a brutish side that I had not experienced before. I expressed hatred I did not know myself capable of in that moment. And, for a brief instant, I saw her terror.

Now the question is, how can I engage my 'inner brute' directly with a target without risk to myself? How can I find this hatred within myself again? I so rarely have deep emotions for anyone. It could be years before someone enters my life who affects me as Catherine did. Then it was months before I allowed myself to remove Catherine.

So far, everything suggests that this experience was target specific. Must it be that way? I am sure much of the excitement resulted from the build-up to that event. Is it possible to compress the build-up in some fashion? Reduce the time involved while intensifying it somehow? Perhaps I could prolong the actual experience in order to allow more time for emotions to emerge within the event under extreme circumstances.

How can I prolong engagement before I complete the act, while minimizing the risk? Minimizing risk is imperative. Time is my enemy. The more time I take, the more chances there are: of being seen, of leaving a trace of myself, of failing to complete the act successfully, of being caught.

Chapter 12

Sunday, September 2

Peter called in a favor and topped it with a case of beer. The tech working that holiday weekend agreed to check for prints and run them while he was there. There were no fingerprints on the capsules. The only fingerprints on the bottle were Bailey's. Peter was disappointed but not surprised.

Chapter 13

Monday, September 3, Labor Day

"Geezelpete, I thought people would be sleeping late today. It's supposed to be a freaking holiday." Lia looked out at the eddying morass of dogs in front of the corral, most of whom were unknown to her. A strange trio lunged at the gate, barking something that sounded like "Come in here and we'll tear your lungs out." Chewy protested with his piercing bark. Honey snarled. CarGo, being many times the size of the challengers, ignored the confrontation.

"Excuse me," Anna called out. "Whose dogs are these? Can you come pull them away from the gate?" She turned to Lia. "We'll be fine as long as we get by the mob."

A string bean of a woman came up, rolling her eyes. "I don't see what the big deal is. There's no reason to be afraid of my dogs."

Anna took a deep breath. "They're guarding, as if this is their territory. You should not let them do that. Most fights at dog parks happen at the gate," she explained patiently.

The woman shook her head. "Whatever." She led the dogs away.

"Idiot," Lia muttered under her breath.

Once the gate was clear, Anna and Lia cut around the furry horde, waving at Roger and Jose as they passed. They headed for the back of the park, which was empty. They joined Jim at their usual table while Lia's dogs ran off to play. CarGo stayed by Anna. Jim was reading on his Kindle.

"Geezel, Jim," Lia said, "I thought you were the mayor of the dog park. What were you thinking, letting all these strange people in?"

"Don't look at me," Jim said. "They just showed up."

"Do you suppose," Anna said, "They just woke up and said, 'My goodness, it's a holiday, I guess I should play with my dog'?"

"And they've got to get it out of the way early so it won't interfere with their beer drinking. I would have gone over to the other side, but it's so small, Honey won't run over there," Lia said.

"Well, we're safe back here," Anna watched the unruly bunch up front. "But I think I'll wait to do my crossword at home so I can keep my eyes on them. Jim, what are you reading?"

"I'm looking up pizza recipes. The kids are coming over later and we're baking pizza in that wood fired oven we built out behind the house."

"That sounds so nice. What about you, Lia? Anything planned with your detective?"

Lia squirmed a little. "Peter invited me to this cookout District Three and District Five are having. They're playing baseball against each other. Peter and Brent are on the team."

"Is Brent that nice boy from Atlanta Peter partners with?"

"That's the one."

"That'll be fun," Anna said.

"I decided not to go."

"Why ever not?"

Lia shrugged. "I figured it was going to be one of those things where the wives and girlfriends all hang out together while the guys play ball. I didn't want a bunch of women I've never met grilling me about my relationship with Peter and asking if we're serious. Does that make me a bad person?"

"Not bad. Chicken, maybe. I imagine you'd feel more comfortable if you knew some of the women," Anna said.

"That, too. It felt like I was going to meet his family or something. I'm just not ready."

"You can join us if you like," Jim said. "You, too, Anna, if you aren't doing anything."

"I'd love that," Anna said. "I hope you'll let me bring something."

"Thanks," Lia said. "I've got my head into a painting right now, so I'd rather stay home and work."

"If you change your mind, just come on over. We're eating around five."

Vicious snarling interrupted their conversation. Honey, Viola, Kita and Fleece started running towards the disturbance. Lia and Jim yelled for their dogs. The errant canines sulked back to the picnic table. CarGo hadn't budged an inch from his spot by Anna.

At the other end of the park, Jose waded through the roiling dogs and fell on top of the main aggressor. Roger pulled a bleeding beagle out of the fray. The string bean woman screeched at Jose to leave her dog alone. Jose shouted back for her to control her dogs.

"I don't believe it," Lia said. "She just stood there and didn't do anything while her dogs attacked that beagle."

They watched as the dogs dispersed. Jose and the woman continued to have words as she collected her dogs and left. Jose called Sophie and headed towards the back of the park. He was muttering to himself as he and Sophie joined them.

"Did you see that?" he asked. "That crazy lady just accused me of stirring the dogs up. She claimed they would have worked it out and been fine if I'd left them alone."

"How is that poor beagle?" Anna asked.

"She's bleeding, but it's not bad. Roger pulled her out before they really got going on her."

"What were you and Roger thinking, jumping into a dog fight?" Lia said.

Jose shrugged. "What are you gonna do when you got a pack going like that? Not like we had a garden hose handy to spray them with."

Jim picked up his walking staff. "If you carried a stick like mine, you could pry them apart."

"I read that the best way to stop a dog fight is to grab your dog by the hind legs and pull back," Anna said.

"I heard that. I never tried it," Jose said.

"Too many amateurs," Lia said. "It's almost enough to make me stay home on holidays."

"At least they ain't been drinking," Jose said.

Chapter 14

Wednesday, September 5

Despite the bad comb-over, the watery, pale eyes and the basketball of extra weight he was carrying under his shirt, Phil Rumsey was as sharp as they came. He grinned when he saw Peter, showing off yellowed teeth. "We've got something interesting here," he announced, holding up a large manilla envelope.

Peter raised his eyebrows. "That so?"

"It is, it is. Come on back to the conference room and I'll explain it to you. Coffee?"

"I'm fine, thanks."

Phil led him to a long, narrow room with a twelve foot oak table surrounded by stuffed leather swivel chairs. Business was apparently good.

"Is this what you do with the money we pay you?"

"One of the things, yes," Phil grinned, unapologetic.

Phil sat at the end of the table and Peter took a chair around the corner. Phil squared-up the envelope to the table's edge, then folded his hands over it. He cleared his throat. Peter found these preparatory gestures annoying, but did not say anything.

"First thing we did was weigh all the capsules." He pulled a report out of the envelope and indicated a column of figures halfway down. "There were thirteen capsules left in the bottle. Each of the weights were different."

"Huh."

"Yep." Phil cleared his throat again. "Now the interesting part. What was in the capsules, do you suppose?" Here he paused for dramatic effect.

Peter would have rolled his eyes, but he didn't want to antagonize the man. He decided to play his part and asked, "What was it?" like a good cop.

"Depakote." Phillip gave him a meaningful look.

"What?" Peter leaned forward. "That doesn't make any sense."

"You wouldn't think so, would you. I'm not the detective, that's your job. But the different weights and misalignment of the capsules suggest they were filled by hand."

"Why would someone fill it by hand just to put Depakote in them?"

"Again, I'm not a detective, but I suspect it would be because something else was in them earlier."

"Makes sense," Peter considered.

"So I went looking for traces of other chemicals, scraped samples off the insides of the caps. Guess what I found."

This time Peter didn't miss a beat. "I have no idea."

"BC Headache Powder."

"Can you still get that?"

"Apparently. And that's not all. BC Powder was in ten of the caps. In two we found amphetamine, and in one we found a hallucinogen, a derivative of LSD."

"So someone dumps out the Depakote, replaces it with other drugs, then later goes back and replaces the Depakote to erase the evidence."

"That would be an appropriate scenario for what we found." Phil smiled at his star pupil. He replaced the report in the envelope, then handed it to Peter. "Interesting case you have here."

"Isn't that the truth."

Chapter 15

Wednesday, September 5

I have been thinking that I'd never experienced primal aggression before Catherine, but that is not true. An old memory has come into focus, like a photographic image emerging in a bath of developer. I could not have been more than six years old. I was playing with the brat next door.

This was not my idea. I didn't like her. She was prettier than I was. She had more toys, and she thought she was better than I was. My mother wished to be friends with her mother, probably because they were better off than we were. So I had to play with the brat.

She only let me play with her old dolls, never the pretty new one. I remember that doll, it had long, silky blond hair in waves held back with a blue ribbon. It was dressed in a pretty, ruffled pinafore. She called it Clarissa. She stroked Clarissa's hair and told me that she only let her very best friends hold Clarissa, and I would have to make do with Dora.

Dora had coarse, muddy brown hair and she did not have a pinafore. She was older than Clarissa. We were playing tea party. I sat Dora down and gave her some tea. The brat said Dora had to be the maid and get tea for Clarissa. Then she sneered at me.

I held Dora by the legs and stood her up, pretending I was walking her. I swung Dora like a bat and hit the brat in the head. While she was howling, I took Clarissa from her and ripped

Clarissa's arms off. I enjoyed the horror in her eyes as I dismembered her favorite toy. She screamed even louder.

Then I smashed Clarissa's face on the floor so she would never be pretty again. I shoved Clarissa back at her and resumed giving tea to poor, unworthy Dora.

My mother was very unhappy about this. The brat was given her choice of my toys, and she picked a pretty palomino pony with a mane as lovely as Clarissa's hair while telling me that none of my toys were as good as Clarissa. I was made to apologize to her. My mother told me that if I didn't act sorry when I apologized, I would lose all my toys and never get another one.

I learned from my mother that it did not matter what other people did. I had to behave well at all times. Getting angry was never permitted, for any reason. She needed to teach me, she said, to be a lady.

I revenged myself for the loss of the pony. The brat had a kitten. It was a pretty white kitten named Snowball. It got out one day when I was playing in the yard by myself. We had a rain barrel in the back. I put the kitten in the rain barrel and held it under until it stopped struggling. Then I buried it in the garbage can. The brat cried when she asked me if I had seen Snowball. I said I was oh, so sorry she lost her kitten. I acted like a lady.

Chapter 16

Wednesday, September 5

Lia opened the door and invited Jim into her apartment. "Come on back, Peter's already here." She led him to her kitchen, where Peter sat the the table with a glass of tea. "I made some guacamole and salsa. Would you like some ice tea? I've got raspberry tea and plain sweet tea, if raspberry is too girly for you."

"Raspberry sounds good, thank you." Lia poured the tea, then set out the chips and dip while Jim looked around the sunny kitchen, "Seems too cheerful in here, considering why we're meeting."

"Sorry, left my cloak at the cleaners, and my dagger is out getting sharpened," Lia said. "I suppose we could meet under a pier at midnight, but that would be inconvenient."

"True," Jim agreed.

"We start acting all mysterious, and people will notice," Lia continued.

"We still have to come up with a reason for me being here, in case anyone asks," Jim said.

"I thought of that. You came by to look at my drawings for Renee. You're reviewing the plans from an engineering standpoint. I want you to do that anyway, so it'll be the truth."

"I guess that'll work."

"That's settled," Peter said. "Shall we get down to business?"

Lia and Jim turned polite expressions to Peter.

"I got the report about Bailey's Depakote back from the lab."

"And?" Lia asked.

"The meds were doctored, and not by Frank."

"How can you tell?" Jim asked. "You said there was no way to know who did the tampering."

"There's no way to tell who did it, but I can say for sure that who ever it was, they didn't want anyone to find out about it."

"What makes you say that?" Lia asked.

Peter laid out the findings for them. He concluded, "So someone removed the Depakote and replaced it with BC Powder to get Bailey off her meds and make her unstable. At the same time, or at a later date, they added some meth and a hallucinogen, possibly buried these down in the bottom of the pill bottle. That way, once Bailey had the Depakote out of her system, the street drugs would set her off in some way. After this was accomplished, they came back and replaced the Depakote in the capsules so no one would find out.

"I'm convinced Bailey's right. I thought she was trying to run a scam to get out of trouble, but she'd want us to find something and this person went to a lot of trouble in an attempt to hide it."

"Poor Bailey," Lia murmured. "Is this enough to prove she was off her meds?"

"At some point, she may need to get hair analysis. That could be helpful. It may also tell us what she was on that sent her over the edge. For all we know, there were additional drugs we didn't find because she'd taken them."

"Why didn't they just replace the doctored capsules with new ones?" Jim asked. "Then we'd have never found this."

"It's likely our perp didn't have access to a prescription for Depakote, or didn't want to leave a paper trail," Peter responded.

"This changes everything," Lia said. "I don't know if I can ever forgive her, but I don't want her to go to jail on my account. Who do I speak to about dropping the charges?"

"We can't do that yet," Peter said. "We've got a bigger problem."

"Officially, Catherine killed Luthor, then drowned by accident. Bailey's assault is being treated as a separate incident. Unofficially, the powers that be believe Bailey killed Catherine and Luthor, but we haven't been able to prove it. So they're hot to put her away with any excuse they can find. They won't want to drop the case. With attempted murder, they can proceed without you. If you don't cooperate, you can be charged with obstruction of justice."

"What do we do about it?" Jim asked

"Whoever tampered with Bailey's meds is still around. It couldn't be Catherine, because she died before Bailey went haywire. The second tampering would have taken place after that. And if we drop the charges against Bailey, it will tip off our perp."

"And we don't want that," Jim said.

"Wouldn't tipping them off force their hand and cause them to make mistakes?" Lia asked.

"This isn't the movies. Playing games like that could get someone killed. Right now they should be feeling pretty safe. We want them to stay that way. It will give us time to do some digging."

"And we should continue to meet here. Nobody thinks anything about me being here because we're dating. And Jim has a plausible reason for being here, to help with your totem pole."

"It's not a totem pole. It's a solar marker."

"Whatever. And you two need to watch what you say at the park. It's too easy for someone to walk up behind you. Our perp is sneaky and dangerous."

Peter turned to Lia. "I'd really rather you weren't involved in this at all. It would keep you safer."

"Whoever it is, they almost got me killed and sent Bailey to the psych unit and maybe prison while wrecking our friendship. You can't expect me to stay out of this."

Peter sighed. "I might expect it, but I don't know what good it would do. Promise me you won't do anything stupid?"

"Stupid like what?"

Peter's head swam with possibilities. "Stay out of the woods, unless you're with your therapist. And no meeting with anyone alone unless it's Jim."

"Seriously? I can't do that. I've got work to do and a client to see."

"You can see Renee. I'm sure she's not involved. Anyone else, you meet with in a public place."

"How do I explain that?"

"Tell them you want to get out because the project is giving you cabin fever and you have to drive in separate cars because you have errands to run. They shouldn't think anything about it."

"What if someone wants to see how the drawings are coming on Renee's sculpture?

"You can say you're not happy with them yet and you don't want to show anyone. Even better, say Renee swore you to secrecy. Then you have an excuse to keep everyone out of your apartment."

"I don't believe this." Lia folded her arms and glared at Peter. "This is like universal precautions. You want me to wear a face mask and rubber gloves, too?"

"Jim, back me up here," Peter begged.

"Sorry, I don't get involved in domestic arguments. Mea culpa, mea culpa, mea maxima culpa."

"What if someone comes to the door?" Lia demanded.

"Don't let them in unless I'm here. Better yet, I'm moving in with you."

"What?" Lia gasped.

Jim placed both hands over his ears. "Mea culpa, mea culpa, mea maxima culpa!" he said louder.

"It'll only be for a short time," Peter offered.

"We've got our lists! I don't have to treat everyone like they're lepers!"

"Lia, the lists pinpoint our most likely suspects. But we don't know for sure our perp is on Bailey's list. Look, can we talk about this later, after we finish our business?"

"Mea culpa, mea culpa, mea maxima culpa!" Jim repeated.

"I guess so," Lia grumbled. "But this isn't over. Geezelpete, Jim, will you take your hands off your ears and stop saying mea culpa, mea culpa?"

"Hoo boy. Are we all still friends? Is the furniture intact?" Jim asked.

"Very funny. I bet you're on his side."

"I'm not on anyone's side. Can I have more of your wonderful tea?"

"I'll get it," Lia said.

When she set down the glass in front of him, Jim said, "So, we're 99% sure Bailey was set up. Agreed?" Lia and Peter nodded. Jim continued, "So far we have a list of names of people that Bailey said knew about her key, and we have a print-out of the posts Bailey made at the Crystal Bridge web-site. And aside from the doctored Depakote, that's all we have, correct?"

"Not exactly. Whoever killed Luthor took Lia's phone, and it only makes sense that they took it that day, after their argument at the park. Back then, Lia made a list of everyone who had access to her bag that day. We think our perp will be on both lists, but that's not a given. However, they have to be on Lia's list." Peter took his wallet out of his hip pocket and pulled out a folded scrap of paper that had been pressed flat from months of being sat on.

"Aw, you kept it," Lia mooned.

"I wished I could say I was being sentimental, but the truth is, I've never been satisfied with the way things went down." He unfolded the paper and put it on the table.

"Hey, I'm on that list!" Jim exclaimed. "Guess that means I can't be alone with you, Lia."

"We can cross Jim off the list." Peter took a pen from a jar sitting on the table and struck a line through Jim's name.

"Why is that?" Lia protested. "How come you get to cross somebody off the list?"

"I can cross Jim off the list because he came to me in the first place. All he had to do was wait awhile, then tell Frank he had the meds analyzed and there was nothing in them."

"He could be playing a very deep game, Detective. Maybe he enjoys toying with you."

Peter looked at Jim. "Do you enjoy toying with me?"

Jim put his hands over his ears again and started chanting, "Mea culpa, mea culpa . . ."

"I thought not." He leaned close, and said loudly, over the chanting, "You can take your hands down now.

"We can cross off Bailey and Catherine. Are we agreed, Madam Artist?"

"I guess so," Lia sulked.

"And Terry was in a wheel chair when Bailey was arrested. I think we can cross him off, too."

"Can't we leave Terry in?" Jim asked. "He squeezes into that kayak of his, I bet he could crawl through Bailey's window in a cast."

"You just want him to be a serial killer because he's a right wing Republican," Lia said.

"Moving along," Peter interrupted, "that leaves Anna, Nadine, Marie, Jose and Charlie."

Jim produced his folder and opened it to Bailey's list. He compared his list with Peter's, calling out names as he circled them. "Nadine, Marie, Jose, and Charlie are on Bailey's list. Anna isn't."

"Jim, didn't Frank say that Jose and Charlie didn't know about the key?"

"Yep, but they're on the list because she figured they'd know how to break in without leaving signs."

"So we concentrate on Nadine and Marie as most likely," Peter said.

"Nadine? Lia scoffed. "You think she pulled this off in between babysitting her grandkids?"

"We can't take anything for granted. No matter how well you think you know them. Whoever is doing this is a pro, a real actor. They're good at getting people to believe they're something they aren't. There's no getting around it. This person is someone you know and like. You can't take your feelings into account here."

"So how do we start?" Jim asked.

"Let's do a little profiling first. What are some things we know about our perp?"

"Can we give him a name," Lia asked, "Or do we have to keep calling him 'our perp.'"

"What do you want to call him?" asked a frustrated Peter. "Goofy? Lassie? Marmaduke?"

"How about DPK, for Dog Park Killer," Jim said. "We could add vowels and call him 'Deepak.'"

"Sounds too much like Deepak Chopra," Lia said. "I can't stand him. I wouldn't mind seeing him as a serial killer, but I don't want to have to think about him. He's too smarmy. Our serial killer is not smarmy."

"How about Cujo," Jim offered. "He's a killer dog."

"Too obvious. Our person doesn't act like a dog. They act like a cat. Cats are sneaky . . . . It should be a cat name. I know!" Lia exclaimed. We'll call our killer 'Bucky.'"

"Bucky?" Jim and Peter asked simultaneously. They looked at each other and shrugged.

"Bucky is a cat's name?" Peter asked.

"From 'Get Fuzzy'. Don't you ever read the comic strips? Bucky has seriously twisted, psychopathic tendencies. He fantasizes about turning monkeys into batteries."

"If you say so. Can you live with 'Bucky', Jim?

Jim shrugged.

"Fine," Peter continued, "let's figure out what we know about 'Bucky.' Who wants to take notes?" He held out a spiral notebook.

"I'll do it," Jim said, "because I don't want to hear an argument about girls having to be secretaries."

"Okay, first, Bucky is smart and organized," Peter said. Jim wrote the two words down, list style, in a column.

"Sneaky," Lia added.

"Good actor," said Jim.

"No access to prescription drugs," Peter said.

"Can get street drugs," Jim said.

"Connected with Lia, Bailey, Catherine, Luthor, and likely Terry," Peter said.

"Terry?" Lia asked.

"We can't count out Terry's accident. Terry was asking around about the gun. If 'Bucky' thought Terry was getting too close, Terry's fall might have been a murder attempt," Peter said.

"Oh," Lia said.

"Which is why I'm so concerned about your safety. Yours, too, Jim."

"Meticulous," Jim said, hoping to head off another argument.

"Could get into Bailey's house without being noticed," Lia said.

"One more thing, the most important," Peter said.

"What's that?" Lia asked.

"He's done it before."

"I think I know the answer to this," Jim said, "but why do you say that?"

"He's too meticulous. This can't be his first time," Peter answered.

"So what do we do with this profile?" Jim asked.

"We keep this all in mind as we look at our suspects. I'll run off the background checks we did on everyone last summer."

"What are we looking for?" Lia asked.

"Whoever our perp . . . er . . . 'Bucky'. . ." Peter emphasized the name, "is, he didn't get that way overnight. Luthor's death was very well planned and executed. As I said, it's likely Bucky has done this before and not been caught. There will be a questionable death somewhere. A family member, a co-worker, a neighbor. Maybe we won't find it. Maybe all we'll find is a questionable attitude. Before Bucky got good at acting, he had to show his true self at some time. Maybe we'll get lucky and hear about missing or dead pets."

"Why dead pets?" Jim asked.

"Serial killers, and I think you'll agree Bucky is likely to be a serial killer, often start by torturing or killing small animals when they're young. So if we can go back far enough, say, to adolescence, we could get lucky there. Or fires. Some serial killers were fire starters as children."

"You've given this a lot of thought," Jim said.

"So, are we just supposed to walk up to Nadine's old neighbors and ask them if she strangled hamsters as a hobby?" Lia asked with an arch look.

"I wish it were that easy. We need to come up with a pretext, something like an award of some kind, and we're looking at the candidates' characters. Or perhaps we're vetting them for some kind of local public office."

"Why can't we just say they're a whozit," Jim said, snapping his fingers, "a person of interest in a case?"

"Number one, there is no case, not officially, and number two, if they still have contact with our suspect, we want to give them a good reason not to tell our target about the interview. If it's an award and it's supposed to be a surprise, hopefully they won't. We want there to be some kind of reward for our suspect, so if they have reason not to like the person, they'll want to spill the dirt and ruin their chance for the reward.

"We don't want to suggest it's a police matter. People often don't want to get involved with police business."

"That's going to take some thinking," Jim said.

"This sounds really complicated," Lia commented.

"If you want out, just say so. I'll keep looking on my own. It'll take longer . . ."

"No, no, I'm in," Jim said hastily.

"Don't be pulling that," Lia said. "I make my own schedule and Jim's retired. We're much more flexible than you are. And you're already working overtime, chasing down creeps. I'm not going to take an easy out on this."

"Even if I wish you would?"

"Even so. Look, with more help, it'll get done faster, right?"

Peter reluctantly nodded.

"And just because Bucky doesn't know we're onto him, doesn't mean he's stopped, does it?"

Peter sighed, "No, probably not."

"So I'm safer if we find Bucky sooner, right?"

"Maybe, maybe not. You could slip up and Bucky would be onto you. Then where would you be? I'd be out a girlfriend."

Jim put his hands over his ears. "Mea culpa, mea culpa . . . ."

"Relax Jim." Lia pulled his hand off one ear. "We'll continue this after you leave. But I'm in, you can count on it."

"You're in if I'm staying here for the time being," Peter bargained.

"If you're staying here," Lia bargained right back, "it's because your plumbing is broken."

"Why is that?"

"Because if you just move in, I'll have to be all lovey-dovey about it, and I'd rather bitch like hell. And you get to sweep up all of Viola's fur. She sheds like she's undergoing chemo."

Peter figured the plumbing ruse wasn't all bad. While Jim could be taciturn, Lia was moody and he expected the investigation to upset her. She wasn't good at hiding her feelings. That was why he would have preferred not to tell her about Bailey's meds. The plumbing scenario allowed her to be as moody as she liked and blame it all on him. Everyone knew she was leery of cohabitation and they hadn't been dating long. Everyone would just figure she was having intimacy issues and no one would think she was being strange. Not that he would tell Lia any of his thinking about this.

They planned to meet again the next evening to put together their thoughts about their list of suspects, and ideas regarding how to pursue their covert investigations. This would also give him and Lia a chance to settle in and get over any jitters.

He watched Jim walk to his car, then shut the door. He turned to Lia and took her hands in his. "You all right, Babe?"

"Babe is a pig. Wanting to protect me from a big bad serial killer does not give you the right to act like a Neanderthal."

"My bad. Is the big, dumb cop allowed to give his best girl a hug, anyway?"

"I don't see any big, dumb cops, but you can hug me if you want to."

He gathered her close and brushed his face against her hair. "I'm really sorry about all this. I can bunk on the couch if you want me to. I just wouldn't ever get any sleep at my place, I'd be too worried about you. Bucky likes to strike at night."

She turned her face so that their lips met, then nipped him. "Ow!"

"Okay, I forgive you for being overprotective, for now."

"Mea culpa," he whispered into her hair. "Mea culpa," he kissed her temple. "Mea maxima culpa," he met her lips, and this time she didn't bite.

Chapter 17

Thursday, September 6

Lia was sitting on her usual table in the dog park when Anna climbed up next to her. "You look awfully grumpy for someone who got to kiss the handsome Detective Peter this morning."

"How do you know I saw Peter this morning?"

"I see Viola chasing Honey, but I don't see Peter. That means you brought her. That means you saw him. That's supposed to put you in a good mood."

"Peter's staying with me for a while. They're redoing the plumbing in his apartment, so he needed somewhere to go. You know these old Victorians. They're quaint, but something always needs work. Apparently the person who originally split the house up into apartments did it the cheap way. He won't have any water at his place for at least a week, probably longer." Lia realized she was babbling, and stopped.

"And this is upsetting because?"

"I already feel like I can't breathe. I'm just not used to having someone around all the time. The two-family I live in doesn't have enough room for all of us."

"You have dogs around all the time."

"They're different. They don't make fun of my television viewing pleasures. I want to watch 'The Bachelor' in peace."

"You watch that trashy show?"

"I always did love a good cat fight."

"Lia, I don't believe you!"

"What? It's not like I'm watching 'Jerry Springer'. Every weekend, he likes to lay around watching grown men get excited over a stupid ball. Why can't I watch a little girl-sport?"

"Well, that's true. What other despicable things does our handsome detective do besides ridicule your choice of entertainment?"

"Oh, he's not despicable. He doesn't have the decency to be despicable. Not yet, anyway. The most annoying thing is that he's so accommodating, I have nothing to complain about. So far, anyway. I'm just not looking forward to thinking about another person. I can't just go into the kitchen and get something to eat, I'll have to ask if he wants something and instead of eating an apple, I'll be fixing dinner. It's going to throw my rhythm off. I'm at that stage in Renee's project where I just want to work for hours and live on carrot juice and green tea."

"Ugh. I'm glad it's him and not me. I think you'll find having him around is not nearly so bad as you anticipate."

"I like my space. And my privacy."

"And you'll get them back. Meanwhile, I assume he's getting a break in his rent, so he can pay for dinner and take some of the burden off you."

"Yeah, whatever." Lia knew she was being bitchier than the situation warranted, but there was so much she couldn't talk about. Since it was Peter's fault, it made sense to use him to dump her frustrations.

"So how is Renee's project coming?" Anna asked.

"Jose and I will be planting the the pole next week. I'm still working on the design. I'm hoping to get the main part done before it freezes. If not, we'll have to wait until spring."

"I'd love to see what you're working on."

Lia used the pretense of watching Viola and Honey play to avoid looking at Anna. She mentally crossed her fingers. "Renee's sworn me to secrecy. I can't show the drawings to anyone."

"Goodness, that sounds extreme."

"Renee's great, really. She's having so much fun with this, like it's Christmas or something. She's paying me well enough. If she wants to be eccentric, that's fine by me."

~ ~ ~

Peter sat, bleary eyed, over his cereal bowl. He winced at the grinding of Lia's blender. "That sounds like an airplane taking off. Where did you buy that, army surplus?"

"I need a powerful motor to grind up greens," she stated primly. She poured her concoction into a glass and sat down at the table across from Peter. He eyed the smoothie with suspicion. It was a deep shade of swamp green.

"What's in that glop? No, don't tell me. It looks like pond scum."

"Smarty pants. I'll have you know it is pond scum."

"Please, I'm eating."

"And banana and avocado and cacao. Oh, and some romaine and frozen cherries." She sipped delicately. "Yum."

"How can you stand to do that to yourself at the crack of dawn?"

"The crack of dawn was two hours ago at the dog park. It is now officially mid-morning."

"Are you going to expect me to kiss you after you drink that stuff?"

"You roust gang bangers for a living. You're afraid of a little algae?"

"Yup," he said, looking back into his cereal. "You start ribbiting and I'm sleeping on the couch."

"Good. Now I know what to do if I want a little privacy. How do you keep from vomiting at crime scenes, with all the brains and guts splattered all over the place?"

"Nobody is eating the brains and guts."

"You're so cute when you're nauseous."

"Thanks. How did it go at the park this morning?"

"I said bad things about you. Anna asked about my project. Nobody dropped a smoking gun."

"I knew it couldn't be that easy," Peter mumbled into his corn flakes.

Chapter 18

Thursday, September 6

Peter opened the meeting. "We have five names. We've got to start with impressions about each of them." He opened the spiral notebook to a new page. "Who do we want to start with?"

Lia shrugged. "Nadine?"

"Okay, Nadine. Jim, what are your thoughts about Nadine?"

"Nice lady. Never heard her say a bad word about anyone. Always well groomed. Disciplined, she always walks a mile at the park ever day. Not like us lazy lugs sitting on the picnic tables."

"I don't see her as Bucky," Lia added. "She's got at least ten grandkids and she's always talking about things she does with them. She and her husband are always playing bridge or cooking some exotic cuisine for that dinner club they belong to. When would she find the time?"

"I think Nadine is just like she seems," Jim said. "She's a simple woman who enjoys her family. This serial killer has to be walking around with a lot of dark thoughts."

"What do we know about her background?" Peter asked.

"She's lived in Cincinnati all her life. Married young and started having kids. Her husband works for P & G," Jim said.

"If she grew up here, doesn't that mean there's a good chance she's still in touch with people we would want to talk to?" Lia asked.

"That's something we have to consider," Peter said. "It also means we need to be very careful with our cover story, because they're more likely to realize it's bogus if we say we're with some non-existent organization."

"This is going to be harder than I thought," Lia said.

"Moving along," Peter continued, "what about Marie?"

"Marie's a first generation Chinese American. Gay, but no partner right now. She grew up in D.C., went to college at Oberlin. From the stories she's told, she traveled around a bit in her twenties and wound up here. She works as a freelance technical writer," Lia said.

"Jim, anything you want to add to that?" Peter asked.

"Not about her background."

"How about impressions of her?"

"Marie's . . . unusual," Jim temporized. "Her sense of humor takes some getting used to."

"How so?" Peter asked.

"I can't explain it. Lia, can you?"

Lia considered for a moment. "If Marie yelled, 'Five points for a dead nun,' you wouldn't know if she meant it or not. She can be confrontational, too. Jim, you remember the day Roger was talking about wanting to shoot himself, and Marie started giving him advice on the best way to commit suicide? That was a little strange."

"Sounds like it," Peter said.

"You would have thought she was telling him how to bake chocolate chip cookies, she was so matter of fact about it. I think it was her way of not buying into his attention seeking, but I don't know for sure. What if she really wanted him to do it? What if she was pushing him to do it?"

"Good point," Peter said. "How well do you know Marie?"

"She's a hard person to know. She doesn't talk about herself much. She prefers talking about her Schnauzer, Nita. She shows Nita, so she's very particular about Nita's grooming and who Nita can play with at the park."

"She's meticulous?" Peter asked.

"Very," Lia said. "She's also very smart. She's the one person who will go head to head with Terry when he's on a political rant."

"So she disagrees with him?"

"Frequently," Lia said.

"What do you think, Jim?" Peter asked.

"We get all kinds of eccentric people at the park, so I've never thought about it. But if you take her seriously, she could be disturbing."

"So maybe we move her to the top of the list," Peter concluded. "Who's next?"

"Charlie," Jim volunteered. "He's another one who's meticulous. He restores old cars. Sometimes he sells them, sometimes he doesn't. He's got this place in Price Hill like a compound with a six foot privacy fence around it. He calls himself a redneck and admits to disliking black people."

"I think his racism has to do with the way Price Hill has deteriorated over the past twenty years," Lia added. "I think he can deal with a black person in a fair way, if he had to work with one, but he can't stand looking at the houses around him, and seeing trash and drugs all over the place."

"No doubt," Jim said, "But there's still something wrong with hating a whole group of people."

"Has he ever married?" Peter asked.

"Not that we're aware of," Jim added.

"Do you know how long he's lived there?" Peter asked.

"Don't know for sure," Jim said, "but it takes awhile to accumulate that many cars. Maybe he has a dead body or two buried underneath the cars. Nobody would see you digging the hole behind that fence."

"Charlie works part time for Fed Ex, making Next Day Air deliveries, so he's off early in the afternoon," Lia commented. When he's working, he's driving a route. That might give him an opportunity to watch people, depending on where his route is. Who thinks anything about seeing a Fed Ex truck parked somewhere?"

"That's worth considering," Peter said. "Mobility would be an asset for our perp . . . "

"Bucky," Lia interrupted.

"Bucky," Peter repeated while rolling his eyes. "Mobility, little supervision, a lot of privacy. Space? How big's his place? Does he have a shed or any outbuildings?"

"He has a huge, old garage in back," Lia said. "I saw it when I borrowed his generator. I think it used to be a barn."

"I don't know if Charlie is Bucky," Peter said. "But he's sure got a sweet setup for a serial killer. We move him up the list. That leaves Jose and Anna. Let's do Jose next."

"Okay," Lia said. "Jose's married, so that gives him less freedom to skulk around and commit evil acts. He's got a really soft heart. He's got Sophie, three cats and a pair of ducklings, that I know of. All of his animals are rescues. He's always fixing something for somebody. He grew up on the west side. He's got a really big family."

"I don't think it's Jose," Jim said firmly.

"Why do you say that?" Peter asked.

"First, he's a really busy guy. He's maintenance supervisor for an apartment complex, and even when he's not working, he's almost always on call. He also does side jobs. And I think it would be hard for him to slip out in the middle of the night to shoot Luthor, having Karen in the bed next to him."

"You could say the same about Nadine," Lia pointed out.

"Older couples often have separate bedrooms and that would make a difference," Jim said. "Is there anyone who's been to Nadine's house? They might know."

Peter put a note on Nadine's page to check this out.

"But," Jim continued, "that's not my main reason for thinking Jose isn't our guy. I'm thinking Bucky thinks he's smarter than everyone else, or else he wouldn't believe he could get away with murder. Jose's just an average Joe. And he thinks he's an average Joe, and I think he likes being an average Joe. There's nothing grand . . . grand . . . What's that word?" He turned to Lia.

"Grandiose."

"That's it. There's nothing grandiose about him. That, and he doesn't hold grudges. I think Bucky is the grudge king."

"So maybe we move him down the list."

"If we move him down, we have to move Nadine down too," Lia said.

"Nadine doesn't work," Peter pointed out. "She's got more opportunity to pull something like this off. And she's a very intelligent woman. If she and her husband have separate bedrooms, she could do it easily. But quit stalling. We need to talk about Anna now."

"Do you need me for this?" Lia asked. "My head is spinning. I need a break. You already know my opinion about Anna from last summer."

"No, that's okay. Jim and I will finish this up," Peter said.

"Thanks. I'll take the dogs out back. You come get me when you're done." She left the table, opened the back door and called the dogs. She closed the door more firmly than necessary.

"Hoo boy," Jim said resignedly, as he gusted a sigh. "I don't think she likes talking about her friends this way. But we gotta do what we gotta do."

"Yep," Peter said. "So what's your take on Anna?"

"She's a smart woman."

"And?"

"She worked in advertising when she lived in Pittsburgh. Now she works part time for a foundation. She really enjoys the charitable work."

"Huh," Peter considered.

"Anna's a good friend. She does crossword puzzles all the time, and she uses them to distract people when their differences of opinion get too hot."

"So she knows how to manage people."

"I'd say so. She's very supportive to Lia."

"What else?"

"She's very even-tempered. Like Buddha. Except I don't think Buddha made smart remarks."

"So she lives alone, and works part time. Plenty of opportunity there," Peter said.

"And one more thing. She couldn't stand Catherine."

"So we put her at the top of the list."

"To be fair, a lot of people couldn't stand Catherine. Marie didn't like her much, either. Charlie thought she was plain nuts, and Jose called her the 'Princess from Jupiter.' As many times as he went over to her big fancy house to fix something for nothing, he had just as much reason to want to conk her on the head as anyone."

"But Jose had limited opportunity. He works days. If we factor in Terry's fall, our person had to be available during the day, before noon. That's Nadine; Marie, because she works at home; possibly Anna, depending on her schedule; and possibly Charlie, depending on his route."

Peter went to get Lia. She sat on the back porch, tossing a chewed up tennis ball for Honey, Viola and Chewy to chase. Peter leaned over, put his hands on her shoulders and dropped a kiss on top of her head.

"You going to be okay?" he asked.

"Yeah," she said, sullenly.

"You're a good friend. I know it's hard."

"How can you just put all your feeling aside like that? As if they aren't people you know? As if they're chess pieces?"

"Because you're so much more important to me."

"Oh."

"I don't know how I'd do it if it were people really close to me."

Lia stood up without comment. He put a hand on the small of her back and rubbed. "You ready to go back in?"

"Yeah." She opened the door and called the dogs. "Honey, Chewy, Viola, who wants a treat?" The dogs raced inside ahead of her and sat expectantly while she doled out homemade liver treats. "Good pups." She gave them each a pat, then joined Peter and Jim at the table.

"Getting back to business, I have the beginnings of a plan. We are proceeding as if Bucky were responsible for Terry's fall. Luthor and Catherine died late at night when nobody had an alibi. We have no idea when Bailey's Depakote was doctored. But Terry's fall happened during the day, when people can be accounted for."

"How do we check this out?" Jim asked.

"First, one of you needs to get Charlie talking and find out where his route is. If we're lucky, we can rule him out right there."

"Charlie only comes on the weekends," Jim said. "It'll have to wait until Saturday. It might be best if you do it, Peter. Since you're newer to the park, it would be more natural for you to ask him about his work. Lia and I have known him for years. It would be strange for one of us to ask him where his route is all of a sudden. You could do it like you just want to get to know him better. We just gotta pry you away from Lia so you're hanging with the menfolk."

"We also need to get our five to tell us where they were at the time of Terry's fall," Peter said. "This could be brought up if Terry comes up in conversation, then you could share something about where you were when you heard and what you were doing when it happened. Kind of like people reminiscing about where they were when JFK was shot."

"Terry would like that, except the part where JFK is a Democrat," Lia said.

Peter smiled. "Maybe wait until everybody is together and Terry's there and ask him how his leg is doing and and say something about that day. And if both of you pick up the conversation, others will be likely to share what they were doing. But this has to be natural. We don't want anyone getting the idea you're looking for alibis. Think you can pull it off?"

"I don't know . . ." Lia started

"Best if you don't force it. The opportunity may just present itself and you can go with it."

Lia pondered, but she didn't say anything.

"Think about it," Peter said.

"Another thing we want to know is if Nadine shares a bedroom with her husband. You have my permission to say I snore and ask her if she has that problem, and how she deals with it.

"Brilliant," Lia smirked. "I get another chance to complain about you."

"Use it for all it's worth. It's for a good cause."

Chapter 19

Thursday, September 6

John Morgan was worried. He was a tall, mild-mannered man of middle age with graying hair. His face was kind, with a strong nose and thin lips. He wore oversize round wire-rim glasses. His carriage was stiff due to calcification of the spine that had been progressing for more than twenty years. This condition, ankylosing spondilitus, was thought to have troubled Ramses the Great. Some people believe that the naturally fused spine can indicate a soul of extraterrestrial origins. John was not troubled by this idea. In fact, those who knew him well thought it likely.

John was a part time IT Technologist at the University of Tennessee. He lived in a small, clapboard house down a country lane on the outskirts of Knoxville. He'd been there for more than a quarter century. There was an ancient oak in the front yard where he'd built a tree house shortly after he moved in. At one time he used it for rappelling practice. Due to his infirmity, he hadn't climbed it in almost two decades.

He accumulated things, as people do. He tended to the tiny and his small house was crammed floor to ceiling with miniature objects. His most recent hobby was Legos. He spent hours erecting structures on his dining room table while his five cats looked on, often batting at the pieces while he tried to place them.

He housed many books about paranormal subjects. Small crystals perched on all available surfaces, including on top of his computer. Many were arranged together in bowls of sand placed in specific locations around the house. He had a statue of Buddha, sitting on top of a box. He put things in the box that required divine assistance. The last inhabitant of the box was a fried hard drive a company of Mac specialists had been unable to recover. John had saved all the information on the drive and credited a week with Buddha for this miracle. He performed this miracle for free. The next day he found over one hundred dollars during a walk in the park and he considered himself compensated.

John suspected he might need Buddha's assistance now, or at least in the near future, and he had no idea why. Usually he could tell when the people around him were in trouble. John could see auras and knew the storm-cloud gray of stress, and the muddy colors of rage and depression. No one around him was emitting worrisome colors. That meant it had to be someone he knew online.

John's physical movements were limited, but he had a wide acquaintance over the internet. Some friends of many years he had never met. Some had travelled to Knoxville to see him. He could not travel because sitting in a car, or sitting anywhere, for an extended period caused him excruciating pain.

He could not see his internet friends, but there were ways. His preferred position for meditation was the lotus position. That had been denied him for many years. He apologized to Miko, a Siamese, and Mr. Ray, a tuxedo cat, and removed them from the sofa cushions. He left Diggy and Bear on their perch atop the back of the sofa. He lay down, closing his eyes and going through his ritual meditation exercises with the intent of opening himself up to the knowledge which would clarify his feeling of unease.

His breathing slowed as he went deeper into the meditation. Colors appeared to his mind's eye. A dark, dangerous red. A blackish green he associated with chemical toxicity, some kind of drug. Muddy grays and browns he associated with depression. Depression settled in his chest like lead, anxiety made his heart race. Mixed in were a fogginess of the mind and a warm, healing glow. He allowed himself to experience this cacophony of colors and emotions. There was trouble, but also help, support of some kind. Whoever it was, they were not alone. He stepped back from the emotions and waited patiently for some hint of identity. He saw flower beds, and smelled roses and rich earth and mulch. He saw hands, tending.

GreenThumb. The name floated into his consciousness. Bailey, the landscaper. He ended the meditation, thanked Buddha and booted his computer. He logged in to the Crystal Bridge forum, where he'd met Bailey several years earlier. He went to his messages and opened an old one from Bailey, then clicked on her name to open up her profile. According to the dates on her most recent posts, she hadn't been on since early July. He checked out her last posts. Half of the thread was deleted. It was hard to follow, but it looked like Bailey was having a conversation with someone about a fringe theory of reincarnation. John was of the opinion that it was never acceptable to commit harmful acts, no matter your motivation. He wished he could see the other side of the conversation. From Bailey's responses, the other poster's arguments must have been compelling. *Bailey, Bailey, Bailey,* he thought, *what have you gotten yourself into?*

Something was calling Bailey to his attention. That must mean there was a way he could help. What was it? And how to contact her? He didn't have anything but an email address. That was useless. If she was online these days, she'd be posting in the forum.

He got on his computer and checked telephone listings for Bailey Hughes and came up with a blank. He found a B Hughes and looked up the address on Google Maps. The location was near Mount Airy. Hadn't she mentioned Mount Airy to him? That's right, she took Kita there, to the dog park. He dialed the number. It was Bailey's voice on the answering machine, but there was no more room for messages. What did that mean? What to do next?

Miko jumped in his lap and he scratched her head absently while she purred like a Maserati. Pushing wouldn't help. He set the cat down, then went into his dining room and surveyed the Lego castle covering the table. It needed some work on the drawbridge. He lost himself in the details of construction and let his mind wander as his cats gathered, eyeing the small, colorful pieces.

The memory emerged slowly, teasing. A project Bailey worked on a few months ago. She built a garden labyrinth with an artist. She'd posted pictures on Facebook. Who was her partner? He went back to his computer, disappointing his menagerie. He logged into Facebook and went to Bailey's profile, clicking on her photo albums. The last album she uploaded contained pictures of the labyrinth.

It was there in the album description. Lia Anderson. He checked Bailey's list of friends to see if Lia had a Facebook page. He saw the photo of the pretty artist and felt a jolt of certainty. This was her partner. He clicked on her face. Her profile was public, as he hoped it would be. He was not lucky enough to find a cell phone number.

He could message her, but her posts appeared to be infrequent. She looked like an irregular user. This was a small obstacle to someone with his talents. He noted the information she gave about herself, then set to work tracking her down.

John rubbed his forehead and stared at the information on the screen. Something was nagging him, telling him not to call yet. There was more he needed to find out.

He ran a search on Bailey and came up with two different items. The first was a newspaper article in June which named Bailey as the person who discovered a drowned socialite. The second took more time and trouble to obtain. It was a police report from July, charging Bailey with attempted murder in an assault on Lia Anderson.

No wonder he'd felt that warning tingle when he considered calling Lia. He wasn't likely to get cooperation from Bailey's victim. He went deeper into the police archives and pulled the file.

Lia's statement about the attack dovetailed neatly with the posts Bailey had made on the Crystal Bridge forum. Still, he knew there was more to the story than was in the report, or his guides would not be asking him to step in. The arresting officer was a Peter Dourson. Also present at the scene was Jim McDonald. He felt a pull as he read this name.

Chapter 20

Friday, September 7

Jim was pursuing an all time high score on Angry Birds when the phone rang. "McDonald," he answered.

"Jim McDonald?" Jim heard a Tennessee twang in the unknown voice.

"Yes, who is this?"

"My name is Trees. I'm a friend of Bailey Hughes."

Jim sighed, mentally. "What can I do for you, Mr. Trees?"

"I'm sure it must seem strange, calling out of the the blue like this."

"How do you know Bailey."

"We've been friends online for years. Mr. McDonald, I found out she's in a jam right now."

"You can say that." Jim, suspicious, fell back on his taciturn nature. He repeated himself, "What can I do for you?"

"I'd like to help her."

"What, exactly do you want to do?"

"Whatever I can. I'm stuck where I am, but I think there must be something. I'm good with computers. I can do research."

"How good are you?"

"I found you. I'm good enough that I'm not giving you my real name, and I'm using a prepaid phone."

Jim nodded to himself, conceding the point. "Why did you come to me?"

"Just a feeling. Was that a mistake?"

Jim tried to think like Peter. "Maybe, maybe not. Where do you know Bailey from?"

"I see her on Facebook sometimes, but before that I met her at the Crystal Bridge online community."

"You post there, do you?"

"Not lately. I went back there yesterday and saw that Bailey was having an odd conversation with someone. It worried me."

Jim took Trees' number and asked what his screen name was at Crystal Bridge. He found out that Trees went by the moniker, "ClimbTrees." He said he'd give it some thought and call back in a day or two. Which would be after he'd had a chance to talk to Peter.

~ ~ ~

Friday Evening, Late

Peter was exhausted and frustrated. He and Brent had spent the evening interviewing witnesses in a domestic violence case where an estranged husband and wife got into a fight when they ran into each other at a cookout. Though the husband remained in jail, it was looking increasingly like the wife had started hostilities. Witnesses stated she'd she swung a beer bottle at his head. She'd apparently objected to him parading his new girlfriend around in front of her friends.

Peter mentally shook his head. Chances were, this couple would continue to antagonize each other until one of them moved out of state or else ended up dead. At least he had Lia to come home to, for now. It was the one bright spot in a long day.

The living room was dark when Peter opened the front door. Moonlight entered through the window and painted Lia's face where she lay sleeping on the couch. It crawled up the arm she'd flung over her head. It lingered on her throat and left intriguing shadows below. She looked so pretty, with her lashes resting against her cheeks, her mouth soft, relaxed and slightly parted, and her hair splayed in whirlpools and eddies around her face.

Peter crossed the room quietly and sat down on the edge of the couch. He feathered his fingers up the underside of her arm, feeling the softness of her skin. She did not wake. He ran his hand up her wrist, felt her fingers as they entwined with his reflexively. He leaned over and nuzzled the juncture of her neck and shoulder. She murmured in sleep. Then her other hand came up and stroked the back of his neck. He didn't know if she was awake or dreaming.

Warm breath caressed his cheek. Then panting, rapid and shallow. He turned his head and met Honey's tongue with his nose.

"Aw, fuck."

Lia jolted awake. "Peter? You're home. What time is it?"

"Past Honey's bed time."

"Hey, Girl." Lia removed her hand from Peter's neck and stroked Honey's head. "She probably wants to go out."

"Can I toss her out and leave her there?"

"No," Lia said primly. "You're an officer of the law. You know that people steal dogs."

"That was the idea," he muttered.

"You go clean up. I'll put her out."

He was toweling off his head when he heard the bathroom door creak open. Cool air from the hallway startled goose-bumps on his skin. He smiled to himself, anticipating the touch of Lia's hands on his back. A small tongue flicked his calf. He looked down to see Chewy licking water off his leg.

"Scram!" Peter yelled.

Chewy looked up at him and whined.

Lia poked her head in the door. "Don't yell. It encourages aggression."

"Get the rat out of here," he ground out.

"You'll hurt his feelings. Come here, Little Man, let's go find some treats."

He tossed on pajama bottoms and went into the kitchen. The trio of dogs sat grinning while Lia handed out treats. He sat down at the kitchen table and scowled.

"Do you always reward them when they behave badly?"

"Don't be such a grouch. They're just being dogs."

"What about me, don't I get a treat?"

She sat down in his lap and rested her hands on his shoulders. "Poor baby. Bad day?"

"Anyone ever tell you that five's a crowd?"

"Just ignore them. They'll go away."

"They're panting like the audience in an x-rated movie. I can't ignore them."

She kissed him. "That better?"

"They're still watching."

She sighed. "Honey, Chewy, Viola, go to bed."

The trio stared at her.

"Now!"

The three slunk off into the other room with whines and grumbles.

"We're alone now," Lia said.

"Kinda killed the mood."

She teased his mouth with her finger. "What mood was that? I was asleep."

"I came in and you looked so pretty with your hair all swirly around your face. You had your arm up with your wrist against your forehead like an actress in a silent movie. I was going to kiss you awake when Honey stuck her nose in."

"I'm sorry I missed it. Maybe you could show me?" She cajoled.

He stood up with her in his arms and headed for the bedroom. "Maybe I could." He kicked the door shut and placed Lia on the bed. "It was like this." He rearranged her arms with one stretched over her head and the other across her forehead. "You pretend to be asleep. I'll go out and come back in again."

She shut her eyes. Maybe she drifted off. She never heard him enter. She became aware of twin touches, gentle as a wish, delicate as fairy wings, on the insides of her upper arms. She kept still as the sensation floated up both arms to her wrists, then off her fingertips. Fingertips traced down her neck to the front of her shirt, slowly unbuttoning, smoothing the fabric back as each button was undone. She felt his breath, softly blowing on the thin, exposed strip of flesh from her collarbone to her waist. He followed this with soft kisses back up to her collarbone, then nuzzled and kissed the inside of one arm, then the other. He continued this torturous assault up to the palms of her hands. Then it stopped. She felt the loss of him then, and considered opening her eyes. Suddenly she felt cold steel around her wrists, heard it ratcheting shut.

Her eyes flew open as her arms jerked reflexively. The steel bit into her wrists. The cuffs were wrapped behind a post in her headboard, preventing her from moving her arms more than a few inches. She felt a frisson of helplessness and opened her mouth to protest. He silenced her with a kiss, deep and probing.

His breath warmed her ear. "Trust me?"

She nodded desperately as she felt his hand on the button of her jeans.

Chapter 21

Saturday, September 8

Lia, Jim, and Peter sat atop a picnic table at the rear of the park. It was early. A light mist overlay the park in the predawn. There was a crisp feel in the air. Honey and Viola were playing tug-of-war with a stick while Chewy refereed, making calls in shrill yips from the sidelines.

Peter shook his head. "Six A.M.? It's still dark out. How do you do this every day?"

Lia bumped him companionably with her shoulder. "Sunrise is so pretty. Drink your coffee and enjoy the morning."

"Artists," Peter snorted.

Lia screwed up her face in a mock-quizzical expression. "Jim, who was it that said we needed to meet first thing?"

Jim pondered. "It wasn't me. Nope, wasn't you. Must have been our leader, here."

"Our fearless-except-when-it-comes-to-waking-up in-the-morning leader?"

"That would be the one."

"Oh, almost fearless leader," Lia batted her eyelashes, "How may we serve you?"

"Jim, hold onto my coffee for a minute, I think somebody needs a good swat."

"Can I interrupt," Jim asked, "or is this a private moment?"

"Sure Jim," Peter said. "What's up?"

"I got an interesting call yesterday. A friend of Bailey's from out of state. Somewhere South, from his accent. I can't figure out how he located me. Said he found out she was in trouble and he wants to help."

"How strange," Lia commented.

"Huh," Peter said. "What does he want to do?"

"He says he's good with computers and research. I'm thinking, if he checks out, we could use some help with background information."

"What did you tell him?" Peter asked.

"Not a thing. I just said I'd get back to him." Jim shared the rest of his conversation with the man called "Trees." ". . . He says he's a member of Crystal Bridge, under the name 'ClimbTrees.' I went and checked out his posts. Mostly stuff about white light and crystals and spirit guides. I don't know about all that, but he seems pretty harmless."

"I think I know who you're talking about," Lia said. "Bailey said something about wanting to go down to Tennessee and meet him. She's been friends with him online for ages. He saved her hard drive a few years ago."

"How did he do that if she's never met him?" Jim asked.

"She mailed it to him. Said she owes him her life. He saved all her financial stuff, everything."

"I wish I could run a background check on him. There's no way to do that, if he won't give you his name," Peter said.

"First Frank, now this guy," Lia said. "You're like a 'help Bailey' magnet."

"I don't know what I am," Jim groused.

Soon after, Charlie and Jose arrived, followed by Nadine, Marie, Terry, and a host of other weekend regulars with a horde of dogs.

Jim and Peter wandered off to hang with the menfolk. Nadine and Marie migrated over to Lia's table.

"What are you doing all alone back here?" Nadine asked. "I can't believe that nice boyfriend of yours just abandoned you."

"'Fraid so. Too much togetherness lately, I guess."

"How's that going," Marie asked. "Thinking about making it permanent?"

"We're tiptoeing around each other a bit. He works a lot of evenings, so it's not like we're in each other's hair all the time. But I still like having my own place. It's the snoring, for one thing."

"That handsome young man snores?" Nadine asked.

"Like a freight train." Lia crossed her fingers and privately begged forgiveness for the lie. "You ever have that problem with Lou, Nadine?"

"You get used to it, in time. But we finally opted for separate bedrooms. Too many midnight bathroom trips after he started having prostate problems. I can't say I miss the noise."

"Another reason I don't date men. Women have such delicate snores. No hairy, sweaty bodies, either," Marie volunteered cheerfully.

"Oh, I don't know, a hairy, sweaty body might be fun," Lia said. "Not that Peter is either hairy or sweaty."

"You girls make me blush," Nadine said.

Lia did not see a good opening for talking about Terry's fall. She figured she'd done well with her first foray into covert action, and was feeling smug by the time Peter rejoined her. "How'd you do?" She asked.

"Charlie is not our guy," Peter said.

"What did you find out?"

"His route is on the east side of town, over in the Kenwood area."

"Sounds like torture for Charlie and his red-neck, West Side roots."

"Maybe so, but it puts him out of the area for Terry's fall. Did you get anything out of Nadine?"

"Separate bedrooms. I still can't see her as a pistol packing granny, but I guess she has to stay on the list."

Chapter 22

Saturday, September 8

I had an epiphany of sorts. It occurred to me that there may be a way to make a stranger killing more satisfying. I thought it must be the eyes. If I could watch the eyes as someone was dying. To see it in their face as the life force fades out.

It would have to be someone whom I could physically overpower, in a relatively safe environment. While it would be handy to remove those with worthless lives who live on the fringes, such people are close to animals. Having animal instincts, they are likely fight back. Such people have to fight to maintain their miserable place at the bottom of the food chain. I decided someone with a soft, suburban background would be best.

The trick was to isolate them, remove the risk of getting caught. This part stymied me for several days. Then I thought back to my trip to Red River Gorge, and I realized there was an easy way to accomplish this.

I thought about taking Baby with me. Baby could be an asset in diverting apprehensions. But managing a dog along with other logistics could be troublesome. Baby whined at being left behind. I promised that if this time worked out, I would consider taking my darling along on another outing.

It was midnight when I left. I stopped several streets from my house and pulled up behind a new car. I put on my wig before I got out. I used a screw driver to remove the license plate. I chose a new car because the screws had not been on long enough to freeze in place. I replaced my license plate with the one I removed. I had already removed the plate from the front of my car.

I drove out I-74, past the Indiana border, to the westbound rest area near Batesville. This was only forty miles on the highway, but a state away, in another jurisdiction. The building was an ugly, blocky thing in the middle of a prairie. It was surrounded by young saplings. The only attractive attribute of this place was the view of the night sky, which I quite enjoyed. It was good to have something beautiful to look at, since I did not know how long I would be there.

I contemplated parking my car in the back, where it would not be seen. I decided that seeing a person at a rest area with no car out front might alarm someone, so I left it in front. My car is generic enough, and I had borrowed plates. I was safe enough, in this regard.

I sat on a picnic table to wait. It was twenty minutes before a car pulled up. I knew this by looking at the cheap watch I had purchased to replace the phone I left at home. I would not chance being traced to this spot at a later date.

A couple exited the car. This would not do. I needed a single woman, someone older than myself, if possible.

I waited another two hours and fifteen minutes. In that time, a family with a dog and two children in an SUV stopped. The parents were arguing. A large, burley man in a truck stopped. Two young men stopped, with the back of their car crammed with boxes. I imagined they were going to college.

In all that time I stayed at the picnic table, in the shadow of the shelter. I only got up on occasion to stretch my legs. I did get a cup of coffee from the vending machine. I was careful to wipe my prints from the coins I used and wore gloves while drinking my coffee. My wig was hot and uncomfortable, so I allowed myself to take it off when the rest area was vacant, and put it back on when a car approached up the access road.

Finally, a woman got out of an old Toyota with Kentucky plates. I could not tell her age, but her posture was bent and she looked tired. I felt, in that moment, like a predator about to cull the herd.

I strolled up the walk to the main building and went into the rest room ahead of her. I entered a stall and waited. She took her time. Eventually, she finished up in her stall and went to the sink to wash her hands. My heart pounded as I exited my stall and walked behind her.

I held a wire that I had bought at a craft shop. It had a toggle at each end, so the wire would not cut my fingers. She was looking down at her hands when I crossed my arms. I raised them up over her head and brought them down, looping the wire around her neck.

She looked up in surprise as I pulled the wire tight, garrote style. She stared at me in the mirror, not comprehending. She did not know me. I watched confusion and fear play out on her face while I pulled the wire tighter and tighter.

First she scrabbled at the wire, but that was useless. Then she batted ineffectually over her shoulders, at my hands. Her eyes popped and her tongue bulged out and slowly, she began to sink to the floor.

I kept the garrote tight as she went down in a heap on the floor and I pulled her head back so I could watch her eyes. Her eyes stayed locked on mine as I examined her face, looking for that moment when everything ended for her.

I never did see the light go out. I gradually became aware that her expression had frozen. Whenever that moment had been, the moment of life departing the body, I had missed it. I stood there and stared down at her, absorbing her face, thinking I should be experiencing something more. But she was gone. I did not need to linger.

I took a deep breath, willing my heart-rate to slow. I stripped off my gloves, turning them inside out. I shoved the wire into them and the bundle into my pocket. My wig had twisted around during our struggle, so I straightened it.

I walked out into the lobby and saw a man standing there, watching the bathroom door. He walked over to me.

"Was anyone else in the bathroom with you?" he asked.

"No, why do you ask?"

"I was meeting my wife, Karen, here at the rest stop. That's her car out front. But I can't find her. I thought she was in the rest room."

"I haven't seen her. Do you suppose she's walking around outside? It's easy to miss someone in the dark. Maybe she was around back when you drove up."

He grabbed onto this suggestion gratefully and followed me outside. As he walked around back, I got into my car and drove away. I got off the highway at the next exit and took the backroads to Cincinnati. I could not chance being seen by the highway patrol after he found his wife.

It was four-thirty when I got home. I finally realized that the couple must have been transporting a second car. It was a mistake that could trap me. I considered this as I showered to wake myself up, then got ready to take Baby to the park.

I arrived at the park earlier than usual, before any of my friends. I sat and sipped my coffee while I took stock of my situation. I had to believe that if they did not find me in the first hours, I would escape detection.

I had the wig and the borrowed plates to protect me. I was in a different state. I had no connection to this woman. I built a shield out of these facts, and I eventually calmed. I would get rid of the wig, the wire, the gloves, each in a separate place. Then there would be nothing to connect me.

I had thought it would be best if I did not talk to my target at all before I killed her. That was wrong. I should have chatted to her long enough to make sure she was traveling alone. Who would guess this one woman was being followed by her husband?

He might be able to describe me to the police. He at least knew my height and build. He probably knew the color of my car, maybe the make. It was doubtful that he had the license plate number. If he did, that would pull him into Cincinnati. On reflection, If I needed another license plate, I should get it away from Cincinnati. Perhaps I could have stopped in Harrison.

I do not believe I will be repeating this experience. I felt adrenaline, but no exultation. For the risk I took, it was not the reward I wanted.

Chapter 23

Sunday, September 9

Lia and Anna were sitting on their usual table, amid the regular morning crowd while the dogs milled around. It was a chilly morning, with the promise of a beautiful afternoon.

"What's the word, what's the word?" Terry asked as he strolled up.

Anna looked down at her newspaper to the clues she had circled. "Che Guevara's first name. Two, four, six, seven letters. Second letter is 'r.'"

"Che Guevara, man, what a prick. He liked to conduct executions himself. He once shot a six year old kid for stealing food out of the garbage. Said he had to make an example out of him. Fucking Liberals."

Marie arrived in time to catch Terry's rant. "Gee, Terry, how would you like it if we lumped you in with every psychopath who bombed abortion clinics?"

"That's not a valid comparison."

"Extremists are extremists."

"No Republican leader ever condoned . . ."

"Terry," Anna interrupted, "do you know his first name or will you pass?"

"I'm gonna pass on that one."

"Ernesto," volunteered Marie.

"Thanks," Anna said. "How about the name of an island in the Hebrides? Four letters?"

"Iona," Terry said, triumphantly. "What's next?" He strolled up to look over Anna's shoulder.

Maddie plodded up and shoved her head into Lia's lap, looking for a scratch. Lacey jumped up on the table beside her. This caused Viola to raise her head, warning Lacy out of her territory. Lacy ignored her. Viola pretended she didn't care. Lia looked up to see Roger and Jose approaching. "Hey, Roger, Jose, how are you?"

"I'm good!" Roger said. "Dija hear? Gina's back."

"I didn't know," Lia said. "How did that happen?" She felt a nudge in her side. Anna didn't want her encouraging Roger. Too late.

"I tole her about all them girls likin' me at Terry's AA meetings and she got jealous. I was tellin' her it was okay she was gone, but I needed the car back, and she came over an' fixed me a big dinner. I couldn't believe it. She said she didn't want me looking at all them women and she didn't want me goin' to meetings, either. She said I didn't need to be thinkin' about nobody but her."

Jose rolled his eyes. Anna rolled her eyes. Jim rolled his eyes. Marie's eyes nearly rolled into the back of her head. It was an eye-rolling extravaganza. Terry didn't notice because he was busy squinting at Anna's puzzle. "Why do you always do these in ink? I call that the height of arrogance. It makes it hard to read when you've made a mistake and have to cross it out."

Nadine, always polite, did not roll her eyes. She patted Roger on the arm and said, "That's very nice, Dear. I'm happy for you."

"Yeah," Roger enthused, "she was bein' real sweet. She said we needed to get away, just the two of us. I'm taking her to Disney World."

Nadine's polite smile froze in place. "I'm sure you'll have a lovely time."

"I never been to Disney world. Gina said she'd ride the roller coasters with me. They say it's real pretty down there. You ever been to Disney World?"

"Roger," Jose interrupted, "you talk to the boss about taking off?"

"Oh, yeah, I gotta do that. An' I need someone to look after Maddie an' Lacy."

"I'm sure somebody will be willing to do that. I think the trip is a great idea," Marie offered.

"Lia, I'll see you at Renee's later," Jose said. "C'mon, Romeo, I gotta get Sophie home. Don't be late Monday. You don't want to piss off the boss if you want vacation on short notice."

"Right," Roger agreed happily.

As the pair took off with their dogs, Nadine turned to Marie and said, "I can't believe you want to encourage this ship of fools."

"I'm hoping ten hours in a car with Gina will knock some sense into him."

"Dammit," Lia said, "I thought I was helping him out by conning him into those AA meetings. Now she's got her Lee's press-on nails into him even deeper than before."

"You never know," Anna said. "Marie may be right. Nothing like a vacation together to break up an unhappy couple."

Chapter 24

Sunday, September 9

Roger is taking Gina to Disney World. Such a ridiculous couple, and such a ridiculous place. As soon as I heard, I knew this was my opportunity. The plan emerged, full blown, Athena from the head of Zeus. A way to pursue my hobby. Ideas and particulars continue to shower like spring rain. I want to dance, like Gene Kelly, as it pours. It would not do to let my elation show. I must act normal. I have a lot of work to do in a very short time.

Chapter 25

Sunday, September 9

Lia held the PVC pipe upright while Jose tamped dirt around the base. Renee stood off to one side, watching. A breeze rising above the edge of the overlook flirted with her hair. Jose's knees cracked as he stood up and dusted off his hands. "I just want to check one more time with the level to make sure it's straight."

"Sure, Jose," Lia said. "What do you think, Renee?"

Renee eyed the ten foot tall piece of four inch diameter pipe. "Will my sculpture be that tall?"

"You betcha," enthused Jose.

"It might make sense to make it a little shorter, depending on what the shadow does on the equinox," Lia said. The women walked away, the better to take in the whole site.

"It will be bigger around, won't it?"

"Of course, this is just to give us an idea how the shadow will fall. I had an idea." She gestured to the poster-board cone attached to the top of the pipe, forming a pointed tip. "What did you think of the drawings I left with you?"

"They're wonderful. I love all the colors. I was wondering about the one with the flat sides and pointy tip. What did you call that?"

"The obelisk."

"Yes, that one. What made you come up with that?"

"I was thinking that we needed the point so that the tip would line up exactly with our marker on the equinox. The marker itself would be larger, of course. but the point would connect with a certain spot in the design on the right day. I know we were thinking about a shape that was more organic. But I don't see another way to get the precision you would want for a solar marker."

"Hmm. I don't know . . ."

Lia glanced over, saw Jose still taking readings with his four foot level. "It will still be quite phallic, you know," she said confidentially. "But it's early days, yet. I'll keep thinking on it. We'll create the penis of your dreams for you."

Renee laughed. "I haven't enjoyed myself this much since I don't know when. So are we going to have a bit of Egyptian flavor to this?"

"Only in the shape of the standing piece, if that's the one you decide on. I'm not aware of the Egyptians having solar markers, though they did lay out their pyramids and temples in a map of the sky."

"Really? How fascinating. So you'll be back on Saturday, the twenty-second? "

"Absolutely, I'm looking forward to Esmerelda's eggs Benedict."

Renee went back into her house as Jose packed up his tools. "You carry the level," he directed, "I've got the post hole digger and the rest of it." They loaded everything in the back of Jose's van.

"Thanks for helping me with this. I know you've got a lot on your plate," Lia said.

"I like doing your stuff, it's always real interestin'."

"So tell me, was today the first time you heard about this trip to Disney World?"

"It sure surprised me. The only reason she's being nice is she wants to keep that car."

"I figured that much out. I wish he'd keep going to meetings a while longer."

"Fat chance of that with Gina back. I hate to say it, but I think the only thing that will help the guy is finding another girlfriend. You know Gina won't ever give him any respect. I swear, there's no talkin' to the guy. But he still comes to work every day. He's a hard worker. I don't know what I'd do without him."

"He's a nice man. It's a shame he's willing to live that way."

"Yep, I don't get it. I don't get it at all."

~ ~ ~

Peter put down the phone and considered the tablet in front of him. He tapped his pen on his notes, thinking. With a sigh, he dropped the pen and sat back. He stared out the kitchen window into Lia's tiny back yard, where the dogs were enjoying the sunshine. Lia had gone to Renee's with Jose and wouldn't be back for hours.

He wondered if he was asking for trouble. He had no business creating an ad hoc team of amateurs. Trees seemed okay, from the conversation they'd just had. He wasn't too sure about the man's woo-woo inclinations, but he seemed to know his way around the internet, better than a law-abiding citizen should. Which was why Trees wasn't giving him his real name and insisted on using a prepaid cell-phone. Well, if he was getting into bed with a hacker, the less he knew, the better. He decided this would be his only contact with the him. In the future, he could deal with Jim, if Jim was willing. Hopefully, Mr. Trees' contribution would allow them to solve this quietly, without having to ask a lot of questions. He'd see how the man did. At the very least, he was out of the state, so there was no question that he was involved in the murders. And no chance that he would let something slip to the wrong person.

Jim was smart and honest, but with his unruly beard, rumpled clothes and gruff manner, might not be the best person to send out making inquiries. Still, he had an excellent mind and it was never a bad thing to have a good mind to bounce things off of.

Then there was Lia. She was personable and could look professional. People responded well to a pretty woman. But Lia was still fragile and lacked objectivity. At least she realized that about herself. He wasn't crazy about tip-toeing around her emotions. And what if she got into trouble? He'd never forgive himself.

He had a cracked team of Keystone Kops going up against an experienced predator. Not his idea of good odds.

He wished he could bring Brent in on this. Brent was on the case last summer, when there was a case, and he knew the history. But at some point, there would be explaining to do, and he would not be doing Brent any favors by involving him in a shady investigation. He was going to be too busy keeping his own ass out of a sling to protect anyone else.

Chapter 26

Monday, September 10

Peter and Jim sat alone at one of the tables in the back of the park. Lia was tossing balls with Kita, Honey and Viola. Fleece was leaning against Jim's leg and Chewy was making his usual rounds, checking for reckless squirrels, abandoned meat trucks, and possibly, alien invaders.

Jim nodded to the other end of the park where a crowd of regulars watched the canine rodeo in progress. "Hard to grasp that one of those folks has been taking down my friends. Doesn't seem possible, does it?"

Peter shook his head. "Have you had any new thoughts since the last time we met?"

"I've been wondering why we don't talk about the victims. On the cop shows, they always talk about a victim profile."

"I've been thinking about that myself, and I haven't come up with any good ideas. You've known them a long time. What do you think?"

"Catherine and Luthor were a lot alike, very self-centered. Terry's very outspoken about his political opinions. Bailey didn't always express her opinions, but she has those New Age beliefs."

"A real mixed bag. What did they have in common? What would make someone go after them?"

"One thing I could say about all of them is they were different. They didn't always play well with others. If you didn't have a sense of humor, any one of them could rub you the wrong way. You might say they're all odd ducks. Maybe something about that made them targets."

So you think our killer doesn't like people who are different? Sounds like bullying in grade school."

"It does. And this place is full of odd ducks. None of us fits into a nine to five routine."

"So that makes everyone a target?"

Jim pondered. "Well, there's odd ducks, then there's odd ducks. We've had a few out here that had real mental problems, but they either tend to isolate themselves or people knew to avoid them. All of the folks we're talking about are social enough to be a regular part of the crowd. It's just sometimes any one of them could be hard to take, first thing in the morning."

"Huh. So you think all our victims were targeted because they ruined someone's coffee?"

"Coffee is serious. You don't want to mess with someone's coffee. You like someone messing with you first thing in the morning?"

"Good point. So if we look at it that way, who do you think is next?"

"Most folks come here for two reasons. They need to let their dogs out, and they want a little company. We've got a lot of different kinds of folks, and mostly we get along okay. Generally, we're able to look past our differences. Everyone who goes to the trouble to take their dog to the park, they gotta love the dog, and when you can see the love in somebody, it helps you over the rough spots."

"Interesting."

"I don't think it's just being odd. I think our victims were provoking, in a way. I don't know if provoking is the right word, but they seemed to stir people up, whether they meant to or not."

"So who's our next contentious odd duck?"

"Not Lia."

"Why do you say that?"

"She does more listening than talking. And she'll offer an opinion, but she avoids arguments. Her choice of diet makes her strange enough, but it's not like she's talking about her bowel movements at seven a.m. She doesn't push it on anyone."

Peter got a quick mental picture and decided to be grateful Lia was willing to co-exist with his Pop Tarts. "So, not Lia. Then who?"

"The two people who seem to stir things up the most right now are Roger and Marie. Now, Marie mostly picks her target. She waits until someone else is going good, then she'll egg them on or go head to head with them. She wouldn't rile up somebody minding their own business."

"Then if Marie's our killer, she might be her own next target."

Jim chuffed out a laugh. "Something like that."

"What about Roger?"

"Roger complains about his problems, and then he won't listen to anything anyone has to say. The man is a broken record. That can get down right annoying. Then there's all his talk about wanting to commit suicide. Someone might want to help him along."

Lia came back and gave Peter a quick kiss before she sat down. "I can see you two plotting."

Peter took her hand and bounced it on his knee. "I guess we were. Jim's got a theory."

"And what is that?"

"He thinks each of our victims became a target because they spoiled our killer's morning coffee."

"Jim, you can't be serious."

"Think about it. They all stirred people up."

"Not Bailey."

"I know Bailey was your friend, but a lot of people don't hold with her New Age stuff. Some folks think it's crazy, and some folks think it's demonic," Jim explained.

"Oh, and what do you think?" Lia challenged.

"I'm a man. I don't think."

"You got that right," Lia sniffed.

"If Jim's right, who do you think would be the next target?" Peter asked.

"Oh, Marie or Roger, no doubt. Neither of them have any filters. That means I'm not a target, and you can go home, Romeo." She batted her eyes in an act of sarcasm.

"I'm crushed. I still think you're in the middle of this somehow. Luthor was your boyfriend. Bailey was your partner. Catherine was your patron."

"And Terry was my secret lover?"

"Jim, do I need to worry here?" Peter asked.

Lia gave him a pointed look. "Ha Ha."

"Getting back on the subject," Jim interrupted, "let's think about this the other way. Who likes a peaceful morning and can't stand hearing about reincarnation and spirit guides?"

"Cheese it," Lia said. "We've got company coming.

"Hey there," she called out to Nadine and Anna, "What brings you all the way back here?"

"The manly men were getting robust in their conversation. The testosterone was flying," Anna said.

"We're looking for gentler discourse," Nadine added.

"You hear that, Peter?" Jim said. "We're not manly men."

"Jim, I think we've been insulted. We should pick up our dolls and go home."

"Oh, you know what we mean," Nadine said. "They were all guns and carburetors and stinking Democrats."

"They're talking about carburetors?" Peter asked. "They don't make carburetors anymore."

"That's got to be Charlie, working on one of his cars," Lia said.

"Yes," Nadine affirmed, "and since he's having problems with it, Terry offered to shoot it for him as long as he lined up a few Democrats in front of the car. He said he wanted a two-fer on the bullets. Then he said he'd have to use hollow points for maximum penetration. He said it would be poetic justice, since Liberals think we should all use mass transit instead of owning cars."

Lia turned to Peter. "Look at what we missed."

"This is your secret lover?" Peter muttered into her ear.

"No whispering, you two," Anna said.

"Private joke. Sorry, We'll be good, won't we, Peter?"

"Yes, Ma'am," he nodded, looking at two prime suspects and wondering which of them had the nerve to pull the trigger. "So you ladies don't hold with guns?"

"Lou and I used to target practice when we were younger," Nadine said. I haven't picked up a gun in years. It's not the guns so much as all this talk about what they want to do with them. Once they get going, they all talk like they'd eat their young."

"I've never had a taste for guns myself," Anna said. "It's not like you can do anything productive with them."

Marie joined them in time to catch Anna's comment. "Sure you can," she said. "You can produce fertilizer. And some people would do so much more good as fertilizer than they do walking around."

"Marie!" Nadine scolded.

Marie shrugged. "You want me to make a list?"

~ ~ ~

Mr. Ray crouched on a stack of papers, taking the occasional swat at John's mouse for entertainment. Miko curled in John's lap, undisturbed by the machine-gunning of computer keys.

John's favorite guilty pleasure was breaking into the IRS. Always for a good cause, of course. Tax returns could be so informative. After the tax records, he pulled police records. Then came credit reports and credit card records. Then phone records. Last, just for fun, he tapped into an online record check site, so he could pull up names and addresses of former neighbors without much sweat.

He downloaded all of it onto two thumb drives to keep it off his hard drive. Everything was nicely organized into a folder for each target. It was a good evening's work.

His back was aching more than usual from the hours of sitting. He popped a chicken dinner into the microwave, then ate it while walking around the kitchen to ease his back. He fed tidbits of the chicken to the cats while they sat at attention, licking their muzzles.

He and Peter had agreed that Peter needed to stay away from these documents. John had offered to review everything and not send any documents, but that made little sense since John didn't know the events or the people.

After dinner, he packed up one of the thumb drives, being sure to wipe his finger prints first. Tomorrow he'd overnight it to Jim McDonald from a non-existent address. But now he would meditate with the packaged thumb drive. He felt an ugly smudge on the thumb drive, a darkness that might not be reflected by the records themselves. Maybe Buddha would help him figure out what it was.

John placed the packaged thumb drive under the Buddha. He lay on his back, on the sofa with his knees raised to ease the pain. He figured Buddha would understand. He closed his eyes and requested a vision that would shed light on the killer's identity. Eventually it came, floating in his mind. A yellow cupcake. Only this was flat on top, like it fell in the oven. And the bottom was brown. There was no icing. Literal? Metaphorical? He asked for more but didn't get it. Should he share this with Jim? No, Jim would think he was crazy.

Chapter 27

Wednesday, September 12

Lia pulled a chair beside Jim so she could look over his shoulder as he opened the flash drive he'd received that morning. She jolted as Kita nosed her arm. "Geezelpete. You got a paper towel around here somewhere? Kita just landed a streamer on me."

"Kitchen counter," was Jim's terse reply.

"Poor baby," Lia said, scratching Kita's head. "You can't help it, can you? Don't you worry, we're going to get your mom back for you." Jealous, Fleece nosed in under her hand. Kita snorted and went to curl up in the corner. "So you're the boss around here. Okay, I'll pet you, too." She got up and went into the kitchen.

"What am I looking for?" Jim yelled from his office.

"Credit card reports. We're hoping someone was dumb enough to buy ammo and leave a record." Lia returned to Jim's office and they started poring over a year's worth of charges for more than twenty cards.

"Geez," Lia said. I have exactly one credit card, and it's tucked away in a drawer. Then I've got one debit card. How many do you have?

"I've got a debit card and three credit cards."

"Check out Marie. She's got her LL Bean card and her Shell card, a BP card and a Kroger's card. Next thing you know, she'll have a White Castle card that gives premium points you redeem for sliders."

Jim grunted. "This type's too tiny for my eyes. I'm going to zoom in."

"I can't believe he was able to pull up all the receipts."

"I suspect this thumb drive could get Mr. Trees put away for a long time. Which is why we're looking at it, and not Peter. Peter needs deniability."

"Then what do we do when we find something and it's time to go official with it?"

"If we find anything on these records that the police need to have, we print it off on a public computer and send it in anonymously. We make sure we don't leave any fingerprints. No licking envelopes, either."

"Been watching CSI again, have you?"

"I'm old, not stupid."

"Geez Louise. Marie spent two hundred and seventy dollars at some place called Fiona's Playpen. Do we even want to know what that's for?"

"Nope." Jim pulled up the receipt anyway.

"Thigh high boots, a patent leather corset, strawberry flavored edible underwear. . . . What's a ball-gag?" Lia turned to look at Jim and noticed his face was bright pink.

"Nothing you want to know about. Nothing I want to know about." Jim pushed away from the computer. "Hoo boy. I don't know about this. We could end up with more than we bargained for. We have to look them in the face tomorrow. How are we going to do that?"

"I don't know. But I'm starting to understand what Peter was going through when he couldn't tell me everything he knew about Luthor. Look, we don't have to go through every receipt. We'll look at the charges on the statement and just pull up receipts for places that might sell ammo. We ought to look at book stores, too. Reading material could be important."

Jim pulled up a book order and started reading. "*Advanced Cabinet Making, Mac OS X, the Missing Manual, Velvet Handcuffs, Lesbian Space Sluts from Planet Libido. . . .* Here, you read this." He rolled his chair away from the monitor.

Amused, Lia took over. "*Pussy Tales, House Mouse, Backdoor Girl, Taming Talia . . . .*"

"Don't tell me, I don't want to know anymore."

Lia scanned the rest of the list. "Nope, no guides to butchering the human body, no *Murder for Beginners*."

"Aren't you embarrassed?" Jim asked.

"Nope. At least we know Marie has a life."

"I wish I didn't know."

"Look at it this way. We'll never have to wonder what to get her for her birthday."

"I don't give her anything on her birthday anyway."

"Take a break. Take the girls for a walk. I'll keep going through this. By the time you return, I should be done with Marie. Nadine's charges should be tamer."

There were no bullets on any of the credit cards. They finished up without anymore surprises. Nadine had a fondness for cookbooks and Diane Mott Davidson, as well as a taste for thrillers. Jim wondered if this indicated a blood-thirsty nature.

Lia said, "With *The Hunger Games* out, Nadine would just have to stand in line behind every fourteen year old girl in the country."

Anna ordered a lot of puzzle books. She preferred mysteries to thrillers, including Jeffery Deaver, Patricia Cornwell and Nevada Barr.

"Considering how Luthor and Catherine died, don't you think our killer would be more the mystery type?" Jim asked.

"Let's see. Marie's into torture. We don't know if that's on the giving or receiving end."

Jim winced.

Lia continued, "Nadine's blood-thirsty and Anna likes sneaky stuff. I'd say that makes them all equally inclined to be murderous, wouldn't you?"

Jim's computer beeped to alert him to incoming mail. "I need to look at this. Do you mind staying in the living room for a few minutes?"

"No biggie. I can take a break."

When she returned, Jim had closed out his email and returned to the credit reports.

"What was that all about?" Lia asked.

"It's private," Jim mumbled as he ducked his head.

"What, you got a secret girlfriend?"

Jim blushed.

"You do! You have a cyber-girlfriend! Is she pretty?"

Jim shrugged, not meeting her eyes. "I think so."

"Where did you meet her?"

"There's this Catholic dating site," he admitted.

"Have you met her yet?"

"What is this, Twenty Questions?"

"You going to meet her?"

"I hope so. Now can we get back to work?"

"Whatever you say. I think it's awfully sweet."

"Well, don't tell anyone."

"Scout's honor," Lia swore, crossing her heart.

They continued pulling up receipts for another twenty minutes. Jim rolled away from the desk and sighed. "We've got that part done. It's going to take days to go through the rest of it, and I don't know if it's going to give us what we want."

"Okay," Lia said, "I'll bite. What do we want?"

"What we really want are suspicious deaths happening around Nadine, Anna, and Marie."

"How are we going to find those?"

"I've been reading up on serial killers."

"You have, have you?"

"And you've got two kind of killers," Jim continued. "Killers with random victims, usually thrill killers, and killers with specific targets. Now, our killer . . ."

"Bucky."

"Okay, Bucky. He's . . . ."

"She's. We're investigating women."

Jim huffed. "She's gone to a lot of trouble to target specific victims, using different methods. One thing I think we can say is that Bucky knows her targeted victims very well to pull that off."

"I'll go along with that."

"So the events we know about, the ones from the dog park, they started this past summer. Where was Bucky getting targets before then?"

"Good question," Lia said. "So we're looking at this from a sociological point of view, in a way. Everyone belongs to all these little groups. Family groups, work groups, dog park groups. For example, none of the evening dog park regulars are being picked off, as far as we know."

"Yep. Terry goes up in the afternoon sometimes. He'd hear about it and tell us if anything happened."

"Then you have neighbors. I'm thinking they'd have to be really close neighbors for Bucky to know enough about them or to even care. And if you go to school, there are the people you have classes with and then there are clubs and organizations."

"These people we're looking for," Jim said, "they would have had extended regular contact with Bucky. So I don't think it would be someone who was in a class with Bucky unless they had the same major and took a lot of the same classes. School's a really long time ago for everyone on our list. We're looking for people who were a regular fixture in Bucky's life. So where are we going to find the highest number of people in close contact to Bucky over the longest period of time?"

"Oh!" Lia said, "That would be work. Except Marie works at home and Nadine's retired. So how does that help us?"

I'm thinking we can get Trees to help us here. One person who knows if we're living or dead is Uncle Sam at the IRS. Uncle Sam also knows everywhere we've ever worked. And Mr. Trees seems to know a thing or two about Uncle Sam. Or maybe he has other ways to find out who worked where and when, and if they're living or dead."

"Oh, I see, he can go through the work histories and see what he can dig up on the people working around them. If he could go through the payroll records for the school where Nadine taught, he could identify the people who stopped working there while she was there and figure out if their payroll stopped because they quit or because they died," Lia said.

"He'd know the easiest way to go about it, but that's the idea. With Marie, I don't think work is our best bet."

"I guess not, since she's a freelancer. So where do we look?"

"That's easy," Jim said. "Her dog club."

~ ~ ~

Peter's Blazer was parked in front of Lia's place when she returned from Jim's. She bounced in the door. The apartment was dark. She called, "Peter? Where are you?" She got no answer. She spotted two empty beer bottles on the counter on her way out the back door. He was on the back stoop, staring at his bottle of Beck's. She sat down beside him and gave him a shoulder bump. "Hey, Roomie."

Peter grunted but didn't look up.

"Bad day?"

"Yep." He took a swig of his beer and remained silent.

"I'm sorry. Wanna tell me about it?"

"Might as well, you're going to hear about it anyway." His voice was full of disgust and futility, something she hadn't heard from him before.

"What happened?"

"I hate when it's kids." He continued staring at the bottle dangling from his fingertips.

"I'm sorry. How young?"

"She was four. Pretty little girl. Killed her, wounded her mother in a drive by. And everyone swears they saw nothing. The house they were shooting at is a meth lab, we're sure of it, but we have no probable cause for a search warrant. And the bozos living there were like, 'No, Mister Policeman, we don't know why anyone would empty a clip into our house and our cars. They must'a took us for somebody else. We were all watching Judge Judy when it happened and we didn't see nuthin'.'" He rolled his eyes and shook his head as he sing-songed in imitation of the dopers.

"Where was this?"

"Less than half a mile from here. Sometimes I hate being in the city. Fucking bangers."

"How will you catch the shooter if there are no witnesses?"

"Oh, somebody will get arrested and make a trade, or his girlfriend will get mad at him and turn him in for the reward. Or he'll use the gun again, and get caught. Eventually it will happen, but it always takes too damn long. And Brent and I get to keep banging our heads against the same doors until it does."

"Isn't there anything you can do about it?"

"Narcotics is going to push on the meth lab. If we have something on them, they'll give up the shooter fast enough."

"So what do you want to do?"

"I could just sit out here and drink."

"Doughnuts for breakfast, beer for dinner. Must you be such a cop?"

"I yam what I yam," he intoned.

"Why don't I tuck you in with a Three Stooges DVD while I make some dinner? I was thinking shrimp, but this calls for burgers. You want I should grill you some cow?"

"You're going to make me eat whole wheat buns, aren't you?"

"White flour is just wallpaper paste waiting to coat your intestines."

"Great image, Anderson."

"I'll make coleslaw," she wheedled. She stood up and dropped a kiss on his head. "Would you like to keep me company while I cook, or would you rather go watch Moe twist Curly's nose?"

"Those guys are really ugly. You're prettier."

"I should hope so. Can you get the charcoal going?"

"Yes, Ma'am."

Lia watched out the window as Peter fiddled with the grill. Sometimes she forgot that when Peter went to work, he was down in the trenches, dealing with all the ways people hate each other. Being an artist meant she was in her own little world much of the time. She dealt with ugliness by shutting it out, and there was Peter, down in the mud wrestling with it.

He was in a mood she'd never seen before tonight. He didn't often talk about work. She hoped encouraging him to talk helped, like talking helped her in therapy. She'd do what she could to make things easier for him.

She'd resented being expected to baby Luthor out of his sulks, but this was different. Peter was hurting over something real. She'd thought she didn't like playing the little woman. Maybe it was as simple as context.

Peter wound up grilling the burgers, and it seemed to pull him out of his funk. They plowed through two apiece, topped with home-grown tomatoes and slices of cheddar cheese. Honey, Chewy, and Viola lined up for mini-burgers.

Peter was stacking dishes. He looked over at Lia and asked, "How did it go at Jim's earlier?"

"I wasn't going to mention it. You've had such a rough day."

"That's okay. I'm bringing it up."

"Jim's scandalized."

"Why is that?"

"We ran across a mail order charge of Marie's for a patent leather corset, thigh high boots and edible panties."

Peter barked a laugh that had Honey and Viola alerting in response. "What an image."

"You think it might be for Halloween?"

"What? And she's handing out edible panties for trick or treat? What flavor?"

"Strawberry."

"You mean strawberry, like the ice cream we just ate."

"Um . . . yes?" Lia said carefully.

He started laughing again.

"It's not that funny!"

"Oh, yes, it is. I now have this vision of the dog park as *Rocky Horror Picture Show*. All the dogs are howling while everyone sings 'The Time Warp.'"

Lia shook her head. "Out of all the cops in Cincinnati, I get the one with the weird imagination."

"No bullets, then?"

"Nope. Not even a BB. But Jim and I have a plan."

"Really? Let's hear it."

Lia explained how they could use Trees to identify possible murders.

Peter beetled his brows as he listened. "I'm not crazy about getting in too deep with a hacker, but it sounds efficient. Go ahead, if he's up for it. While he's doing that, you and Jim keep reviewing the information he already sent us."

"I owe you a big apology."

"Oh, you do?"

"Jim and I were looking at all this personal information about people we know, and now there's no way to un-know it. And I can't talk to anyone about it but you and Jim. I see what you must have been going through last summer. And I'm sorry I didn't understand."

"How sorry?"

"Sorry enough to borrow Marie's patent leather corset."

"That's pretty sorry. I'd ask you to put your money where your mouth is, but then the mysterious Mr. Trees would wind up in jail for acquiring that tidbit of information. You'll have to come up with something else."

She took him by the hand and pulled. "Come with me. I'm sure I can think of something."

Chapter 28

Thursday, September 13

The internet is truly a marvel. You can find anything there. Physical restraints, Ball gags, Rohypnol (Popularly known as Roofies) for chemical restraint, cases of Ensure, hospital gowns, a cattle prod. I made my list. Shopping on the internet does leave a trail. I can't have that, so I purchased a Visa gift card at Walmart and paid cash for it. I did my research and made my purchases while using the Roselawn branch library computers. I am not known there. I used guest passes instead of my library card to log in.

I set up a gmail account and used it to open new online accounts, using a neighbor's name and mailing address. I ordered everything 2nd day air, so that it would arrive while my neighbor was in Elkhart. I'll stop by early Thursday morning and leave a note on the door, asking the Fed Ex man to leave the packages on the stoop. These should arrive in the middle of the day. She is always getting packages, no one will think anything of it.

Chapter 29

Friday, September 14

"Did you know Nadine had an early marriage?" Lia looked up from the records she was scanning.

"She never mentioned it." Jim was sitting at his other computer looking at the Marie file.

"Aw, geez. Looks like there was a child, and an accident. Her husband and daughter both died. Her husband was disabled in the accident, then died a few years later. Poor Nadine. No wonder she doesn't talk about it."

"None of my business," Jim said.

"Aren't we the ironic pair, as we run amok through private files."

"Can't be helped."

"That's the NSA's excuse."

Jim stopped what he was doing. "Do you want to help Bailey?"

Lia sighed. "I just wish this wasn't the way."

"You think of a better way, let me know." He returned to his monitor. "Meanwhile, the sooner we get this done, the sooner we can forget everything we've read."

They continued plowing through megabytes of trivia.

"Hoo, boy," Jim said.

"What? Did you find something?"

"Marie's got a juvenile record. It was sealed. I guess we can thank Mr. Trees for this."

"What did she do?"

"Says here, arson. There was a fire at her school." Jim continued scanning the page. "Looks like she wound up in a juvenile facility. Court records show she went through years of therapy."

"Isn't arson one of those things Peter told us to look for?"

"That and bed-wetting. Don't think we'll find that in these files."

"We can always poll everyone at the park."

Jim snorted. "I'm sure everyone will want to answer that question."

"We'll have to follow up on the arson, won't we?" Lia asked.

"It'd be a good idea."

"Jim?"

"What?"

"What did you find out about Anna yesterday? I know you went through her file then."

"Nothing we don't already know. A couple fender benders, that's about it."

"Seriously?"

"Yes, Ma'am."

~ ~ ~

Friday Evening

The pizza had been sitting on the table, growing cold. That's where it was when Peter left the kitchen. Now the box was shredded on the floor and three guilty pairs of eyes were looking up at him. There wasn't a crumb in sight, though a few olives were scattered around. He guessed dogs didn't care much for olives.

It fired his seething temper. "Bad dogs!" he yelled. The trio slunk away. He grabbed another beer from the fridge and sat out on the back stoop. It wasn't their fault. He'd been distracted and hadn't put the pizza out of reach.

He'd come home to find the apartment empty. Lia hadn't taken the dogs, hadn't left a note, and wasn't with any of her friends. She wasn't answering her phone. The last person to see her was Jim. She'd spent the afternoon reviewing files with him, but had left around four o'clock. Hours ago.

He was torn between anger and fear. Anger that Lia hadn't let anyone know where she was, and fear that something very bad had happened, was happening at this very moment, and he couldn't do anything about it. That, along with a fruitless afternoon with Brent interviewing reluctant neighbors in the drive-by, had put him in a foul mood.

By the time the beer was half empty, he'd cooled down enough to decide it was cruel to sit out back and keep the dogs locked up in the house. Rationalizing that they deserved it did him no good. He let them out and tossed a couple of tennis balls for Viola and Honey.

It was ten o'clock when he heard the key in the lock. He waited until she came in the door and he could see that she was unharmed.

"Where the hell have you been?"

"Excuse me?"

"You heard me."

"I wanted to be alone. I had to think."

"You had to think with your phone off?"

"My phone was off? It must be dead." She had the nerve to appear unconcerned.

"I've been going crazy. Nobody knew where you were. I thought Bucky had you and was at this very moment, cutting you into very small pieces." Peter ran his hand through his hair as he paced.

"You called my friends? I can't believe you did that!" Lia's voice started to elevate.

"What was I supposed to do?"

"You could have just trusted me."

"Dammit, Lia, it's not about trust. Not when people are being murdered."

"Peter Dourson, I've been getting along just fine for my entire adult life without you. I think I can handle a few hours by myself."

"For Christ's sake, why do you think I moved in here? It's not for the pond-scum smoothies!"

"You mean, why did you blackmail me into letting you stay? I was never crazy about this set-up. I hate digging into my friends' lives, and right now, I'm not happy with you, either."

"Well, that sure makes two of us."

"And if you're going to keep yelling, you can leave. You don't get to stand here in my apartment and yell at me."

He heaved a big sigh and lowered his voice. "You know I can't leave."

"Well, if you hadn't been here in the first place, you wouldn't have known I was gone, and you'd have no reason to be angry." Lia walked to the linen closet and pulled out a stack of sheets and a blanket. She shoved them at Peter. "You can have the couch and the television. I'm getting something to eat, then I'm going to bed." She stomped into the kitchen. "What is this mess?"

"I brought home a pizza," he explained. "You weren't here and the dogs got it."

"You let them have a whole pizza? Crap. If any of them gets diarrhea, you can clean it up."

"If you'd have been here, I wouldn't have been so stupid with worry that I left it where they could get it. Aw, forget it. The salad's in the fridge. They didn't get that."

"Have you eaten?"

"I had some beers."

"That's not good enough, Dourson. Between the doughnuts and the beer, you're going to make yourself hypoglycemic. You need some protein." She dug through the fridge "I'll make some tuna salad to go with the greens. If you clean up this mess, I'll let you have some."

Lia set a hard boiled egg and celery on her cutting board. "You aren't here for my green smoothies?"

"I am so not here for the green smoothies."

"If you apologize for yelling, I'll apologize for not charging my phone."

"Will I still have to sleep on the couch?"

"Let me think about it."

Chapter 30

Monday, September 17

Lia and Jim spent more than an hour arguing over the best cover story for their phone interviews. They finally realized it would work better with a different story for each suspect. It was decided Lia had the most professional voice.

Lia geared herself up for making the phone calls by reviewing her notes and drinking some ginger tea to calm the queasiness in her stomach. She glowered at Jim, who was sitting at the other end of the kitchen table. "Stop staring at me."

"Yes, Ma'am. I will look out into the back yard and pretend you aren't there."

"Thank you." She took a deep breath and dialed the first number on her list. It was disconnected. An answering machine picked up the next three calls, one of them identifying the number as belonging to someone different than the person on Lia's list. She finally got a hit on the fifth call.

"Hello?" The voice was creaky with age.

"Is this Margaret Kovach?"

"Why, yes, it is. Who am I speaking to, please?"

"My name is Lia Anderson. I'm a volunteer with the Cincinnati YWCA. We're in charge of vetting nominees for this year's Turn Around Role Models. I understand you used to be neighbors with the Woo family?"

"Oh, my, that was years ago. What's this about the Woos, dear?"

"Marie Woo has been nominated as one of this year's Turn Around Role Models. We're looking for women who have successfully built productive lives after a troubled youth. We were hoping you could give us some background on her."

"So this is about Marie? Is she in Cincinnati, now?"

"Yes, Ma'am."

"What is she doing these days?"

Lia rolled her eyes and prepared to fib a little. "She has a very successful business doing technical writing. She's also very involved in animal welfare, and shows her Schnauzer at national dog shows."

"Goodness, all of that. Well that's nice. I always felt a little sorry for her."

"How so, Mrs. Kovach?"

"Her parents, they were immigrants, you know. And they wanted all their children to succeed. She rebelled against all that pressure, and the more she rebelled, the more they pressured her. She was a smart enough girl, but I think she was bored with everything they wanted for her. She liked excitement, that girl."

"What kind of excitement, Mrs. Kovach?"

"I don't want to cause her any problems. This was all a long time ago."

"No problems. We're looking for women with a troubled past."

"Well, then. She used to climb out her window at night. She and her friends would steal cars, mostly their parents', but they were too young to drive. I know she drank. I imagine she smoked marijuana, but I don't know that for certain. It was just something young people did back then. Do they still do that?"

"Do what?"

"Smoke marijuana. They called it grass back then."

"Yes, I believe they still do."

"Well, she and her friends crashed a few cars and got into trouble that way. One of the cars wound up in the bottom of a swimming pool. Can you imagine that?"

"No, Ma'am."

"It cost them plenty to haul that car back out. Cost them even more to keep her out of trouble. That car they picked up on the street. Neighbors left their keys in the visor. Asking for it, if you ask me."

"Mrs. Kovach, do you remember anything about the fire?"

"My goodness, I forgot all about that. You mean the fire at the school?"

"Yes, Ma'am."

"She sure got the blame for that. All her friends broke into the science lab and were fooling around with the chemicals. I heard it was some other boy who set the place on fire, but she was the one who got caught, and she wouldn't tell who was with her. You can imagine that really upset her parents."

"What happened?"

"This time they didn't bother keeping her out of trouble. She went to a reform school for a year. Then she ran away as soon as she got out. She was the youngest. All her brothers and sisters were gone to college, or graduated and working. Her family moved. Said they were downsizing since they didn't have any children at home, but I think it had more to do with Marie and everything that happened. You say she owns a business now?"

"She does, and she's doing very well."

"Well, that's good. I always liked her. Some kids get a wild hair, and there's no making them fit in, no matter how hard you push. But I never thought she was a bad girl. Is that what you wanted to know?"

"You've been very helpful."

"Is she going to get that award?"

"I can't say. But she certainly has a chance. Thank you for your time."

Lia hung up the phone. "Margaret doesn't think she set the fire. Says she took the rap for her friends. Everything else was just joy-riding and partying. She seemed to like Marie. She didn't say anything about her being mean or hurting anyone." She stretched her arms over her head. "Do you think we need anymore interviews on Marie?"

"How many more numbers do you have?"

"Three."

"Give them a shot, then let's call it quits for today."

One person hung up on her. One number was out of order, and on the last number she got an answering machine. "If we need to go back later, there are three numbers that might work. I'm glad you want to quit now. If I had to switch up stories right now, I might forget who I am and why I'm calling." She closed the Bucky book. "You sure you don't want to do some of these? You could do Anna's. That's the one where she's dating a very wealthy man, and his children are investigating her. You could be a private eye, couldn't you?"

"You're doing just fine."

"I'll bet."

~ ~ ~

The first thing Peter did when he got back to Lia's after work was pet the dogs. The second thing was pop a beer. The third thing he did was plop down on the couch next to Lia. She was engrossed in the TV screen and did not look at him.

"Sure is nice coming home to a pretty woman after a hard day's work," he said to nobody.

"Tell you what. After you move back to your place, I'll send you a blow up doll to keep you company."

"Ouch. What are you watching? Not 'The Bachelor', is it?"

"'The Bachelorette.' And if you touch the remote, I will break off your fingers and feed them to the dogs."

"There's got to be a ball game happening somewhere in the world right now."

"A great reason not to have cable."

Peter took a resigned pull from his beer. He decided to watch, so maybe he would understand. Watching didn't help. When a commercial came, he said. "Okay, explain it to me."

"Explain what?"

"Why do you watch this show?"

"I'm a girl. We were all raised on Cinderella. This is Cinderella, sort of."

"Is that what you want? Twenty guys panting after you while you wear evening gowns and fly to Tahiti?"

"Are you kidding? Did you see those heels she was wearing? And those nails?"

"Okay, forget the evening gowns. What about the twenty guys with hot jobs and styled hair."

"Nah. Those guys all want a high-maintenance female."

"You know those relationships never last, don't you?"

"Well, duh. I'd swear the girl who got picked on the last show has borderline personality disorder. I'm just waiting for that to blow up. So far it's still lovey-dovey, but he hasn't had to live with her yet."

"So what's the attraction?"

Lia sighed. "Look, I'm female. The Cinderella thing is hard-wired into all females."

"I thought you said it was bullshit."

"It is. So my romantic side gets a Cinderella fix, and my rational side gets to laugh at how unreal it is."

"So you're not buying into it."

"Nah. This show thinks romance is roses and champagne."

"It's not?"

"Anybody can buy a dozen roses and a bottle of Dom. It takes no imagination. Roses are about the most unromantic thing I can think of."

"So you don't want to be that girl dating a dozen guys at once?"

"Dourson," She looked him in the eye. "Do you buy into those 18 year old pin-ups with the silicone boob jobs?"

"Umm - uhh . . ."

"You do know they're airbrushed, right?"

"Well, yeah . . ."

"And you know they're not really real, right?"

"Umm . . . uh . . . right . . .?"

"So why do you look?"

"Uh . . . I'm a guy?"

"Exactly. Not that I want your porno laying around my apartment. Now, shush, the show's back on."

She leaned back against him. This time she gave him a play-by-play. "See that studly guy going off with Amanda? He thinks he's the hottest thing going. He's got a good line, but if you listen carefully, he's really competitive and he wants her to be his arm candy. He's the guy who will start sniping if she gains a few pounds. . . . Okay, this guy with the floppy hair? He's worried that Studly is getting too much time with Amanda, so he's going to interrupt. . . . This guy with the baby face, he's a single dad and he thinks he's more mature than anyone else, but whenever there's a problem in the house, he's in the middle of it. . . . Now that guy hanging back in the corner is the one she really likes, only Studly is too conceited to consider him competition."

Peter shook his head. "This is like a sport to you."

Lia shrugged. "You could say that. Kind of like getting a bunch of your pin-ups to play baseball."

Peter, being a cop, recognized a dangerous situation when he saw one. He decided not to comment. "So if roses and champagne don't do it for you, what is your idea of romance?"

"Hmm. It's not big gestures. I think paying to have the jumbotron flash a marriage proposal is a big waste of money. To me, romance is not about impressing someone."

"It's not?"

"Nope. Guys tend to be competitive, and they think the bigger and more expensive it is, the more romantic it is, and they're wrong. Romance isn't about money. It's about timing and imagination, and knowing someone, paying attention. That orchid you left at the studio for me was awfully romantic."

"I'm glad you think so." He kissed her temple.

"But if you just keep giving me plants, it starts to look lazy. You want to know what I think is romantic right now?"

"Go ahead, shoot."

"It's you trying so hard to understand what I like about this dumb show, when I know it bores you to death."

"How much time is there left on this dumb show?"

"She's about to give out roses, maybe ten minutes."

He slid a hand under her t-shirt and rested it companionably on her stomach. "Maybe after you've had your Cinderella fix, you can let me know what else you think is romantic."

Chapter 31

Thursday, September 20

"Okay, Fearless Leader, where do you want to start?" Lia opened the meeting by batting her eyelashes at Peter.

Peter reached into the fridge and pulled out a beer. "Want one, Jim?"

Jim shook his head.

"Just give me what you've got. Jim, you start."

"I have a list of alibis for Terry's fall. Jose and Charlie were working, like we thought. Nadine was gardening, that puts her outside and out of sight for much of the morning. Marie was working, that means she was at home with no one to verify. Anna was shopping, up by Northgate."

"So the men are out. And all the women are still in," Peter said.

"What if we pull up a credit card receipt for Anna, wouldn't that leave her out?" Lia asked. "It would have the date and time on it."

"That can be misleading," Peter explained. "Terry was up on that roof for over an hour. We don't know exactly when the ladder was booby-trapped, just when he fell. Plenty of time for someone to get from his place to Northgate and make a few purchases. And if she was smart, she would have made a purchase before, ran down to his house, fixed the ladder, and ran back up for more shopping. Unless you have enough receipts to show that she had less than thirty minutes unaccounted for, then it's not enough."

"I'm going back through her credit cards anyway."

"Go ahead, I'll be interested in what you come up with. How did the phone interviews go?"

"Lia should go into acting," Jim said. "I would have believed her if I hadn't been sitting here watching her."

"Aw, shucks. You're sweet," Lia said. "You came up with the scenarios."

"Enough with the mutual admiration society. What did you find out?"

Lia wrinkled her nose at Peter. "Marie was a delinquent, but she was mostly rebelling against strict parents. And the neighbor believes someone else set the fire she was convicted for."

"What about Nadine and Anna?"

"Neighbors say Anna was a straight arrow. Only child of an older couple. Spent a lot of time taking care of her dad after her mom died. Good student. Hard worker. Didn't date much, so the cover story of the rich boyfriend made the neighbors happy. They were sorry to see her move out of the neighborhood."

"And Nadine?"

"The most interesting thing we found out about Nadine was that she had a breakdown after her daughter died. She was doing some strange things, leaving the house half-dressed, walking out of stores without paying. Screaming at the neighbors for no good reason. The family stepped in. Her sister-in-law came to help out and they put her on some heavy tranquilizers. Xanax, and some others. She met Lou in grief therapy. Rumor has it that they started seeing each other before her husband died."

"Good stuff," Peter said, "but nothing points to anyone in particular."

"What's next?" Jim asked.

"We keep our eyes open and see if Trees turns up anything interesting."

"Good," Lia said. "I've got work to do on the solar marker. Jim, I'd like to come over to your house in a few days to look through Anna's credit and debit card records." She turned to Peter. "When I find all those receipts, can we take Anna off the list?"

He kissed her. "Find the receipts. Then we'll talk."

Chapter 32

Friday, September 21

I tsked as I made my way up the walk to Roger's small house this evening. The paint on the clapboard ranch was peeling and the porch listed. I carried a tote bag and a covered Chinet plate of my special goodies.

Roger opened the screen door before I reached the steps. "C'mon in," he said. "Maddie, Lacey, you behave. I was really surprised when you called and said you'd look after the dogs. I was ready to take them to a kennel. They'll like being home better."

The dogs sniffed at the Chinet plate and barked. "Not for you girls," he said to the dogs. He turned to me. "Whatcha got there?"

"I brought a treat for you and Gina. Mini-Cheesecakes. Is she here yet?"

"She'll be here in a bit. You know women," he laughed. "She takes a while to get ready."

"While we're waiting, you can show me where the kibble is and we'll have some cheesecake." I set the plate on the counter and peeled the foil back.

"Those look real good. You didn't have to go to all that trouble."

"No trouble at all. It's just a store-bought mix, no baking. Here." I pulled out one of the cupcake sized treats and handed it to him. "Try this."

"You have one, too."

"Of course." I smiled as he took the first bite.

"This is real good. I might not save any for Gina."

"Oh, but you must."

"Well, I gotta have one more, anyway."

He showed me the dogs' food and explained their routine. As he went on, his voice started to slur. I knew it was time.

"Roger, I'd like to see the basement."

"Huh? Yeah, sure. This way."

He clung to the hand rail on the way down. "Feeling woozy. Don't know what's wrong with me. Mus' be tired. Guess Gina'll have to drive. Anyway, here's the basemen'. Why'd you want to see this, anyway?"

"You look pale, Roger." I pulled up a chair. "You sit down. I'm going to get you a glass of water."

"'Kay," he mumbled.

I didn't get him a glass of water. Instead, I went back to my car and pulled out a pair of rolled-up cot mattresses. I carried these to the basement. I unrolled one on each side of the main room. By this time, Roger's head was drooping.

"Roger, Roger, wake up."

"Huh?"

"You need to lay down." He obeyed like a little lamb. He didn't question the presence of the mattress. "Now you need to take off your clothes."

"You wan' my clothes? Gina ain' gonna like that."

"Here, I'll help."

"Better 'n' better. But I'm awful . . . tired." He let me remove his shirt and pants.

"Gina . . . not . . . gonna . . . like . . . it," he half yawned, half sing-songed.

I pulled a hospital gown out of my tote bag and dressed him in it. By this time he was turning into dead weight. Once the gown was on, I pulled out handcuffs, a ten foot tie out cable for a dog, and a lock. *I handcuffed Roger, ran the cable through the cuffs and around a pipe in the wall, then locked it to itself. Satisfied, I gave the dogs cheesecakes and put them in the bedroom. I waited for Gina.*

Gina was put out that Roger had decided to take the dogs for a walk. But she took the cheesecake.

Chapter 33

Saturday, September 22, Autumn Equinox

Lia and Renee sat on the patio with a pair of lattes, watching the eastern sky as the gray gave way to blue. Dakini lay on the flagstones at Renee's feet.

"It must be amazing, having this overlook to yourself every morning. What a great way to start the day," Lia said.

"I'm blessed, and I know it. Harry and I were a couple of broke scholarship kids when we started out. Neither of us ever imagined we'd wind up here. I feel an obligation to enjoy every minute of it." She eyed the tent stakes and string lying on the table. "I thought you'd need more equipment than this. Last time you brought Jose and all his stuff."

"Today is easy. Look, here it comes."

The sun lifted over the rim of hills on the eastern horizon, spilling light and casting long shadows across the landscape. The shadow of the post stretched ten yards across the ground. Lia jumped up and quickly planted the spike at the apex.

"What do you think, Renee? Imagine a circle, this far from the post, all the way around. Is this too big?"

"It's bigger than I imagined. The shadow certainly stretches out, doesn't it?"

"Doesn't it, though? We can make this shorter, if you like."

"Not on your life! This is going to be wonderful. What do we do now?"

"I'm going to mark the other side." Lia tied one end of the string around the central pole, then walked it out to the tent stake, pulled it straight. She took a Sharpie from her pocket and and marked the distance on the string. "You stand right here, with your foot on top of the tent stake."

She walked around to the opposite side, then pulled the string tight. She visually lined up Renee's foot with the center pole, then using the string to mark the distance, planted the other stake.

"Okay, you can move now."

She rolled up the string and untied it from the post.

"Why did you have me stand here?"

"I couldn't see the tent peg in the grass, but I could see you. When the post blocked your foot, I was in the opposite spot."

"Oh, I see. Do you suppose they did it like this ten thousand years ago?"

"I wouldn't be surprised."

"So, are you ready for some breakfast?" Renee pulled out her cell and called Esmerelda in the kitchen. Esmerelda came out with two glasses of mixed orange and grapefruit juice, freshly squeezed.

Lia took a sip. "Renee, will you adopt me?"

"Oh," Renee laughed, "absolutely! I plan on it. So, how are your ideas coming for the final piece?"

"I have something to show you." Lia reached into her tote bag for a drawing pad, then flipped through the pages. She laid the open pad on the table in front of Renee. There was a three dimensional rendering of a pair of standing wedge shapes, as if someone took a slice of watermelon, cut it in half, then upended the pieces so the curved ends formed an arch that had a slit in the middle.

"This is very different from the other ideas we talked about," Renee said cautiously. "Tell me about it."

Lia mentally took a deep breath. "I kept thinking about the monolith and I wasn't happy with the things we'd talked about so far. Then it occurred to me that I wanted to mark the seasons with light, not shadow. So I created an arch with a slit in it."

"Interesting. Why is it made of wedge shapes?"

"With a slit in a square slab, you could line it up for the equinoxes, but the slit would be blocked on the solstices. So I cut away on both sides so that when the sun hits it at an angle, you'll still see the slit of light in the middle of the shadow."

"Fascinating."

"Now," Lia paused to take a sip of juice, warming to her subject. "Since the shadow elongates so much in the morning and evening, we can go for a stumpy shape in the sculpture, which prevents the sculpture itself from looking phallic. It's the shadow which will embody the . . . uh . . . male energy. So you can invite every art snob in the world to see it and none of them will make sexual references."

"Aren't you clever!"

"Better yet, if you like, we can make a removable frame to fit in the slit, set with cut crystals to represent life force."

"Or little sperm?" Renee's eyes twinkled.

"And when the sun hits it, you'll have rainbows all through the shadow. This is for special occasions. The rest of the time it can be displayed on its own stand in your house."

"Be still my heart. I knew you were a genius when I met you at Catherine's, but I never expected this. This is fantastic."

Lia flipped through the other drawings, showing Renee the sunburst design for the standing sculpture, and the leaf designs for the ground markers. They continued talking about options for the mosaic designs while Esmerelda served her famous eggs Benedict. Renee was right, Lia thought. The smoked salmon was fabulous.

Lia was still giddy with excitement when she arrived at the park that morning. Anna and Jim were still there. Anna was still working the crossword. The rest of the Saturday crowd was gone.

"Look, Jim, our girl is late, and she's smiling. Do we blame Peter for this?"

Lia laughed. "You can put your filthy minds back in the gutter. I was working this morning. It's the equinox."

"Work," Anna commented dryly, "has never made me giggle. Has it ever made you giggle, Jim?"

"Not like that."

Lia rolled her eyes and heaved a good natured sigh. "Okay, I'm excited," she bubbled. "This project is going to be huge. Renee has the imagination to understand what I'm trying to do and the money to make it happen. And she's a delightful woman. She had her cook make us eggs Benedict, fresh squeezed juice and lattes."

Anna's smile froze, just for a moment. "How wonderful for you dear."

Chapter 34

Saturday, September 22, Autumn Equinox

Roger woke with his head pounding. He was cold and his entire body was sore. He was laying on his side. In bed? Something was hissing. Were there snakes? As he clawed through the fog in his brain, he became aware that the hissing was not a snake. It was a voice. Maybe a really smart talking snake, then.

"Roger, you idiot! Wake up!" The snake hissed.

He tried to bring his left hand up to rub his eyes, but something bit into his wrist and held it back. He opened his eyes to see Gina glaring at him. Gina with her fried blonde hair in Medusa tangles. Mascara smeared under her eyes like an NFL lineman. The mascara smears matched the roots of her hair. She wore a pale blue hospital gown and sat on a mattress in an unladylike sprawl, creating an intriguing crevice under the hem. She was handcuffed, with a cable looped around the cuffs and behind a vertical iron pipe. He realized he was in the same state.

"I'm awake. Don't yell at me."

"I'll do more than yell at you, you stupid ape. Stop staring at my crotch and get us out of here."

Roger was slow to gather his wits. "What are we doing here?"

"What do you think we're doing here? Handcuffs? Basement? We're prisoners, you jackass. What's with Broomhilda and her magic cupcakes? Did you put her up to this? Is this your idea of some kinky sex trip? Disney World, my ass. I never should've listened to you."

"Gina, I don't understand any of this."

"Understand this, Bozo. You get me out of this right now."

"Such virulent invective. Where does all that anger come from?" The calm tone commanded attention.

Roger looked up to see her at the foot of the stairs, carrying two open cans of Ensure with straws in them. Gina's screaming had covered up the sound of her approach.

"What is this?" Roger asked.

She ignored him and looked at the fuming Gina. "Dear girl, I could hear you call me 'Broomhilda' all the way upstairs. That really wasn't nice."

"I'll call you worse than that, you bitch. Let me out of here!"

"Manners, manners," she chided.

Roger repeated himself. "What is this?"

She turned to Roger now. "Think of this as therapy. Couple's therapy. In your case," she looked at Gina, "a bit of shock therapy, I think."

"I'll shock you, you dried up old hag!"

"And here I came to offer you breakfast."

"That? Breakfast? You gotta be kidding me."

She sighed. "Okay. Therapy before breakfast. She set the cans down on Roger's workbench, then picked up a thirty inch rod with two short prongs on the end. "You will apologize for your behavior."

"Says you and whose army?"

She extended the rod, pushing the tip against Gina's exposed thigh. Gina shrieked.

"Don't hurt her," Roger yelled.

"I don't need an army, dear," she said mildly. Gina whimpered.

She turned to Roger, shaking her head. "This is who you've been pining over? Really, Roger? Very sad."

"Who are you talking about, Bitch," Gina sneered.

She continued to shake her head as she turned back to Gina and raised the cattle prod.

"Don't hurt her!" Roger yelled again.

"All right, Roger. I'm reasonable. I won't hurt her if you agree to take her punishment."

"Just don't hurt her," Roger repeated.

She pressed the cattle prod into his leg. Roger yelled.

"See how he loves you?" she said to Gina.

"Miserable jackass deserves it for getting me into this."

"Well, Roger," she asked, "you? Or her?"

Roger couldn't bring himself to ask for more pain He just repeated, "Don't hurt her."

"So, so sad. She really isn't worth it, Roger." And she shocked him again.

Roger passed out. When he woke up, she was looking down at him with a concerned look on her face. "This will never do. Gina would just let me shock you to death."

"I'm not the one trying to kill him, you old bat."

"See, all the pain I've caused you, and still she has no manners. She doesn't care what her behavior will cost you. It's pointless to punish you for anything she does. She'll never learn that way. It's okay, Roger. You just lay there and rest, and think about how pointless it is to give her anything because she just takes and takes and the only thing she ever gives back is abuse."

Roger lay on his side, curled into a fetal position. "Don't hurt her," he groaned.

"Yes, Roger, I'm going to hurt her. But that's how people learn."

Chapter 35

Monday, September 24

"I don't believe it!"

Anna looked up from her crossword puzzle. "What?"

"It's Renee. She's been threatening to bring her dog to the park, but I never thought she'd do it."

Lia jumped off the picnic table and ran to the park entrance, followed by her furry trio. She stopped twenty feet short of the corral. "I'd come closer, Renee, but I don't want these hooligans to crowd Dakini when she comes in."

Renee entered the corral with her beautifully groomed collie. Dakini sat and waited to be unclipped from her leash. "Look at that well mannered young lady. Do you think you could do that?" Lia asked her pack. The look they gave her had 'you've got to be kidding' written all over it.

Renee opened the inner gate, and still Dakini sat. Then Renee said something and Dakini bolted through the opening and raced to greet Lia. Lia patted her head, then Dakini set about the business of greeting Lia's motley crew, which was getting motlier by the second. The four dogs completed their round of sniffing. Honey made a play bow and raced off. The others ran after her.

"Geezelpete, Renee, if I had known Dakini was going to come here and show everyone up with her fine education, I never would have invited you. I'm going to put a sign on the gate, 'Obedience School Dropouts Only.'"

Renee laughed. "She doesn't do it on purpose."

"Yeah, yeah, yeah. She's so gorgeous. Look at her run. You must spend hours brushing her."

"It's not too bad if I do it every day. I've got to keep her coat up. If I don't, she sheds everywhere and Esmerelda would leave."

"And no more eggs Benedict," Lia concluded.

"And that would be so sad," Renee pouted.

The pair walked back to the picnic table where Anna consulted Terry about her crossword and CarGo lolled. Jackson busied himself digging a hole under the table.

"Anna, Terry, meet Renee," Lia said.

"Hi," Renee said, "I've heard so much about you."

"Thank you," Anna said. "So you're Lia's new patron. Nice to meet you."

"So, how's the crossword coming?" Lia asked.

"We're stuck on Hans Christian Anderson's birthplace. Six letters," Terry said.

"Not a clue," Renee offered.

"Me neither," Lia said.

"And who is the lovely young lady you brought with you, Renee?" Terry asked.

"That's Dakini," Renee answered.

"Ah, Dakini, the feminine embodiment of enlightenment, also known as the sky dancer. A popular Hindu figure."

"Only you would know that," Anna groused to Terry.

"You know your comparative religion. I'm impressed," Renee said.

"So," Lia said, turning to Renee, "you see Anna sitting on the top of the table. This is standard practice here, since it's the best way to avoid getting body slammed."

"Does that happen?"

"Often enough," Anna said without lifting her eyes from her paper.

Lia climbed up beside Anna, and Renee climbed up on Lia's other side.

"When in Rome," Renee said cheerfully. "How long have you been coming here, Anna?"

"Years. Since CarGo was knee high to a greyhound."

"That's knee high to a greyhound bus," Lia amended.

"Aren't you funny," Renee said.

"I discovered this lovely spot three years ago," Terry said.

Renee leaned forward so she could see past Lia. "So, has Lia told you about our project?"

"No, she said she was sworn to secrecy," Anna said.

"Oh," Renee laughed, "there's an aspect that is . . . um . . . personal. That I didn't want Lia to discuss. But I didn't mean to execute a gag order. Lia, you should show the latest drawings to Anna." She turned towards Anna, "They are simply brilliant. I've decided to adopt her and make her famous."

"And what project is this?" Terry asked.

"Lia's creating a solar marker for my property. Girl," she turned back to Lia, "you've been hiding your light under a bushel basket too long."

"Um . . . ah . . . geezelpete, Renee. I don't know that my stuff is what anyone would call 'high art.'"

"Nonsense. Look at the Impressionists. Pretty pictures marketed under a snazzy concept. All we have to do is find you the proper label and plenty of curators will eat it up. A number of them are secretly relieved when they can find an excuse to hang something pretty. . . . I know, we'll call it 'Ironic Naturalism'. What do you think?"

"Uh, Renee, there's no irony in my work."

"Oh, but that's the best part! I love it. Don't you love it, Anna?" Renee turned back to Lia. "Tell you what, when my sculpture is finished, I'm going to send pictures to some people I know. There's this curator for a lovely little museum in upstate New York. Seems a bit out of the way, but they're well endowed and totally connected. They need something for their grounds, and this is going to make them green with envy. Don't you think, Terry?"

"I'm sure it will," Terry said.

"Renee, are you planning to ship me off to New York?"

"Only temporarily, Dear. Cincinnati's a much more pleasant place to live, but it's a backwater for artists. You'll just have to commute. Of course, we could bypass New York and go straight for the Japanese. They do love a nice flower painting. They've paid millions for Van Gogh canvases. Imagine!"

"Renee," Lia protested, "we haven't talked about any of this."

"Poor Lia," Renee commiserated, "I'm overwhelming you. I just got inspired. I'm getting ahead of myself. Don't worry about it, it's not happening tomorrow. But anyone with half an eye can tell you'll wind up going places. Seriously, Anna, how can she not?"

"Renee," Lia pleaded, "lets just get your sculpture done first."

"Certainly." Renee patted Lia's hand. "When the time is right, we'll talk about it again. For now, just put it out of your head."

Dakini pranced up, and rearing, braced her forepaws on the bench. She dropped a dirty tennis ball in Renee's lap and woofed softly, with a winning expression.

"Well," Renee said to the dog, "since you asked so politely." She turned to Lia. "Would you like to come toss some balls with me?"

"Sure." Lia and Renee walked their furred ones to the back of the park where there were fewer trees. They picked up several tennis balls along the way.

Anna watched as they started launching balls for the pack.

Jim sat down next to Anna. "Who's that with Lia?"

Anna rolled her eyes. "That's Renee. She's decided to adopt Lia. Next thing you know, she's going to buy Lia a rhinestone studded collar and start walking her on a leash."

"Anna! That's a terrible thing to say," Jim said.

"She's only known Lia for a few months and already she has grand plans to make her famous. The woman is half Jack Russell Terrier. I thought I was going to have an aneurism. She's decided Lia's going to storm the Japanese art market."

Jim pondered this. "It's nice for Lia to have someone like that in her corner."

"I know," Anna sighed, "but that woman is tiring. Wait till you meet her. Terry, how about eight letters for 'irksome'?"

"Hmm," Terry said. Try 'annoying.'"

~ ~ ~

Peter was still in bed after Lia got home from the park. She stood, leaning against the doorjamb and indulged in aesthetics. The artist in her appreciated his unconscious pose, arms and legs haphazardly consuming as much of the queen-sized bed as possible. Her eyes followed the splay of hair against his forehead, echoed by the lashes against his cheek. The unburdened countenance contrasted by rumpled bedclothes. The woman in her enjoyed the arrow of crisp curls marching under the sheets, and the pectorals peeking beneath them.

She sat down on the edge of the bed and gently stroked his cheek. He opened his eyes and smiled at her. "Hello."

"Hello, yourself," she said. She tried not to be obvious as she watched him stretch.

"You could climb back in here, if you wanted to." He traced a finger on her arm.

"Uh huh. And make you late for work? I don't think so. I don't want to get on Brent's bad side."

"Will you at least sing me to breakfast?"

"You heard that? I thought you were asleep."

"Lucky dogs, getting serenaded while they eat."

Lia shrugged. "Beats yelling at them to come get it. They hear the song, and they know what to do."

"If you sing to me while you fix my breakfast, I promise I'll know what to do."

"Sure, as long as you don't mind getting dry cereal on the floor."

"Such a hard, hard woman. What is the hard, hard woman up to today that's so important it's keeping her out of bed?"

"I'll be working on Renee's drawings. Later I'm going over to Jim's to check out Anna's receipts."

He leaned over and kissed the inside of her knee. "You won't sing to me." He kissed her again, a little higher on her leg. "You won't come back to bed." One more kiss, an inch north. "What am I going to do with you?"

~ ~ ~

Lia fixed a stern expression on her face when she rang Jim's bell so she wouldn't have to explain why she was feeling so cheerful. Still, he gave her odd looks. He did not, thankfully, comment.

It took her less than an hour to pull up the receipts she needed for Monday, May 16. There were four of them, all debit card receipts. The first, for Michael's, was time stamped at 10:47 a.m. Anna had bought some dried flowers. The second was time-stamped at 11:33 a.m. for used paperbacks at Half Price Books. The third was a Kroger receipt for $121.43, stamped 12:17 p.m. This was slightly outside the parameters Peter had set. She figured it still worked because it would have taken a long time to pick up that many groceries. The last was a gas receipt. She'd bought fifty dollars worth of gas, a bottle of water and a small bag of chips. The time on this receipt was 12:39 p.m.

"Look at this, Jim. Anna's off the hook. There's no way Peter can say she caused Terry's fall."

Chapter 36

Tuesday, September 25

I'm very disgusted. I invested a lot in this experiment, and it is not working. Tending to this pitiful pair is a time-consuming burden. After all this effort, the only emotion they arouse in me is revulsion. It is nothing like I hoped. The thought of killing them does not excite anything like blood lust. Instead of anticipating their deaths with manic glory, I find that I just want to get it over with.

Gina did show some fight on the second day. I won't repeat the foul language she used to describe me. She sat on her mattress, calling me crude names. The woman is nothing if not vulgar. I reached down to shock her. She got her hands on the shaft of the cattle prod and yanked it away from me.

I was careless, I admit. I will say it was somewhat humorous to watch her waving the cattle prod around while she was chained to the wall. Roger still had the ball-gag in his mouth. His eyes were bugging out, but there was nothing he could do.

To remedy this situation, I stood well out of her reach with a broomstick. I wore rubber gloves and rubber soled shoes to avoid getting shocked. She attempted to sword-fight, as if we were playing light sabers. It took a few tries, but I placed the tip of the broomstick in the hollow of her throat and shoved. She dropped the cattle prod immediately. As a bonus, she had difficulty speaking after that.

They have been very submissive since then. I administer random punishments to remind them to behave. I thought I might enjoy causing pain, but I was mistaken. They mean nothing to me. Their pain means nothing to me. I suspect their deaths will mean little beyond exterminating vermin.

They say that every failed experiment increases your knowledge. In this case, I fear I have discovered that the only thing which will evoke the necessary emotions will be personal involvement. Apparently, the emotions must be pre-existing. I cannot induce them by artificial means. I cannot use substitutes. I must target someone close to me.

Chapter 37

Wednesday, September 26

Lia sat between Anna and Jim on her favorite picnic table. She sipped delicately at her hazelnut flavored coffee while she watched the canine social hour at the park. Honey and Kita were playing keep away and tug of war with a stick. Chewy was refereeing. CarGo lay atop the picnic table, a king surveying his realm. Jackson was busy digging a hole in the mulch.

"How is Renee's project coming?" Anna asked. "You've been very quiet about it."

"It's coming. I had a hard time developing a concept that I liked, but I think I'm happy now. The trick is going to be making it work."

"What all is involved?"

"It's turning out to be quite an engineering feat to pour vertical slabs of concrete the size we want, and then shape the top. Jim's helping with the structural planning, and Renee's husband is hooking us up with a contractor he knows, someone with a cement truck.

"Will Jose be helping you again?"

"He says he wouldn't miss it. He's going to help me build the forms for casting the concrete. They have that curved wall in the lobby of the Contemporary Arts Center. I thought I would do some research on how that was done, it might help."

Anna tsked. "That building is like a parking garage. I don't know who had the idiotic idea that it would be a good place to show art."

"And yet it's one of the most important examples of third millennium architecture."

"Not to me."

"Me, neither." Lia drained her cup. "Excuse me while I go toss this."

Anna looked at Jim, "I suppose you've been eating eggs Benedict, too."

"Not me," Lia heard Jim telling Anna. "I'm just a structural consultant."

On her way back from the trash can, Lia spotted Honey and Kita running straight for her. They were looking at each other and not paying attention to anything else. Lia stepped sideways to avoid a collision. Right into the hole Jackson was digging. She sat down, hard.

"Ow!" She surveyed the mulch particles embedded in her palms, then dusted her hands off on her jeans. "Dammit!"

"Jackson! No dig!" Terry yelled.

"A little late," Anna commented. "Let me give you a hand up."

"I don't know if I can stand on this foot."

"Marie," Anna called. "get on Lia's other side. Terry, Jim, get those dogs out of Lia's way. We're going to help you over to the table . . . Easy now, on three. One, two, three."

Anna and Marie hauled Lia up and held onto her as she staggered over to the nearest table. Lia punctuated each step with a soft "Ow." Nine steps. "Ow . . . ow . . . ow . . ."

Honey trotted up and sniffed at Lia, finding this unusual behavior more compelling than Kita and her stick. Kita stood there, bouncing on her front paws, hoping Honey would resume the chase. When it became apparent that Honey had defected, Kita dropped the stick, whuffed in disappointment, and stalked away.

"Dammit," Lia said, "I won't be able to drive. How will I get the dogs home?"

Jim came trotting up. "How's your foot?"

"I think it's sprained."

Jim kneeled down and gently felt her ankle. "I don't think it's broken. But you should still go to the E.R., just in case."

"No insurance. I don't need a big bill right now. If someone can take me home, I'll put ice on it."

"But a doctor should look at it," Anna insisted.

"I'll go see a doctor if it doesn't improve in a couple days."

"If you insist. I can take you home. There's plenty of room for the dogs in the back of my Explorer. Marie, can you follow me in Lia's car?"

"Looks like Peter's going to be on park duty for a few days. Serves him right for dumping it on me since he moved in."

Anna and Marie helped Lia down to Anna's SUV while Jim and Terry corralled the dogs and loaded them in back. CarGo, miffed at the crowd in his personal domain, moodily looked out the window and refused to acknowledge their presence.

Jim eyed the four dogs. "Are you sure you can handle this by yourselves? I can follow behind."

"Marie and I will be fine."

"Shit. Shit. Shit. Damn." Lia kept muttering under her breath as she leaned her head back against the headrest. Honey poked her head between the seats and gave Lia a lick on the cheek and a worried look. Lia reached a hand back and stroked Honey's head. "Thank you. Sweetie. I know you didn't make me fall on purpose." She resumed muttering. "Shit. Shit. Shit. Damn."

The tailgate of the SUV slammed shut and Anna climbed into the driver's seat. She caught Lia muttering. "Hurt much?"

"Enough."

"I really think you should see a doctor."

"Thank you for your opinion, Mom. I'll be okay with an Ace bandage and some ice. Just get me home before my foot swells so much I can't get my shoe off. Can we just go?"

They drove in silence punctuated by Lia's mutterings. Anna helped Lia into her apartment and settled her on the couch while Marie brought the dogs in and fed them. Anna propped Lia up with pillows from the bedroom, behind her back and under her ankle. Following Lia's instructions, she found an Ace bandage in the bathroom closet.

"Thanks, Anna. I can wrap this myself, if you'll get the bag of frozen peas out of the freezer."

"Certainly. Let me make you a cup of tea while I'm at it. What would you like?"

"Chamomile would be great, thanks."

Anna went into the kitchen. Lia could hear her putting the kettle on to boil. Marie brought her the much abused bag of peas.

"Are you hungry?" Anna called to Lia. "I can't make your glop, but I can fry up an egg sandwich."

Lia listened to the homey sounds as she wrapped her foot and draped it with the peas. She lay back and shut her eyes, drifting off. The smell of chamomile woke her up. Anna was standing over her with a cup of tea.

"Marie," Anna called, "what are you doing?"

"Looking for aspirin."

"Ibuprofen, in the medicine cabinet," Lia called back.

"Bring a towel for the peas, would you?" Anna yelled.

"I'm already on it."

~ ~ ~

"Anna and Marie what?" Peter exploded. Honey and Chewy started from their naps. Viola crawled under the couch.

"You don't have to yell. You're scaring the dogs.

"I wish I were scaring you. What were you thinking?" His voice, though lower, was still harsh.

"What do you mean, what was I thinking? I couldn't think. I damn near broke my ankle. I was too busy hurting."

"I can't believe Jim let you do this."

"Let me?" Lia forgot herself as her voice rose. "Since when does Jim 'let me' do anything?"

Honey whimpered. Lia took a deep breath.

"What was I supposed to do? Tell my good friends, 'Excuse me, but my boyfriend thinks one of you might be a serial killer, so you can't help me'?"

"You were supposed to bring Jim along."

"Oh, right, bring a man along. Well, he must not have thought it was a big deal either, because if he had, he would have come anyway. This is ridiculous."

"This is Bailey in an institution, Terry in a cast and two people dead. You need to take *this* seriously."

"Well, it's not Anna. We know that from her receipts. I don't think it's Marie, either."

"How do you know?"

"I just do."

Peter heaved the mother of all resigned sighs. "Maybe it's okay. How long were they here?"

"I don't know, they helped me in, Marie fed the dogs. Anna made me some tea and a sandwich."

"They were in the kitchen? Were you with her?"

"Of course not, I was camped out on the couch."

Peter strode into the kitchen. He returned, pinching the bridge of his nose.

Lia, you know what was on the kitchen table?"

"No, what?"

"The Bucky book."

"Oh," Lia said in a tiny voice.

"How long, exactly, were either of them alone in the kitchen."

"Marie was in there long enough to feed the dogs. Anna, just long enough to boil water and fix me a sandwich. Peter, they didn't look at it," Lia pleaded.

"You know this how, exactly?" Peter forced himself to be calm.

"Either one of them would have said something. They would have asked me about it. But they were perfectly normal."

"Lia, Baby," Peter sat down and put his arms around her. "I know you're hurt, and I know they're your friends, and I know you want your friends when you're hurt. But please, listen to me. Bucky has normal down to a science. I wish I felt as sure of them as you do, but I don't."

"Just hold me, okay?"

Peter obliged, and privately considered all the ways he was going to wring Jim's neck.

Chapter 38

Friday, September 28

It was time. There was nothing more to be gained from this situation. It had been my hope that interacting with these two daily would raise the emotional stakes, as it were. I needed to break through my usual detachment if I was going to experience another death like Catherine's. But these two were pathetic. After three days I was bored, even with Gina's histrionics. I needed to cut my losses and clean things up with as little fuss as possible.

Gina's car, the car Roger bought her, the one they had supposedly driven to Florida, has been hiding in plain sight at a hospital parking lot. It's now in the drive. I left my car around the corner. The most vulnerable part of this plan was the possibility of being seen with Gina's car. I believe I avoided that problem by wearing a hat and sun glasses. Everything went as planned and there should not be much in the way of evidence. Still, they do so much with forensics these days. Maybe not as much as on those shows, but enough.

I carried Roger and Gina's slop buckets up to the toilet and emptied them. I rinsed them out, then stacked them and placed them in the broom closet. Roger and Gina were well out from their last dose of Rhohypnol. I unlocked Roger's cuffs first, and dressed him in the clothes he had been wearing when I first drugged him. The handcuffs, hospital gown, chain and lock went into a plastic garbage bag in my tote bag, where I'd placed the ball gags I'd removed when I gave them breakfast. Then I unlocked and dressed Gina, though I did not go so far as to put make up on her.

The pair were heavy and hard to maneuver but it was important for them to appear as normal as possible. I disliked touching them. Bodies are so ugly. I'd had enough of caring for bodies a long time ago. In a way, this brought it all back. Those months of caring for him. I'd gotten tired of it. And I did something about it.

Distasteful or not, I am experienced at maneuvering dead weight, and I made short work of dressing them.

I'd removed the empty Ensure cans every evening in my very roomy tote. The stained mattress couldn't be helped. I could have left Roger and Gina on the floor, but I was afraid the cold concrete might penetrate their drug-induced sleep. I needed them to stay out. Someone might wonder about the mattresses. Or they might not.

I looked around to see if I'd left any other evidence of Roger and Gina's incarceration. I carried my tote bag upstairs and left it by the front door. Another bag sat there. I picked this one up and carried it down stairs. Back in the basement, I pulled a pair of latex gloves out of the bag. Perhaps not worth the effort, but you never knew.

I picked up Roger's bolt cutters from the jumble on his work bench and carried them over to him. I wrapped his fingers firmly around the handles to create fingerprints. Then I carried the bolt cutters over to the water heater. I bent low and opened the panel that protected the pilot light. I turned the dial to 'off' and waited for the flame to go out. I stood up, and reaching behind, clipped a tiny hole in the gas line. I bent the line to open the hole up so it would flow freely out into the basement.

I had one more thing to do. I had found conflicting information on the internet regarding whether natural gas was lighter or heavier than air. Apparently, there was more than one kind of gas and I wasn't sure which this was. If it was lighter, it would fill the room from the ceiling down. If it was heavier, it would fill the room from the floor up. In that case, Gina, that nasty piece of work, and Roger, would asphyxiate.

So I carried my bag back to the steps. I pulled out a twelve-hour votive candle and placed it on the steps, halfway up. I figured whether the gas was light or heavy, there would be half a basement full of gas before it blew up. It should be enough.

It should take a couple hours for the gas to build up. I knew there was a chance that there would not be the correct mixture of gas and oxygen to produce an explosion. In that case, Roger and Gina would simply asphyxiate. So I counted on asphyxiation and hoped for an explosion.

I collected Maddie and Lacy and put them in the back yard, then locked the house. I stashed the tote bag behind the driver's seat of my car. I mustn't forget to wipe the cuffs and chains down and dispose of them later.

I decided on an extended visit to the dog park. Roger's house was about a mile and a half from the park. I was sure you could hear a house explode from that distance. I should take along a book. It could be a long morning.

Chapter 39

Friday, September 28

Roger cracked an eye. This wasn't the first time he'd played dead. In 'Nam, there had been a time when he'd kept still amid the gore of shredded bodies for more than three hours, waiting for the Viet Cong to move along. It had saved his life then, though forty years later it still gave him nightmares.

He continued to lay there as she walked across the floor upstairs, until he heard the front door closing. It had been harder this time, playing possum while she removed the cuffs and dressed him. He'd had to stay limp while she struggled to pull on his pants and shoved his arms through the sleeves of his t-shirt. It brought back memories of the Viet Cong prodding bodies with rifles. They'd somehow missed him with their bayonets, but the dreams followed him home and never left.

This time, he pretended unconsciousness, not death. He had concentrated on staying calm. While he was supposed to have a pulse, an elevated pulse might give him away. It had been hard to hold the excitement at bay. He was free. He thought about rising up and attacking her then. But he was too weak from inactivity and a starvation diet. So he waited, feigning unconsciousness until he heard the door shut.

Roger was barely conscious. The drug swam in his blood, leaving him groggy as a teenage boy at his first frat party. Except his joints were stiff and screamed as he moved. He had to think. He smelled gas. He pushed himself upright, sitting. Roger spotted the candle on the steps. He shoved up on his hands and knees, carefully stood, then stumbled over to the stairs and blew it out.

He had to get out. He had to get Gina out. The basement door, the one to the back yard, was blocked with piles of junk. He couldn't get out that way. The gas valve was also obstructed with piles of junk, so he couldn't turn it off. Roger cursed the laziness that created this disorganized mess of things he had no use for. He staggered over to Gina and dragged her limp body up into a fireman's carry. It bowed his back, and his joints screamed in further protest, but Roger could not leave her behind.

Now was the tricky part. He'd have to go up the steps, carrying Gina. Gas floated. It would be collecting at the top of the stairwell. They could still asphyxiate. He stumbled to the stairs. Roger hung onto the rail with one hand, the other arm wrapped around Gina. He hauled himself from step to step by sheer force of will as unused muscles sent daggers of pain through him each time he put one foot in front of the other. It was taking too long! Gas was still pouring out with every foot of progress he made.

As Roger neared the top of the stairs, he grew dizzy from holding his breath. He fumbled for the knob, shoved the door open, and dropped Gina on the floor. No longer able to carry her, he dragged her to the kitchen door, his lungs bursting. He unbolted the door and flung it open, sobbing fresh air.

Chapter 40

Friday, September 28

Anna was looking for an eight letter word for 'monster' when they heard an explosion. "Goodness!" She flinched. "What do you suppose that was?"

Lia cuddled with Viola next to her, stroking the silky black fur. "That sounded like an M-80. What direction was it coming from?"

Nadine put down her book. "That's too loud for a car backfire."

"Cars don't backfire anymore, Nadine," Lia said.

Marie gestured to the Southwest, where a dark mushroom cloud blossomed above the trees.

"Roger and Terry live over there," Lia said. As they watched, black smoke spread, growing denser until a malevolent haze hung in the distance. Sirens shrieked in a cacophony of alarm, signaling the approach of emergency vehicles.

"I wonder what caught fire," Anna commented. "Do you suppose that's near either of them?"

"I don't know. When are Roger and the ever-unpopular Gina due back, anyway?" Marie asked.

"Any time now," Nadine said. "He was vague about their plans. I imagine it depends on how well they're getting along."

"Geezelpete," Lia said. "A week alone with Gina. After all the stories Jose has told, I wouldn't wish that on anyone."

"I'm sure you're right," Anna said. "So what is an eight letter word for 'monster'?"

"Do you have any letters?" Lia asked.

"First letter is 'b', maybe."

"Behemoth," Marie offered.

"Of course! Perfect!"

Chapter 41

Saturday, September 29

The sun was barely over the horizon when Lia pulled into the park that morning. Jim's was the only car in the lot.

"How's your ankle?" Jim asked as Lia hobbled to their regular table.

"It's there. That's about as much as I can say about it. It's better than yesterday." She sat down next to him.

"Here. Read this." He handed her a newspaper. Lia scanned the page, then settled on the headline, "Westwood Explosion No Accident"

Lia read aloud, "'In an apparent murder/suicide, Roger Gilmore of Westwood cut the gas line to his basement water heater. It is believed the house exploded when the gas was ignited by the pilot light on the kitchen stove. Firefighters were at the scene within minutes. However, the resulting blaze took several hours to control. The house is a total loss. Firefighters were able to protect neighboring houses from damage.

"'Two bodies, believed to be Roger Gilmore and his girlfriend, Gina Thomas, were found at the kitchen door. It is possible Gilmore changed his mind at the last minute and was attempting to escape when the house blew up. Neighbors were not surprised, citing the couple's volatile relationship and Gilmore's frequent threats of suicide. Gilmore's two dogs were in the back yard at the time. They have suffered serious burns and are currently under care . . .'

"Oh, Jim, how awful! And we never believed he'd do it."

"I'm not sure I do believe it."

"What do you mean?"

"Roger was our candidate for Bucky's next victim."

"Seriously? You think one of our friends blew up a house because Roger annoyed them in the morning? And that Roger and Gina would just let them do it? That's insane."

"You may be right. We still need to tell Peter."

"Great. This will have him putting me on house arrest with an ankle bracelet. The dogs will have to learn how to use the toilet, because I won't be able to walk them, ever again. Did I tell you how he blew up over Marie and Anna being in the house?"

Jim sighed. "You didn't but he did. He was right. I should have gone with you."

"Not you, too? I know you both want to look out for me, and I appreciate it, but this is getting to be too much. We haven't turned up proof of anything, and the less we turn up, the more suspicious you and Peter get." Lia stood up. She would have stomped off, but her sprained ankle was still too tender. She settled for wincing every time she put her weight on that foot as she crossed the park.

Charlie and Oggie were coming in as she arrived at the gate. "Where are you off to?" Charlie asked. "It's a bit early to be burning flags."

"Bite me." She took the dogs to the small park, hoping to avoid company while she brooded. She sat on the bench, sipping her coffee and staring at the woods.

Honey and Viola found this side of the park uninteresting. It was bare of trees and squirrels. There were no dogs to chase.

There were no people to charm. Disgusted, Honey lay at Lia's feet and closed her eyes. Viola climbed up on the table and curled against her back. To Chewy, a fence was a fence. He went on his border patrol. Lia decided Chewy was revoltingly well-adjusted.

She reached back and stroked Viola absently while she silently railed against the unfairness of her situation. She tired of this and recalled Asia's suggestion that when she was upset, she take time to listen to her gut feelings. What was in there? Her first thought was anger. Asia said anger was a secondary emotion, that it covered up a fear of some kind. What was the fear? What was there to fear? Fear of a possible killer? Fear of being suffocated by Peter? Fear of her own inability to identify what was happening around her?

"Is this seat taken?"

She looked up at Peter, shrugged. "I guess you heard."

"Jim called me." They sat in silence.

"Say what you came to say."

"I didn't come to say anything. I was worried about you. Jim's worried about you. I think even Charlie's worried about you."

"What are you going to do?"

"I imagine I'll call the arson investigator and see if there's anything hinky about this, give him a heads up to look beyond the obvious. It may be just what the papers said. Then again, any possible evidence may have been destroyed by the fire. We won't know until I look into it."

"You think Bucky could deal with two people at the same time?"

"There's a lot we don't know about Bucky. Bucky could have a friend. Or maybe Bucky is just an excellent planner."

"We knew that. If there is a Bucky."

"There's something. No matter how impossible it seems that someone we know has been fooling us, we have to remember that Bailey didn't mess with her own drugs. I'm certain of that."

"I wish you weren't. I wish this would all go away. I just can't see anyone I know doing this."

"I know. I wish it would go away too." He put an arm around her and she leaned into him.

Lia turned and eyed the crowd that had gathered in the large park. "So how am I going to explain my melt-down?"

"You're a sensitive artist. You're entitled to be upset that you didn't take his suicide threats more seriously and try to do something about it. Will that work?"

"It's as good as anything." She shrugged.

"You going to be all right now, Babe?"

"Babe is a pig."

"Babe is a fox."

"Says you."

"I love you and we're going to get through this."

Lia stood up and walked away. She stopped and turned around. "Dammit, Dourson, don't drag love into this. I'm not ready for it."

"You don't want me to love you?"

"I didn't say that."

He sat back and gave her a steady look. "What exactly did you say, then."

She walked back and took his hands. "I'm sorry. Luthor used to say he loved me right before he would try to manipulate me. I guess I'm a little sensitive."

"I'm not Luthor. I wish you wouldn't compare me to him."

"I know you're not. You're not anything like Luthor."

"I'm not going to unsay it. It doesn't mean I want anything. It just means I'm here for you."

"Is that all it means?"

Peter shook his head. "You're some piece of work, you know that?"

"Have pity on me. I'm in therapy for a reason."

"True. I only hang out with you because I feel sorry for you."

Lia punched him in the arm. "You don't have to be a jerk about it."

He tugged her hand. "Come back here." She climbed up on the table and he put his arm back around her. "It means a lot more than 'I'm here for you,' but I don't think today is the day to talk about it. Just get used to the idea, okay?"

Chapter 42

Sunday, September 30

Lia placed the two sheets of half inch plywood side by side against the wall of her studio, making an eight foot square with a four inch vertical gap. She tapped in a few roofing nails around the edges to hold the boards in place. Taking a piece of chalk, she traced curves on the upper corners, following the same template she used when making the mold for Renee's sculpture. She grabbed her cup of cooling coffee and drank while she considered the arch shape in front of her.

Renee had decided on a mosaic pattern that incorporated the gray concrete in sinuous negative shapes. The sunburst mosaic would be inlaid. To achieve this effect, Lia needed to create the channels for the tile by cutting the shapes out of plywood, then screwing them onto the insides of the mold. The concrete guy had told her that they would vibrate the concrete as it was poured into the mold and this would ensure that the shape of the channels would be preserved.

She studied her drawing, then free-handed the flames onto the eight foot arch. Lia stood up and studied the effect. She grabbed a blackboard eraser and removed part of her drawing, redoing it until she was satisfied. Finally, she redrew the design with a Sharpie marker to preserve the lines.

She looked out the window. It was probably around 7:30 a.m. She thought about calling Peter to remind him to get the dogs to the park. Nah. He was a big boy. He knew the routine, and he owed her for all the days he'd slept in while she took Viola with her crew. He'd offered to perform this task so she could get some extra time in at the studio. Best not to spoil it by checking up on him.

She placed several two-by-fours on the floor, then lay one of the plywood sheets on top. She used a jig-saw to cut out her shapes. It was slow work, following the flowing lines. When she finished cutting out both sheets of plywood, it was lunch time.

She drove home. The dogs met her at the door, and they were happy but not desperate. She let them out in the back yard and made a quart of blender gazpacho. She sat on the back stoop and drank the gazpacho while she tossed balls for the dogs. She took a thirty minute nap and headed back to the studio.

That afternoon, she traced off another set of shapes onto two more sheets of plywood for the western side of the sculpture. By the time she'd finished cutting these out, it was almost 6:00 p.m., and she was exhausted.

Monday morning she was due at Renee's, the concrete guys were going to pour the footer for the sculpture. Thursday, they were due to pour the sculpture itself. Tuesday afternoon she would refine her shapes with the drum-sander attachment on her power drill. Wednesday she would screw the shapes into the molds. Then she would pray.

For tonight, she'd go home and take a long, hot shower, maybe talk Peter into a shoulder rub. There were advantages to having a room mate.

~ ~ ~

Peter was stretched out on the couch when Lia arrived home. One hand held a beer on his stomach, the other stroked Viola where she lay on the floor. He sat up when he heard the key in the lock. Lia walked in, covered in sawdust from her pony tail to her sneakers. He noted that she had wiped the sawdust off her hands. She bent down to pet Honey and Chewy.

"Hey, Gorgeous."

"Uh, huh, that's me."

"You look exhausted. I'm not much of a cook, but we can go out, or I can pick something up."

"Something intravenous sounds good. I'm taking a shower. Whatever you do, don't kiss me. This stuff loves to migrate."

She came out twenty minutes later, wearing pajama pants and an oversized tee. Her head was wrapped in a towel, turban-style.

Peter handed her a large glass of carrot juice. "I don't know how to make those concoctions you like, but I figured I could pull this off."

She took the glass and went up on her toes and kissed him. "You're sweet. Tell me how it went at the park today." She plopped down on the couch.

"Everyone was talking about Roger. About what you'd expect. Marie thought it was a waste of a perfectly good house. Jose said he didn't have any family."

"He didn't. That's what's so sad."

"Nothing set off my spidey-sense. I talked to the arson investigator. I gave him an unofficial heads up to look for anything that suggests there was more going on than a murder/suicide."

"How did that go?"

"Not great. I couldn't say much, since there is no case. I suspect he thinks I'm a whack job. There wasn't much left of the bodies, nothing much to go on."

"Poor Roger."

"I notice nobody is saying 'poor Gina.'"

"Your point?"

"Jim and Jose were taking up a collection for the dogs. I gave them twenty."

"Good. I hate thinking about them in pain. I hope they find somebody nice to adopt them."

"Jim said people were already calling in because they saw them on the news. I don't think you have to worry. Are you in the mood for eggs? I could scramble them up with veggies."

"That sounds perfect," Lia said. "I came home for lunch today. You weren't here. What were you up to?"

"I went to see my other girlfriend. I figured it was all right, since you were busy."

"Oh, really?" Lia folded her arms and sat back.

Peter laughed. "I went back to my apartment, and I stopped by Alma's for some pecan pie."

"That nice old lady who gave you those plants for me?"

"That's the one. She wants to meet you. She sent you some pie. It's in the fridge."

"Gimme."

"Nope. Not until after you've had your eggs."

Chapter 43

Monday, October 1

Lia was fascinated. She was supposed to be supervising, in a way. It was her sculpture. But this was well out of her experience. It was amazing what money could accomplish. She and Renee sat on the patio and watched as a backhoe tore into Renee's pristine lawn, digging out a six foot hole for the foundation of her sculpture. Then the concrete workers set the bow-tie shaped mold for the base, and installed rebar that would stabilize the sculpture when it was poured. Last, they poured the concrete. All this from a drawing and some numbers she and Jim had worked up.

Renee was giddier than a four year-old boy at the sight of all that heavy equipment. Dukini, good girl that she was, remained watchful at Renee's feet. This morning Esmerelda plied them with omelets to go with their lattes. Lia warned herself not to get used to being spoiled like this. She was unlikely to run into more patrons as open and generous as Renee. She'd met too many who treated artists like hired help.

Peter had park duty again. She imagined he was absorbing every detail of everyone's behavior. She didn't know what he expected to find. She was just about convinced that Bucky was a myth. Yes, something weird had happened with Bailey's meds, and someone had pulled some posts on that web-site.

But there had to be another explanation. This wasn't like the quiet neighbor that nobody knew who buried bodies in the basement. She knew all these people, and there wasn't a killer among them.

And she was tired, tired of living with the suspicion, tired of digging into secrets. It just wasn't her. She believed in seeing the best in people. That philosophy had worked well for her for years. Now she was trying to live with conflicting world-views, and it was making her crazy. Peter was really sweet, and thoughtful, and he genuinely cared for her, and geezelpete, the sex got better all the time. But she needed more air. Time to step back a bit. She needed her own space again. Once she had that, she could figure out if she could deal with his cop's perspective full time.

She didn't look forward to the conversation. This week was going to be crazy with the sculpture going in. And Peter was totally convinced Bucky had blown up Roger's house with Roger in it. He wouldn't listen to reason right now. Better to let him dig around and not find anything. She'd let it ride until the weekend. By then, maybe things would be calmer.

By mid afternoon, the cement was setting and spires of rebar formed a vision of her intent. It was real, and it was happening.

"Look at all that wet cement, Lia. Don't you just want to go and scribble your name in it?"

Lia smiled. "Yeah, but we don't want to upset the concrete guys."

"I think you should put your signature in the base. I'll ask them."

Lia shook her head as Renee strode across the yard and approached the foreman. He shrugged, and Renee came back grinning.

"He said, 'Lady, you're the one who's paying.' Find a stick, Lia, we're going to christen this thing."

Chapter 44

Thursday, October 4

Peter came home to a dark apartment. Lia was lying on the couch, one hand drifting indolently over the side, tangling in Honey's long fur. Chewy and Viola met him at the door, seeking attention. He petted them absently. "Hey," he said, "aren't you the soon to be world-famous artist, Lia Anderson?"

"Smart ass."

He sat down next to her legs and placed a comforting hand on her thigh. "Did something go wrong with the pour? I thought you'd be dancing on the roof when I got home."

"It went fine. I hope it did, anyway. We won't know for sure until the mold comes off. That will be a few days. I get spacey when something big happens, and I don't know what to do with myself. So I just came home and tried to take a nap."

"We should celebrate. It's not every day you make a major sculpture."

"It's not done yet. We still have to polish the concrete, set the mosaics and create the ground markers. I've got months of work left to do."

"Yeah, but you've now got this big, honking pile of concrete to play with. It wasn't there before this morning."

"Well, yeah. . ."

"We need to do something to mark the occasion."

"Putz's."

"That's it? I was thinking steak or sushi. You sure you wouldn't like something with a little more class?"

"I'm exhausted. I want a banana split for dinner, and I don't want to get out of the car. We can toss the dogs in the back of your Blazer. Besides, who said Putz's isn't classy? It's the classiest soft-serve on the West Side.

The dogs got cups of soft serve. Peter had a couple chili-dogs. Lia ate every last bite of her banana split, then discovered she was hungry and had a chili-dog.

"I don't understand your diet," Peter said. "One day it's algae and raw food, the next it's processed meats and white bread."

"I'd be an insufferable bore if all I ate was a raw, vegan diet. How would it be if someone, with love in their heart, baked a big triple chocolate mousse cake for me and I said, 'Oh, I'm sorry, I can't eat that, it's got to be a dehydrated raw cake made with freshly ground cacao nibs and raw local honey.' I'd be a jerk if I didn't have at least three pieces."

"And your banana split and chili dog dinner?"

"Was so exactly what I wanted. There's something about eating junk food in your pajama pants when you're fried. Only this is Putz's, so it's high class junk food. I think I may live."

He took her home and tucked her in. Then he sat at the kitchen table with a beer and the Bucky book. Lots of notes, nothing solid pointing in any specific direction. Trees was still working on those payroll records, looking for deceased employees. That was a time consuming project, and one that might not bear fruit.

Peter was worried. It had been a month, and they were spinning wheels. Worse, they were losing momentum. He'd been working overtime and hadn't had much time for off-the-clock sleuthing. Lia was caught up in her project and didn't seem to be taking Roger and Gina's death seriously enough. They needed to talk about this, but not now.

Chapter 45

Friday, October 5

"Very good."

Lia opened her eyes to see Asia smiling at her from the other end of the log.

"Take note of how you are feeling inside. Are your muscles tense or relaxed? Feel your pulse, is it fast or slow. Is your heart beating normally, or is it pounding?"

"I feel pretty relaxed," Lia said after she'd taken stock. "It's amazing, really." She looked up into the trees, the interlacing of partially bare branches, felt the sun on her face. "I feel like I have my special place back."

"That's excellent. I noticed your dogs are not staying so close today. Do you suppose they sense that you aren't anxious?"

Lia looked across the creek to see Honey rolling in . . . something, while Viola and Chewy watched. "Oh, God, I don't even want to know what that is."

Asia laughed. "Do me a favor and keep her away from me, I have more clients to see today, and I don't have time to go home and change.

"One thing we never talked about," Asia started. "We've never talked about what you were doing in the woods that day. You've mentioned that you were upset and came down here to think and then met Bailey."

"That's right."

"What had you upset that day?"

Lia blinked. "You know, I don't remember. Someone said something that set me off. Why do you ask? Do you think it's important?"

"It could be. It's part of that experience. On some level, you're probably still reacting to it. If you don't remember it, you have no way to deal with it. If you want, I can help you remember."

"You can? How can you do that?"

"I can hypnotize you."

"Hypnosis? Seriously?"

"It's not like in the movies. You won't become Kevin Bacon channeling dead girls. I do a relaxation exercise and put you into a very light trance. You probably won't feel different. You'll be totally aware of everything around you and you'll remember everything that happens. Would you like to try? I promise I won't make you cluck like a chicken."

"Why not," Lia shrugged.

"You can sit there, or you can lay on the ground if you like. That might be more relaxing."

Lia stretched out on a bed of leaves. The three dogs came over to examine this strange development, sniffing at her as if she were a strange life form. Viola licked her face, then lay down near by. Honey snuggled up to her side.

"Is this all right?" Lia asked.

"They can stay with you. Okay, now close your eyes. Take notice of the tension in your body, starting with your toes. Put all your attention into your toes, and relax them. Move your mind up to your instep, notice any tension or stress there, now relax your instep . . ." Asia proceeded in this fashion up to the crown of Lia's head, where Lia was asked to "relax your hair."

"Now I'm going to count to ten. As I'm counting, imagine you are walking down a spiral stairway. The higher I count, the deeper you go. When I reach ten, you will be in a light trance . . . now there is a door in front of you. Notice the size of the door, what materials it's made of, how old it is. I'm going to count to three, and when I reach three, you will open the door. When you walk through, you'll be back at the day Bailey attacked you. You will enter the time before you went into the woods. One . . . two . . . three . . . . Now open the door and walk through. . . . Where are you?"

"I'm in the dog park." Lia didn't actually think she was in the dog park, but the thought popped into her head in answer to Asia's question.

"Who do you see?"

"I see Anna." Again, this was an impression more than a memory.

"Where is Anna?"

"She's on a picnic table, next to me."

"How do you feel?"

"I'm angry."

"Angry with Anna?"

"No, Peter. I'm telling Anna about it and she's defending Peter. She says I need to be reasonable." The conversation came flooding back, almost as if she were there. "Now she's saying awful things about Catherine, and she says Catherine did me a favor when she shot Luthor. She's saying Luthor's death is a gift."

"How does that make you feel?"

"Confused . . . I don't understand why she's saying these things."

"What is it that bothers you?"

"It does't sound like Anna. It sounds like someone else, someone I don't know."

"What do you do?"

"I leave. I go for a walk in the woods."

"Okay, you're doing great. Now I want you to close your eyes. On the count of three, open your eyes. Leave the fear and anxiety behind. You'll feel fully refreshed and relaxed. . . . One . . . two . . . three . . . . How are you feeling?"

Lia blinked. "Um, fully refreshed and relaxed?"

Asia laughed. "Smart ass. What about the memory?"

"I can't believe I forgot that conversation with Anna. It was so unlike her. It was a bit creepy, the way she was talking."

"Sounds like you saw something you didn't like."

"I didn't understand it at all."

"I know Anna is your good friend. Does remembering this conversation affect how you feel about her?"

"I don't know. I'll have to let this settle and see how I feel. I don't know what I should do."

"What's the problem?"

Lia struggled to find a way to speak to Asia about her dilemma. "Peter . . . he's not crazy about Anna, and if he knew about this conversation, well, I'm hearing a big fat, 'I told you so' in my head. It would give him ammunition. But Anna's my friend and I don't like being told who my friends are."

"You, yourself, said the conversation made you uncomfortable."

"It was one conversation. We've been friends for years."

"It sounds like it was an important conversation. Your gut was trying to tell you something. It's important to honor your gut. Right now, I hear you rationalizing the experience away, discounting your own perceptions. It's important to own your truth. The more difficult it is to face, the more important it is to face it. Remove Peter from the equation. Listen to the non-verbal part of you, the feeling part. What is it saying?"

"I can't remove Peter from the equation. There's a bit more to it than his opinion. There's something I can't talk about, not yet."

"When you're ready, I hope you'll tell me."

"It's not like that. Someone trusted me to keep something private, so I can't share it with you. I'm sorry I'm being so confusing. I'm pretty confused myself, right now."

"Don't apologize. This is your time to use however best supports you. Let me make just one suggestion, and then let's call it quits for today and enjoy a nice walk back up the hill."

Lia laughed. "Since when do 'nice walk' and 'up the hill' belong in the same sentence? Okay, what are your parting words of wisdom?"

"The more complicated things feel, the more important it is not to let outside issues cloud your perceptions. Forget Peter, forget everyone but you and Anna, and that one conversation. Isolate that and feel it until you understand what it was about that conversation that made you want to get away from Anna. This is your truth, and it's important for you to accept it. You've told me that you're not sure you can trust yourself where Peter is concerned. When you learn to honor your gut and really listen to what it's telling you, you'll be able to trust yourself."

Lia said goodbye to Asia at the parking lot, then walked her furry crew up the hill to the park. The hypnosis session had given her a peek behind a curtain, a glimpse of inhumanity in Anna that she didn't like. Anna had always been a practical woman, but her comments during that conversation went beyond practicality to something Lia couldn't quite name.

Her mind was frozen. It was as if to think would be to see something she couldn't bear. Behind the wall of ice was the thought, "Could it be Anna?" Anna, her friend, who babied her and watched over her like a mother after Luthor was shot. Anna who fixed her a scrambled egg and cheese sandwich when she sprained her ankle, Anna who for years made her laugh with caustic observations about people and life in general. As Honey, Viola and Chewy towed her up the drive, she chipped away at the ice, carefully. If it were Anna, then that meant Anna stole her phone, shot Luthor, booby-trapped Terry's ladder, framed Catherine and drowned her, then set Bailey up to have a nervous break-down, endangering Lia's life.

But why? It was true, Anna had no love for Luthor, Catherine, or even Terry. But she was always so rational and dismissive about it. And Bailey, Anna liked Bailey. That's what she'd always thought, anyway.

The park was empty except for Terry at the far end. He was still in a walking cast, and couldn't drive. He must be waiting for Donna to pick him up.

As far as Terry knew, his accident had been the result of his own carelessness. He wasn't aware of Peter's suspicion that it had been staged. She remembered something she'd seen on television on a cop show. They said that when you have a string of connected events, and one of those events broke pattern, that event is the most likely to reveal something.

The other events involved meticulous planning, likely over a period of time. But Terry had only decided the day before to work on his roof. If Terry's fall was staged, and not an accident, this must have been a crime of opportunity spurred by his determination to find the source of the gun that killed Luthor. Perhaps it wouldn't hurt to talk to Terry again.

"Hail," Terry called out as she approached.

"Hey, Terry. Chewy! Off! No jumping on Terry's cast! Sorry about that, he's such a brat."

"Not a problem. The limb in question is impervious."

"How's the leg?"

"Getting better. I should have this thing off next week."

"That's great news. You must be getting tired of having people drive you everywhere."

"Indeed, that I am, though the conk on the noggin is causing more problems."

"I'm so sorry. I didn't realize. What is it doing to you?"

"Headaches, fatigue. Sometimes I can't concentrate, and the brain doesn't process as fast as it used to. Short term memory problems. It's quite annoying."

"I'm so sorry. What do the doctors say?"

"Bah! They want to put me on anti-depressants. Damn Liberal medical schools think everyone should be on anti-depressants. I'm not depressed, I'm concussed! So far I'm holding out. They have no idea when or if this is going away. Don't know why I should listen to doctors who can't tell me what to expect."

"That sounds awful."

"They say the best thing I can do for myself is keep from going crazy while I wait for it to heal. Could be six months, could be two years, could be never."

"So what have you been doing?"

"Watching movies, sleeping, reading sometimes, but that's hard these days. I do Sudoku."

"That must be frustrating."

"It is, it is."

"Say, Terry, I was wondering, back then you were talking to a lot of people about the gun that killed Luthor."

"Guns don't kill. People kill. Did they ever decide if it was Catherine or Bailey?"

"It's still a mystery."

"Bizarre, that was."

"How so?" Lia asked.

"I thought I saw a Luger several years ago. I asked about it, but she said it was this odd brand of air pistol, a Schimmel. I don't see how I could have made that mistake. Plastic has a distinctly different sheen from metal. I can't believe I didn't notice. That's neither here nor there. Even if it was a Luger, I can't imagine her allowing Catherine to have access to it, and Bailey was not around the dog park long enough, she was a newcomer. She wouldn't have known anything about it, I imagine."

Lia struggled to get a word in. "Who, Terry, who had the air pistol?"

"Didn't I say? It was Anna, of course."

Chapter 46

Dammit, dammit, dammit. If it could have been anyone but Anna. Lia fretted. What to do? She helped Terry load Jackson and Napa into the back of his truck when Donna arrived, then returned to the park to toss balls for Honey and Viola. The exercise loosened her up and the repetition was soothing.

If only there was a way to take Anna off the list entirely. Her phone interviews and Trees' report had revealed a life that was unexciting and perhaps unfulfilled, but there was no evidence of anything evil.

If there were evidence of any kind, wouldn't it be in Anna's house? She'd been in Anna's house dozens of times, and even looked after CarGo once. She'd never run across anything remotely weird.

What she'd really like was a peek in Marie's house. Marie was very private and no one that Lia knew had ever been inside her house. But that was a pointless wish, Marie worked at home and how would she get in?

She could, however, get into Anna's. She still had a key. CarGo wouldn't mind her being there. She would be trespassing. It was a rotten thing to do to Anna. But surely, if she was able to rest her mind, it would be a good thing?

Would she know evidence if she saw it? What would she look for? A day planner that said "kill Luthor" on the appropriate date? A detailed plan of some sort? That seemed unlikely. But Bucky, if there was a Bucky, had visited Crystal Bridge. It had been a few months, so it was doubtful that it would still be in Bucky's browser history. But browser windows had an autofill function. If she went to Anna's computer and started to type in the URL, wouldn't the rest of it pop up if she'd been there? And that wouldn't involve ransacking Anna's house, just turning on her computer. It wouldn't be the same as rifling through her underwear. And it would be almost definitive whether Anna was innocent or guilty.

Should she tell Peter or Jim? No, they would be dead-set against it. Her mind made up, she tossed the dogs into her Volvo and drove home. She continued thinking while she made herself carrot juice for lunch.

Anna usually worked half-days, in the afternoon, but her schedule could change. So she'd call Anna at work on some pretext to make sure she was there. Should she dress in black? What an idiotic thought. But a hoodie wasn't a bad idea.

Lia parked around the corner, put on sunglasses and pulled up her hood. She pulled out her cell, looked up Anna's work number on the contact list and hit send.

"Lieberman Foundation, Anna speaking,"

"Anna, it's Lia." Lia's palms were sweaty and her voice sounded stilted and too cheery to her own ears.

"What a nice surprise. I missed you at the park this morning. Were you in the woods with Asia?"

"Yes, when we came out, Terry was the only one there."

"Waiting for Donna, I imagine. So what's up?"

"You remember that recipe for liver treats you told me about?"

"Yes, of course. What about it?"

"Can you tell me the recipe again? I forgot to write it down and I'm at the grocery store, I thought I would pick up the ingredients, that is if you remember." Lia winced. She sounded idiotic, like she was in tenth grade and asking some boy to a Sadie Hawkins Day dance.

"Certainly. One pound of beef liver and a box of Jiffy cornbread mix. You puree the liver in your blender and add enough water to combine well with the cornbread mix. Pour it into a greased pan and bake about 30 minutes at 350 degrees. Let it cool in the oven. You can use two cups of flour instead of the mix, and you can also add two teaspoons of garlic powder. If you want a grain-free snack, you can use yam flour instead. I get that at Francis International, that's around the corner from you. And don't forget to freeze anything you can't use in a week. Is that all you wanted?"

Lia didn't bother listening, she'd already used the recipe several times and had it committed to memory. "Yeah, that was it. See you tomorrow."

"You take care."

"You too."

Lia pressed 'end' on her phone. It was now or never. She took the key to Anna's house from the dashboard cubby and gripped it tightly. She checked her hood and left the car. Too much walking today, she was starting to favor the sprained ankle. Forcing herself to walk normally, she proceeded up the street to the nondescript 1950's brick house where Anna lived.

She felt jittery, as if a thousand eyes were watching her as she turned the key in the lock, which was silly since overgrown yews hid the porch from view.

She entered the living room. It was a grandmotherly sort of living room, with traditional furniture in varying shades of beige. The only spot of color was a blue pansy Lia had painted for Anna a few years earlier. There was a fireplace with Rookwood tiles that had been converted to gas. On the mantel were pictures of Jim, Anna and Lia at the park. CarGo was a black and tan lump on the floor. He had a tan corduroy dog bed that filled the corner in front of a set of bookshelves. He lifted his head when he saw Lia and thumped his tail.

"Good CarGo. Look what I have for you." She patted his head and pulled a pig's ear out of the pocket of her hoodie. CarGo would make short work of it but it would at least keep him busy long enough for her to examine Anna's computer.

Anna had converted the dining room into a home office. Lia sat at the desk and turned on Anna's monitor. She reached down to the HP tower sitting on the floor and pressed the power button. As she waited for it to boot up, the house was silent and overloud, with the humming of the refrigerator and the sound of CarGo gnawing his pig's ear.

The system whirred and chimed. Lia double-clicked the Firefox icon. She clicked on the browser history. Nothing interesting, just the Lieberman Foundation and a number of educational web sites, LL Bean and Amazon. She clicked the nav bar and keyed in "c", "r", "y", and "s". Nothing. She continued to type out "crystal bridge" and no links appeared. She heaved a sigh of relief. Just to be sure, she navigated to the Crystal Bridge site and clicked on "forum." Normally, an autofill function would add user log in information. Nothing. The blanks remained empty. She took a quick look through the computer's directory. There were no files referring to guns, drowning or psychotropic medicines. She clicked on Anna's picture album, and by this time she was feeling creepy for digging through Anna's files. She scanned the thumbnails, many pictures of CarGo and other dogs and dog park regulars. Some scenes from a fall drive. Pictures from a Caribbean cruise she'd taken, when Lia had babysat CarGo.

Some photos from Lieberman Foundation events. No staring corpses, no bloody knives. The creepiest photo there was a snapshot of an aging lounge lizard on the cruise with his arm around Anna. Anna had told her all about "Mr. Hands" and his inexplicable determination to hook up with her.

So very normal. Lia snorted. She didn't know what that feeling of alarm was during her session with Asia, but it was apparently baseless. The business with the gun a coincidence. She checked the clock. 2:07 p.m. Time to go. She'd been there for more than 20 minutes. She shut down the computer and walked over to CarGo and scratched behind his ears. "No harm done, right?" She asked the big dog. "You won't tell on me will you?" CarGo twitched his eyebrows and continued to gum the pig's ear.

Chapter 47

Friday, October 5

Peter loved the smell of roasted garlic on fresh pizza. He loved it almost as much as he loved living with Lia, temporary though the arrangement might be. Which was why he was currently enjoying the aroma of an extra large Edgar Allan Poe from Dewey's Pizza as he drove to Lia's. Domesticity suited him. Sure, their hours didn't quite match, and her place was a bit cramped, especially with three dogs. And she ate some pretty weird stuff, like sprouted sunflower seed pate rolled up in sea weed and kale juice with lemon. But she was sweet and funny and beautiful and warm and a welcome change from a fruitless and frustrating day attempting to track down the shooter nobody wanted to admit they saw.

He opened the door to find Lia lying on the sofa face down, one arm draped over the side, her hand twined in Honey's fur as Honey mimicked Lia's pose on the floor. The pizza mocked him as his vision of a pleasant, homey evening dissolved, wafting away on the aroma of roasted garlic. He walked into the kitchen and placed the pizza on top of the fridge, having learned from his last experience that Honey was an expert counter surfer. He went back into the living room and perched on the edge of the sofa and placed a hand on her back.

"What's wrong?" he asked.

"I don't know how to tell you," she mumbled into the cushions. "I'm afraid you'll get mad and yell."

"Did you kill anyone?"

"No."

"Then we're probably okay. Will pizza fix it?"

She turned her head and eyed him suspiciously. "What kind?"

"I thought there was only one kind in this house."

She sat up. "Pizza first. Then if you decide to yell at me, I'll be fortified."

They ate in silence, tossing crusts to the dogs. When the last slice was gone, Peter closed the box and set it aside. He braced his elbows on his knees and looked at her expectantly.

"I don't know where to start," she said.

"The beginning is always a good place."

Lia took a deep breath, sighed it out. "I saw Asia this morning. She wanted to help me remember why I was so upset when I went into the woods the day Bailey threatened to kill me. So she hypnotized me."

Peter raised his eyebrows but said nothing.

"I remembered having this conversation with Anna. It upset me because she thought I should be happy that Catherine and Luthor were dead."

"Why didn't you ever tell me this before?"

"I forgot all about it when Bailey stuck my own gun to my head."

"Okay, I can see that."

"So then I saw Terry and I was talking to him about the gun, the one that killed Luthor, and he said he would have sworn Anna had an old Luger, but she said it was just an air pistol."

Peter mentally smacked himself on the forehead. Terry had tried to tell him months ago, but he'd been preoccupied and missed it. "Okay, then what?" He had a feeling he wasn't going to like what came next.

"I knew you would say that put Anna at the top of the list and I couldn't stand it so I thought I could find out for sure."

This alarmed Peter. "Lia! What did you do?"

"I knew you'd yell."

"Sorry. What did you do?" he asked again, gently.

"I have a key to Anna's. She gave it to me when I took care of CarGo once. So I went to her house while she was at work."

Peter mentally took a deep breath. It would do no good to yell right now, even though he thought Lia was expecting it. "Why did you go to Anna's house?" he asked, as calmly as he could.

"I figured I could look on her computer and see if she'd been at the Crystal Bridge web site."

Peter was taken aback. As strategies went, it was simple and smart. "What did you find?"

"Nothing. No evidence she'd been at the site. I looked through her directory and her photo albums. Nothing at all strange."

"Huh. It's not conclusive, but it's helpful. I don't want you taking risks like this again. Did anyone see you?"

"Just CarGo, and he can't talk."

"I still want to hear more about this conversation you remembered."

"Is it that important?"

"I won't know until you tell me."

Lia sighed. "Anna was going on about how bad Luthor was for me, and she said Catherine did me a favor when she shot him. She said his death was a gift."

This time Peter's eyebrows rose nearly to his hairline. "What else did she say?"

"There's one thing I remember for sure. She said, 'Freedom from rude, selfish people is always a gift.' But that doesn't mean anything, does it?"

He took her hands in his and chafed the palms with his thumbs. "I don't know. But it doesn't make me happy. Normal people value human life over their own comfort, Lia."

"But this is Anna. She was just trying to get me to stop brooding about Luthor and start being happy with you. She was being nice to you when she said it. You should be okay with that."

"Still, it was a very odd way to put it, don't you think?" Peter said.

"Not as weird as the stuff Marie says. She's the one who was running around showing off the suicide machine. And what about Terry and his arsenal? Jose and his taser? Bailey's in a mental ward! All my friends are weird. That's not a criminal offense, except maybe to you."

"That's not fair."

"Do you mind sleeping on the sofa? I don't feel like company tonight."

"Lia, I don't want to leave it like this."

"You don't want? What about what I want?" The tension of Lia's day finally snapped. "I've been playing by your rules for weeks now. I let you into my home. I have no privacy. I'm keeping my friends out. I'm supposed to act like everything is normal while we secretly pry into my friends' lives, digging up dirt. And we haven't found out a goddamn thing except that Marie had a hard time as a kid, and now has a very kinky sex life. Oh, and Nadine lost her first family."

"I know it's rough. I don't know of any other way to protect you."

"You don't know. It's not your friends we're violating. And did you ever think maybe I don't want or need protecting? I feel like I'm being smothered. Do you have any idea how embarrassed I was that night you called around looking for me?"

"Lia, what do you expect me to do? We still have a murderer out there."

"I don't know that. I don't know what happened to Bailey's meds, but I don't believe any of my friends had anything to do with it. I'm having a really hard time buying this whole conspiracy you and Jim have cooked up. Bailey's the one who believes in little green men, not me. I can't live like this. You're my boyfriend, not my father."

Lia started rummaging around in the linen closet.

"What are you doing?"

"Getting you some sheets and a blanket. I want to sleep by myself tonight. I'd rather you went home. But if you want to guard me so bad, you can do it from the living room."

Chapter 48

Saturday, October 6

"Why so mopey?" Anna asked as she sat down next to Lia on their favorite table.

"I had a fight with Peter last night," Lia grumbled into her coffee.

"I'm so sorry. What was it about?"

"He's a man. Does it have to be about anything?"

"I guess not, when you put it that way. How serious is it?"

"I made him sleep on the couch last night. I'm thinking about telling him he has to go home, remodel or no."

"Do you feel like talking about it?"

"Not really, no." A seed of rebellion took root in Lia's chest. It was time she took her life back. "Are you busy this afternoon?"

"Not today. I was going to put in some daffodil bulbs, but that can wait. What did you want to do?"

"Feel like catching a matinee?"

"I might. Is there something in particular you want to see?"

"Something with loud explosions. Nothing cute. What's in the paper?"

Anna unfolded her paper to the movie ads. They pored over the selection and settled on a heist flick with Robert

DeNiro and Matt Damon. Lia arranged to meet Anna at her house.

"Come early," Anna suggested, "I'll feed you. We don't need to be spending theater prices for junk."

~ ~ ~

"Go ahead and sit down," Anna said as she went into her kitchen. I'll make us some tea. Do you want a sandwich? I have some nice chicken salad."

"That would be great, on whole wheat, if you have it," Lia said absently. Lia wandered around the room, inspecting Anna's collection of figurines and tchotkes. She was uncomfortably aware that she'd been in this room the day before, illegally. CarGo tilted his head and eyed her from his corner bed. His eyebrows were twitching as if he were trying to process profound ideas. Or maybe he was just trying to figure out if he could extort her for another pig's ear.

"What kind of tea do you want?" Anna called from the kitchen. "I have green tea chai and plum blossom. Lemon ginger, too."

"The chai sounds great."

She heard the hissing of boiling water as the kettle was removed from the stove.

"Do you want milk with your tea, Lia?"

"Yes, please."

She noticed her painting of the pansy was off level, down on the left, and nudged it back straight.

"Have you decided to take your painting home?"

Lia looked up to see Anna standing in the doorway, a cup of tea in her hand. "Oh, huh uh. It doesn't seem to want to hang straight. I was trying to level it," Lia said.

"Oh," Anna laughed, "always the artist. Don't worry about that right now. Sit down and have your lunch."

Lia plopped down on the sofa and dove into her sandwich. "I am really looking forward to taking a break this afternoon."

Anna nibbled delicately at her own sandwich. "So what is Renee up to these days? How is the project going?"

"I'll know when we pull the mold off. It's going to be a few more days. I can't stand the wait. This chicken salad is really fantastic."

"It's the curry. This is all so interesting. First it was just pavers, now it's a huge sculpture. I can't wait to see what you do next."

"I have a feeling I'm going to sleep for a month after I'm done with this. Or lay out in the back yard and read romance novels."

"You can't possibly need romance novels with Peter around."

"I may not have the energy for romance when this is done. I may swear off any activity that requires physical exertion. Peter may have to pretend he's a necrophiliac. Maybe I'll need to read a few zombie romances to get in the mood. Better yet, I'll have him read them to me. Less effort involved. That is, if I've forgiven him by that point."

Anna changed the subject. "I know you wanted to see a movie, but I've got another idea."

"What did you have in mind?"

"Pomegranate margaritas in the afternoon are a nice way to handle fighting with a boyfriend. Especially with a couple of female friends. We could call Marie and Nadine, see if they're available."

"You're on."

~ ~ ~

"What are we drinking to?" Marie asked as she pulled out her chair on the patio at The Painted Fish. The afternoon was breezy and warm, just right for sitting out in the sun.

"Lia has been fighting with Peter," Anna said. "She wanted to go to the Esquire. I thought this would be so much better. I was hoping Nadine could come, too, but she's busy this afternoon. She did say she'd stop by if she had time."

"I don't know, Anna," Lia said. "Two hours staring at Matt Damon could cure a lot of ills."

"Oh," Marie said, "but you'd feel so dirty afterwards."

"Would not," Lia said. "Anyway, alcohol never cures anything."

"Maybe not," Anna said, "but at least you'll forget you're sick. You never mentioned what you were fighting about. We're going to get you so drunk, you'll spill everything."

Nick brought out the icy pitcher and set it down in the middle of the table. "Drink up, Ladies," he said. "Sure you don't want anything to eat with that?"

"Better bring some nori fries," Lia said. "We'll need something to soak up some of this."

"I want all the smutty details," Marie said as she poured the drinks.

"What? You don't want the clean ones?" Lia said in mock affront. "I'm afraid all I have are clean ones. You're just going to have to make do."

"Oh, all right." Marie pouted. "I just thought you two were going to spice up my life for a minute. No phone calls from an old lover? No requests for a three-way?"

Lia giggled. "Last time Peter said something about a three-way, we were passing Skyline Chili."

Marie rolled her eyes. "I'm looking for something hot, and she gives me Skyline. You do realize, that stuff bears no resemblance to chili. It has negative alarms."

228

"Let us not digress," Anna said. "Lia, since I'm picking up the tab, you must sing for your supper. You're the only one with a man . . . um, romance, right now. Marie and I must live vicariously through you."

"It's not all that exciting. It's just, well, I've been taking care of myself for a long time, and he's too protective. He's telling me what I should do and I don't like it. And I like living by myself. I'm not used to sharing my space."

"That pig!" Marie said with an ironic expression.

Lia giggled again. "Peter isn't a pig. He's old fashioned, but he's not a pig."

"I thought we were drinking in the afternoon because you'd had a fight with a man. In that case, he's a pig. It's automatic," Marie insisted.

"Perhaps, just for the afternoon, he can be an old fashioned pig?" Anna suggested.

"Hmm," Lia mused. "What makes a pig old fashioned?"

"Well," Marie offered, "a contemporary pig won't perform oral sex because they claim they've got a repetitive motion injury of the tongue."

"Marie!" Anna interrupted.

"But an old fashioned one won't do it because it's unsanitary and leads to damnation," she finished. "So, is he an old fashioned pig?"

Lia made a prim mouth and batted her eyelashes. "A lady doesn't tell. Absolutely no comment."

"We can't be ladies," Marie pointed out. "We're drinking in the afternoon."

I don't think that rationale is going to get our Lia to divulge her secrets, Marie," Anna said.

"You're probably right. So what bad things do you want to tell us about him?" Marie asked.

"Geezelpete, I don't know. Otherwise, he's just so . . . nice."

"He's nice? You're complaining because he's nice?" Marie asked.

"Shocking, isn't it?" Anna said. "How dare he be decent."

"He's always, well, there. Like he could just hang out with me all the time and that's enough to make him happy. I'm not used to it. I don't know if I want to hang out with him all the time. And I think he has the china pattern picked out."

"That brute. Before you know it, he'll be buying you a washing machine," Anna said dryly.

"That's just it. I don't need a washing machine."

Anna shook her head. "Well, you obviously have to tell him. He must go. Tell him to go someplace good, like Newark."

"Oh, Anna, quit it," Lia said. "Help me out here, Marie. I bet you know what I'm talking about."

"If I get this right, he's got a plan, or at least it seems like he has a plan, but you don't know if you're on board, and you're feeling cramped because of it?"

"Yes! That's it! I'm going to tell that to my therapist next time I see her and she's going to think I'm so insightful."

"What? I don't get an attribution?"

"I'm stealing it. Sue me." Lia eyed the dregs of the pitcher. "Looks like I'm tipsy. And I still have my secrets."

"What do you think, Anna? Is it time for the bamboo shoots?" Marie asked.

"I give up. I think Lia may just get to keep her affairs private for now," Anna said. "I've got a couple of errands I have to run. Do you girls mind if I take off? I'll take care of the tab with Nick." She gave Lia a hug. "Hang in there, it'll work out." Then she left.

Lia and Marie continued to nibble on the now-cold nori fries. "I'm really being a bit of an ass, aren't I?" Lia asked. She sipped her water, having finished her margarita.

"Nah. It's easy to feel manipulated when you know someone wants more from you than you're ready to give."

"I don't think he's trying to pressure me. I just think he knows what he wants and I don't, and it feels like pressure. And this remodel is going on much longer than I thought."

"You know, I'm jealous of you."

"Oh, Marie, I'm such a bad friend. We spent all this time talking about me, and none talking about you. You never talk about your girlfriends. You can if you want to."

"Don't worry about it, the entertainment value of watching you squirm is worth it. We've done an excellent job of wasting the afternoon. You ready to blow this popsicle-stand?"

They gave each other a tipsy hug in front of Marie's car on Spring Grove Avenue. Lia continued to the corner of Spring Grove and Cooper, where she'd parked her Volvo. She turned around and waved good-bye.

Chapter 49

Saturday, October 6, 6:00 p.m.

"Damn," Peter muttered to himself as he looked at his cell phone display. Jim. Not Lia. He pressed the "accept" button and held the phone to his ear. "What's up, Jim?"

"Are you busy?"

"Just finishing up some reports. You haven't talked to Lia, have you? I've been trying to reach her all afternoon, but her phone's either dead or off."

"I haven't seen her since this morning. I was just calling to let you know that I heard from Trees. He said he hasn't been able to work on our project for more than a week, but he's back on it tonight."

"I wish he'd hurry up. We're dying here." After Peter ended the call, he sat, tapping his notebook with his pen, agitated. He tried Lia one more time. He broke down and called Anna.

"No," Anna said, "I haven't seen Lia since earlier this afternoon. She wanted to go see a movie at the Esquire, but we wound up going out for drinks at The Painted Fish with Marie instead. I left before they did. Maybe they decided to catch a film after all, and she turned her phone off. She probably forgot to turn it back on again."

"Yeah, I bet that's it," Peter said, but he was lying. "Thanks, Anna." He hung up, and called Marie. She said she'd waved goodbye to Lia in front of the restaurant and knew nothing about a movie. He sat, tapping. It wasn't like he and Lia were joined at the hip, and they'd had that fight. This wasn't the first time her phone had been dead or off. Lia just didn't see her cell phone as the life line most people considered it to be. But lately she'd been better about letting him know what she was up to, and he hoped she wouldn't go off in a snit.

She'd resisted his babysitting. He knew he hadn't given her much room. What else can you do when you suspect your girlfriend is hanging out with a violent offender? He'd take a half hour to finish up paperwork. If she wasn't home then, he was going to look for her, whether she liked it or not. The rest of the reports could go hang.

Lia's car was not on the street in its usual spot. He was greeted at the front door by a trio of housebound canines desperate for a potty break. They barked and raced for the back door, running back and forth, urging him to let them out. The scrabbling of their claws on the hardwood floor echoed his own rising urgency. He watched as they erupted from the house, each making a beeline for their favorite spot in the lawn. This was not good. Lia obviously hadn't been there for hours. He wished it could be that easy for him to get relief as he watched the pack spill their bladders on the grass.

He checked Lia's answering machine. There was a message from Anna, asking Lia to call when she got in. He pondered his options as he fed the dogs. Anna said Lia probably went to the Esquire. He'd ask Jim to make some calls while he looked for Lia's car in Clifton. It could be in the merchant's lot, or somewhere in the residential neighborhood behind the theater.

He grabbed a snapshot of Lia off the refrigerator, snagged her spare car keys out of the dish by the door and dialed Jim on his way out. The dogs abandoned their supper dishes and howled at the window as he pulled away.

Peter eventually found Lia's dilapidated Volvo a few blocks off Ludlow on Telford. It was dinner time, and the street was bumper to bumper with parked cars. Peter parked in the nearest drive, figuring he could flash his badge if he needed to calm an irate homeowner.

He pulled on a pair of rubber gloves and used Lia's spare key to unlock the door. A quick glance showed nothing out of place. He wanted to sit in the driver's seat to see if the seat or the mirror had been readjusted for someone shorter than Lia, but decided he didn't want to foul up any trace that might be on the upholstery. He felt around under the driver's seat and found Lia's cell phone on the side closest the door, where it might have fallen out of her pocket. The phone was off. He turned it on. There were no messages. He turned it off again and placed it back where he found it. He locked the car.

Should he knock on some doors? If Lia was just taking in a movie, she'd freak if she found out he was asking random people about her. And this neighborhood was mostly two income, white-collar families. Little likelihood of anyone seeing anything during the day. While it was way too early for an official missing person's report, he knew Lia would never leave the dogs alone for so long. No matter how angry she was with him. Still, he had to go through the steps.

He moved his car to the first available spot and hiked back to the renovated art-deco movie theater. Of the three clerks on duty, two recognized Lia, but no one had seen her that day. Peter slipped the photo back in his pocket and left. He mentally imagined himself slamming his fist through the community bulletin board at the corner of Telford and Ludlow.

He called Jim. Jim had canvassed Nadine, Jose, Renee. The latest anyone had seen Lia was around 8:30 a.m., at the park. "Meet me back at Lia's," he said, and hung up the phone.

Peter knew from experience that going off on a tear would not accomplish anything. He tamped down his frustration. Food. The hungrier he got, the more likely he was to let anger get the better of him. It was going to be a long night, and forgetting to eat never helped. He picked up a case of sliders at Knowlton's Corner and headed back to the place he was thinking of as home.

Jim was waiting for him when he arrived. Peter let him in and tossed the case down on the kitchen table. They let the dogs out. Peter pulled two cokes out of the fridge. "You had any dinner?"

"Not yet."

"Dig in. Want a coke?"

"Lia's missing and you're thinking about food?"

"I'm about to spaz out like a monkey in a meth lab. So we sit down and talk about what's next." He set one coke down in front of Jim.

"Okay."

"And we fuel up. Have a slider. Or five."

"No fries?"

"Fries require too long to eat."

They sat and ate. Peter concentrated on breathing slowly and chewing his food. After he downed a half-dozen miniature cheeseburgers he sat back. "Do we have any reason to believe it's anyone but Marie?"

"We've never gotten anything significant on anyone else. Why do you ask?"

"Because if we focus all our attention on her and we're wrong, it could cost Lia her life."

"What did you have in mind?"

"We now have genuine reason for alarm, and Marie's the last person to see her. It makes sense to stop by to ask her in detail about her afternoon with Lia. What I really want is to get inside her house, see if she'll let us in, if she's nervous, anything like that."

"You think Lia's tied up in the basement?"

"Could be. But I don't think she'd kill Lia in her own house."

"Why not?"

"Bucky's too smart. If Marie is Bucky, she won't want to chance leaving any blood behind. So if Lia's in the house, she'll have to move Lia before she kills her. And if Lia's not in the house, Marie hasn't had enough time to move her, kill her and dispose of her. She's got to go to her before long. So after we talk to her, we watch the house and when she leaves, we follow."

"Won't she recognize your car?"

"That's why you're going to follow me while I go over and swap cars with Brent. I'll park his car down the block from Marie's. You pick me up, then we go see her. After we talk to her, we'll park your car on the next block, then walk back to Brent's car and keep watch. Scratch that. Are you up to keeping watch on your own?"

"I suppose so. Why?"

"We'd better interview Anna and watch her, too. Just in case."

"What about Nadine? She knew where Lia was going to be this afternoon," Jim asked.

"I think we can cut Nadine out. If I'm right, something happened today to set Bucky off. Lia hasn't seen Nadine or talked to her since the park this morning. Whatever happened, it's not likely it happened at the park, in front of a lot of people. Lia spent time alone with both Marie and Anna today."

"Makes sense. What do I do?"

Follow my lead in the interviews. You act as sincere as possible. We've got to be careful. We don't want either of them to think we suspect them. After that, you park down the block from Anna and keep an eye on her house. Call me if there's any movement."

"You going to call them first?"

"And warn them? Don't think so."

Peter set the house phone to forward all calls to his cell. He packed up two surveillance survival kits.

"What's the mason jar for?" Jim asked.

"Bladder emergencies."

"Oh. Maybe you shouldn't be packing up all the cokes."

"We'll need the sugar and the caffeine. It could be a long night." Peter pulled a baggie of kale chips out of the cabinet, grimaced and tossed it into his bag.

"You really think we're going to need all this?"

"I hope not, but if we do, we're stuck. Better to have it. Do you want me to split the nacho flavored Doritos with you?"

Anna responded to the doorbell with an expression of polite surprise. "Jim, Peter, what brings you here?"

"Lia is missing," Peter said. "Can we come in?"

Anna stepped back from the door. "Come on in. I can't believe she hasn't shown up yet."

"We don't know where else to look," Peter said. "We're hoping you can give us some ideas." Peter kept his eyes on her face, searching her expression for clues.

"What about the Esquire?" Anna asked.

"Her car's down on Telford, but they haven't seen her. Can you think of anything she might have said when you were with her today?"

"I don't know what to tell you. I know you argued last night, but she didn't really talk about it. She wanted an escape, I think. We were just having girl talk and being a bit giddy. She didn't say anything about her plans, except what I told you earlier about the movie. What are you going to do?"

"Until I can file a missing person's report, we've done all we can do. We'll have to hang tight." Peter and Jim stood to leave.

Anna touched his arm. "This isn't like Lia at all. I can imagine how worried you must be. What can I do to help? Have you had anything to eat? I could fix you a sandwich."

"We're fine. If she's still gone tomorrow, you can help us canvass around Clifton. If she contacts you, will you call me?"

"Certainly." Jim gave her a pained expression as he and Peter walked out the door. He looked back and saw Anna's face in the window as they drove away.

Marie looked puzzled when she answered the door. "Hey, what's up?"

"Lia is still missing," Peter said. "Can we come in?"

Marie stepped back from the door and pointed to the couch. "Sit down. Tell me what's happening."

"We've called everyone we can think of," Jim said. "Peter says you're the last person to see her."

"Did you try the Esquire?" Marie asked.

"I found her car," Peter said. "No one working at the Esquire has seen her. We need to know everything you can tell us about this afternoon."

Marie pursed her lips. "Let's see . . . she said you had a fight. We had some drinks and got a little drunk. She seemed more frustrated than angry. We gave her every opportunity to trash you and she didn't, in case you want to know. Are you sure she's really missing? It's only been a few hours."

"The dogs were left in the house all day," Jim said. "You know she wouldn't do that."

"No, she wouldn't. What will you do?" Marie asked.

"I can't file a missing person's report until tomorrow. Until then, I guess we've done all we can. We'll have to hang tight." Peter sighed and stood to leave.

Marie held the door open for him. "Look, is there anything I can do? I'd like to help."

"There's nothing right now. You can help us knock on doors tomorrow if she's still gone. If she calls, will you let me know?"

"Sure." She wrote his number down, then watched worriedly as Jim pulled out of the drive.

Jim drove around the block, then let Peter out on the corner by Brent's car. "Call me when you get into place at Anna's," Peter said.

"You bet."

Chapter 50

Saturday, October 6

It was dark when Lia opened her eyes. She was lying on her side, knees tucked up, arms pulled behind her back. Her head pounded. Something, a cloth, was jammed into her mouth, a gag of some sort. Her hands were numb and her arms were screaming in pain. She realized her wrists were tied together, with something soft. Pantyhose? Same with her feet.

Dammit, dammit, dammit. Admit it, Anderson, you are an idiot. Why hadn't she listened to Peter? He'd said there was a murderer running around. She'd jokingly named him Bucky. Why hadn't she paid attention? Why had she let her loyalties and emotions get the better of her?

She couldn't remember how she got wherever she was. Nothing made sense. She shoved against the cloth in her mouth with her tongue. No good. Whatever was tied around her head was too tight. The cloth tasted like nylon. More pantyhose? She was revolted at the thought and shoved it away. She tried to call for help around the gag. It came out sounding like "el." She kept this up until her throat became scratchy. There was no response.

She reached back into her memory. The last thing she remembered was having drinks with Anna and Marie, Anna leaving, then waving good-bye to Marie. . . then . . . nothing.

She felt the concrete floor and imagined she was in a basement, or a garage. Where else could she be? Then she noticed the pale rectangles of light cast onto the floor from the windows. Large, industrial windows, covered with a dense steel mesh.

Who could have done this to her? Neither Marie nor Anna were strong enough to carry her into a place like this.

It took several minutes of wiggling and contortions. Finally she was sitting upright. She shoved with her feet until she felt a wall behind her. She was still captive but it felt like a victory to get her face off the dirty concrete floor.

She rested against the wall and breathed deeply to keep down the panic. *Think, think, think.* What should she do? What could she do? She had to do something. She wasn't going to be a victim again.

She took in her surroundings as best she could in the dark. She knew she was in an industrial building of some sort, with the concrete floors, steel mesh over the windows and the lingering scent of machine oil. There was a doorway to her left, with the door off the hinges, leaning against the wall on the far side. Otherwise, it was empty. It was a large room, maybe thirty by thirty feet?

She should try to get loose. But how? She needed something sharp. If there was something, anything small and heavy on the floor, could she pick it up with her feet and fling it at the windows with enough force to break the glass? Doubtful.

Maybe she could work her way into a standing position and hop over to the windows and break one with her head. After the way she screwed up, that was about all her head was good for. It might work, but the glass would fall out, not in. With the steel mesh over the windows, she wouldn't be able to angle her head to break off a shard with her teeth. Which she couldn't do anyway with the gag in her mouth.

She looked in the other direction, towards the doorway, and eyed the protruding hinges. She didn't think they would help her get her hands untied, but maybe she could hook the gag over the hinge and pull it off. Would that work? Only in the movies.

Where would she find something sharp? Not here, where the floor was a dirty open space devoid of any objects. She'd have to look elsewhere.

She sat upright and wiggled on her butt experimentally. If she rocked from one hip-bone to the other, she could "walk" forward an inch or two. She turned to the left, facing the door and began her trek. After a dozen "steps" she was two feet closer to the entrance and her heart was pounding. *Geezelpete, you could do an entire aerobics class based on getting yourself untied.* She rested, then began again. After four intervals of butt-walking, she finally reached the doorway.

The next room was a small interior space, like an office. It had no windows. The floor was covered in shag carpeting and there was a dark shape against the left-hand wall. She assumed it was a desk.

There had to be a light switch somewhere. It should be by the door, on the side opposite the hinge. She wiggled up against the jamb, then painfully worked her feet under her and pushed up. Slowly, slowly, thighs and calves screaming, glutes flexing, until her shoulder bumped into a switch plate. Just a little more, up over the lip of the plate, she felt the switch and shoved up. Nothing happened. She felt around with the edge of her shoulder and determined that the switch was on. She leaned sideways against the wall, to avoid crushing her hands. No electricity.

She decided to go for the desk and tried an experimental hop. Her bad ankle gave way. She lost her balance and fell against the wall, sliding down to the floor. Friction from the carpet made butt-walking harder. It took six intervals to get to the desk.

She rolled onto her back, crushing her numb hands, and tried to pull out the bottom drawer with her foot. Her shoe slipped off the pull. Locked or stuck, she couldn't tell. She tried the rest of the side drawers. No luck. Then she tried the middle drawer. Success.

Lia lay on her side and rested for several minutes, stretching her chest in an attempt to ease the pressure on her arms. After her breathing slowed, she rocked and rolled until she she had enough momentum to use her left knee to shove herself back up into a sitting position. Considering each move carefully, she brought her knees up to her chest, then tucked her tied ankles beside her hips and rocked forward onto her knees. She stood on her knees and "walked", an inch at a time, over to the open drawer. This was less comfortable than butt-walking, but do-able on the carpet.

She leaned over and used her chin to pull out the drawer more. Then she felt around inside the drawer with her chin and cheek. She wondered what the point was. With her mouth gagged and her hands and feet tied, how could she get something out of the drawer if she found anything? Maybe she could pull the drawer all the way out with her feet and dump it on the floor?

Then a memory surfaced. An old desk of her father's. You could not pull out the side drawers until you opened the middle drawer. Maybe she could open them now. She rolled back on her haunches, and raised her bound feet, catching the toe of one foot under the pull. She rocked back and the drawer came with her. She pulled again and the drawer tumbled and turned, spilling a small jumble on the rug.

With a few minutes of maneuvering she was able to lean back and feel the pile with her hands. A few pens, paper clips, a pushpin. A push pin! Something sharp! She picked it up, but no matter how she contorted, she could not reach her bound ankles with her hands. Which is what she deserved for dropping out of yoga. She swore that if she got out of this mess, she would go to yoga three times a week, at least.

She rested again, then tackled the other two drawers. No knives, no handy telephones. No joy. Just a couple of phone books. By this time she was exhausted. She wanted to lay down, go to sleep, and forget where she was. But time was passing, and she had no idea what time it was, when her captor would come back, or what would happen when the mysterious "Bucky" returned.

She eyed the other door. This one was on its hinges, but was cracked open. She knee-walked over to the door and shouldered it open. A huge open space, more than two thousand square feet, with a bank of windows on the right. There was a dark hulk along the far wall. It was a long piece of equipment, something with a hood and a conveyor belt, maybe. Looked like some boxes on the conveyor belt part. She eyed the machine. Maybe there would be something, the point of a screw, a piece of metal, something protruding from one of the legs where she could reach it with her hands or feet.

It was an island in a sea of concrete, and Lia eyed the distance and died a little, inside. She would have swallowed, but she had no saliva. She sighed through her nose. She couldn't knee-walk on the concrete. She was back to butt-walking.

It took forever to cross the expanse, and she counted her progress by the pale squares of moonlight that fell on the floor and flowed and bounced over her body as she bumped along. When she finally reached the monstrous contraption, she fell against one of the legs and wept.

As she leaned against the metal monstrosity, she considered her next move. If there were any screw points or other sharp bits of metal, they were most likely to be underneath the long conveyor belt. which was about three feet off the ground. Maybe on one of the legs or braces.

She found it on the third leg she checked. Someone jury-rigged a support with a pointed wood screw that protruded at least an inch from the back side of the leg, about eighteen inches from the ground. She crouched under the conveyor, and maneuvered her numb hands against the point. She suspected she'd scratched herself several times before she felt the tug of the point biting into the cloth. She rocked and tugged and twisted, and finally she felt some give in her bonds. She stretched out her aching arms to keep the cloth tight and continued her work, frenzied now, slamming her head against the bottom of the conveyor. She fell over twice and had to work her way back into position.

And then the last bit parted. *Oh, God, oh, God, oh, God.* She thought the prayer but could not say it because she was still gagged. She brought her arms in front of her and sat on the floor. Her useless hands lay in her lap as she willed the circulation back into them. She wept again, with relief and with anger.

Why would someone do this to her? Kill her boyfriend, kill her patron, drug her partner into insanity. Kidnap her for who knows what purpose. As she sat there and waited for sensation to return to her hands, she had time to think. None of it made any sense. Who except Anna and Marie knew where she was that afternoon? It couldn't be either of them, they had both left. Was it someone random? How could it be with everything else that had happened? Why couldn't she remember?

Sensation stabbed into her hands, reminding her that she had more to do. She began wiggling her fingers and rubbing her hands, shaking them out. When she had some control, she felt for the knot at the back of her head. She tugged on it, sliding it around so that the knot was over one cheek where she could more easily reach it. She picked at it patiently until it loosened, then pulled the gag off. She coughed several times, and tried to work saliva back into her mouth. If only she could have water. Was the water off, too?

She had to take care of her feet next. This knot was much tighter from all her moving around and she could not pick it apart. She scooted out from under the conveyor belt and used her arms to haul herself upright against the machine. She felt around on top of the belt and the hood. There was a screw driver lying by the control panel.

Energized, she sat back down on the floor and began attacking the pantyhose wrapped around her ankles, stabbing and clawing it apart. The screwdriver was an imperfect tool, but once she created a sizable hole in the pantyhose, she grabbed the edges of the hole with her fingers and ripped it apart, bit by bit.

She stood up, stuffing the remains of the pantyhose in her back pocket. There had to be a bathroom in this place. Maybe she would luck out and find running water. She found the bathroom in a small hall. The taps were not running, but when she lifted the lid on the toilet, water remained in the tank. She dipped one end of the panty hose into the tank and used the damp nylon to scrub her hands. Then, disdaining a grimy mug sitting on the back of the sink, she dipped her hands into the tank. She scooped water out of the tank, and it dribbled down her arms and face as she drank it. It ran down her neck, leaving a damp blotch on her shirt. She scooped out more and splashed her face, dampened the back of her neck.

She relieved herself in the toilet, deciding not to flush to preserve the water in the tank. Refreshed, she went in search of a door. At the end of the hall was a short set of steps leading down to an exit. She turned the knob and pushed. Nothing. She felt around for a deadbolt. She found a double deadbolt, one that key-locked from the inside. "Shit, shit, shit, damn!," She told the darkness.

She found two more doors, both locked tight. She continued to explore the building, looking for a way out. It was a two story, at least 100 feet long. The second floor windows were not covered with steel mesh, but they were over twenty feet from the ground. No convenient dumpster full of mattresses to jump into.

She saw no landmarks through the window. She wasn't positive, but thought she might be in the industrial section of Northside, East of Hamilton Avenue, near Spring Grove Cemetery. This was the closest place such a building could be located. *I could scream my lungs out and nobody would hear me, not until Monday morning. Nobody will drive past here on a Sunday.*

She toured the windows, trying to get a better sense of her location, checking for a fire escape, any way to get out. The doors were metal. Even if she found a hatchet, she wouldn't be able to hack her way out. She wondered if she could build a fire somehow, get attention that way. *Sure, that's a great idea, if what you want is a memorial stone at the park.*

An ancient freight elevator was open on the second floor. Non-functional, since there was no electricity. She walked inside and spied the hatch on top. She went through the rooms, found an old oak chair and dragged it into the elevator. By climbing on top, she was able to reach up through the hatch. She could probably pull herself up, climb the ladder on the side of the shaft and get out on the roof. But then what? She'd be stuck until someone drove by.

Think, Think, Think. Bucky has to come back here before Monday morning. Whatever she's got in mind, she can't let you go. So you've got to be ready.

Could she pretend to be tied up when Bucky returned, then attack her when she got close? Too Hollywood. *She'll know something isn't right the minute she sees what I did to the desk. You could fix that. Maybe, but better not to let her get in close. God only knows what she'll bring with her.*

She decided her best bet was the machine, and the boxes on the conveyor belt. She went back downstairs and busied herself hauling the boxes into the pale moonlight so she could root through them for a possible weapon. She found an assortment of small hardware, including nuts and bolts, lock washers and nails. She kept these to the side. Three boxes were full of printed material: order forms, brochures and business cards. The last box held promotional give-aways: imprinted pens, keychains and pocket knives. She held up one of the knives. *Where were you when I needed you?* She shook her head and stuffed it into her pocket.

She went back to the machine and peeked under the hood. There was a three foot long two by four. *That's more like it.* She picked it up, hefted it to get a feel for it, decided it was better with a two handed swing.

A tour of the back offices revealed a spool of phone wire. She picked this up, carried it back to her little arsenal in the main room. Then she sat down to think.

Chapter 51

Sunday, October 7

Bear wanted attention. He stretched up on his hind legs and pawed at John's knee. John kept banging away at his keyboard. Bear dropped down and started chewing the laces of John's cross-trainers. John continued to ignore him. Finally, Bear bit his ankle.

"Okay, Kitteh," John said, leaning back in his chair. He patted his lap and Bear jumped up for a cuddle, purring as John scratched behind his ears and stroked the dense brown fur. John stood up, carrying Bear out onto the porch while he walked out the pain in his back. He watched the quarter moon through the leaves of the tree he could no longer climb.

"This one doesn't feel right. I think I may have found it," he told the cat.

There was nothing to say the death was a homicide. Then again, there was nothing to say it wasn't, either. The overdose was ruled an accidental death. But there were too many ways to make something like that happen.

He should call it a night. Play with the cats. Go to bed. But he had to know. He felt the tingle, the gentle nudge which indicated a push from his guides. So he went further back in time. It was tedious, hacking into payroll files, then HR files, then police reports.

Eventually he found it. Twelve years ago. A bathtub drowning. The decedent had taken sedatives and then fell asleep in her bath and slid under the water. The only questionable part of the report was the source of the sedatives. She didn't have a prescription and no one knew where she'd gotten them. He continued looking. Two hours later he dug up an insulin overdose.

By now it was 2:00 a.m. and his back was screaming. His intuition was nagging him, but surely it was too late to call anyone tonight. He'd call Jim tomorrow on the burner phone. A few hours wouldn't make any difference. He stepped out on the porch and started to pace out the pain.

Chapter 52

Sunday, October 7

Lia crouched in the darkness under the desk. In the tomb-like silence, she heard keys rattle in an exterior lock, then the door squealed open. It shut with a bang. Keys in the lock again. Bucky was taking no chances. She had relocked the door. No chance to make a run for it.

Lia became aware that she was holding her breath and forced herself to breathe naturally. There was a scuffing of shoes on concrete steps, then quick steps across the floor in the large room, then silence as those shoes met the ancient shag carpeting.

Lia froze as the glow of a flashlight spread across the carpet, lapping at the legs of her hiding place. She kept her eyes away from the light, not wanting to lose her night vision. The circle of light moved on, crawled up the wall and fell through the doorway to the room beyond. Lia tensed as the dark smudge that was Bucky passed by.

"Dammit to Hell!" An ugly voice exploded from the next room.

Lia yanked the phone wire, pulling it tight across the doorway. It was tied to the door hinge and wrapped around a desk leg. She wrapped the tail of the wire three times around one hand, placed her other hand on top and braced her feet against the wall for impact.

Bucky flew across the trip-wire, landing face first on the carpet, her flashlight on the floor in front of her, illuminating a gun. Lia burst out from under the desk, grabbed up her two by four and ran for the gun. Before she could kick it away, Anna, quick as a snake, snatched the gun up and pointed it towards Lia. Lia nearly stumbled from the shock.

She threw the two by four at Anna and ran, ducking down at the door long enough to snatch up the small box of hardware. A shot bit into the wall over her shoulder. She dashed up the stairs, scattering handfuls of nuts and bolts behind her.

She heard Anna shriek as she slipped on the trail of hardware. "Don't you think you're smart! It doesn't matter what you do, you can't get out, and I've got the gun."

Lia dashed for the elevator, jumped up on the chair and lifted her arms through the hatch. Adrenaline gave her the boost she needed to pull herself up on top of the elevator. On her way up, she kicked over the chair, hoping that Anna wouldn't see it and realize where she was. She closed the hatch carefully, making no sound.

She knelt there, shaking, as she heard Anna calling. "I don't want to do this, but you've given me no choice. You might as well come out now. Prolonging this isn't going to make any difference."

She waited until her heart slowed, till the sound of Anna's voice grew faint, then quietly as she could, she stepped onto the ladder that ran up the shaft. She climbed up to the room on the roof that contained the elevator mechanism. This door had a slide bolt instead of a key lock. The door creaked as she opened it. She hoped the sound wouldn't carry, or if it did, that Anna wouldn't be able to identify the direction from which it came.

She sat down, leaning against the door of the little room and considered her situation. She wished she'd thought to put a board up here that she could jam under the doorknob. She didn't think Anna could pull herself up through the hatch, but this was not her kind, mothering friend. She didn't know what this person was capable of doing.

If Anna did come up to the roof, she didn't have a weapon except the tiny pocket knife. Anna had a gun. If Anna didn't find her, she could wait on the roof until she heard a car. Then she could go to the edge of the roof and start screaming. She stared out into the darkness, wondering how many hours she had until dawn.

Chapter 53

Sunday, October 7

Peter tapped his fingers impatiently on the steering wheel. He decided to call Jim.

"Yes, I'm awake. No, she hasn't moved." Jim said.

"Nothing's happening here, either."

"How long do we keep this up? It's after two."

"Murphy's law says the minute we leave, she'll act, whichever one she is. So we stay. I figure the next four hours are critical."

What makes you say that?"

"It's the dead of the night. Nobody to see her coming or going. Past history says Bucky works at night."

"You sure it's one of them? All we've seen them do is watch television, take the dogs out for their last pee, and go to bed."

"That's what the pattern of lights going on and off has suggested. For all we know Bucky's really looking up remote places for a body dump on Google Earth."

They pondered this in silence, unwilling to say out loud what that would mean.

"You think Lia's in one of these houses, in the basement?"

"No, I don't. Neither one has made a move for the basement since we've been watching, and both of them were comfortable with us in the house. No scrambling when we knocked on the door. That suggests there was nothing to find.

"I think it's time to stir the pot. I'm going to give them a call, see what they say, how they act."

Peter found Anna's number, hit send.

"Hello?" She sounded groggy.

"Anna, it's Peter."

"What time is it?"

"It's after two. I'm sorry to wake you. I was wondering if you ever heard from Lia."

"She's not back yet? I haven't heard from her."

"I was hoping she called you and made you promise not to tell me."

"No, I'm sorry."

"Do you have any idea where she might be?"

"The only place I can think of is her studio. Unless, maybe . . . oh, probably not."

"What is it?"

"You don't suppose she's at Renee's, do you?"

"I called there. I called everywhere."

"Is there anything I can do?"

"Not right now. I'll let you know when I think of something."

"Call me the minute you do."

"Thanks, Anna. I'll let you get back to sleep."

Peter clicked off the phone. He repeated the process with Marie, with the same results. This time he was able to see her bedroom light switch on when the phone rang. He called Jim back. "It appears I woke both of them up. Whichever one is Bucky, the butter still hasn't melted in her mouth. What's that mean, anyway?"

"You don't know what that means?" Jim asked.

"My mama used to say it, but it never made any sense to me. What does butter have to do with anything?"

"It means being good at acting innocent. They're so cool, butter wouldn't melt in their mouth."

"So it's cold-blooded."

"I guess so," Jim said.

"Like a snake."

They ended the call. Thirty minutes later, Jim called Peter.

"Peter?"

"Yeah?"

"What's to stop Bucky from leaving out the back door?"

"She's gotta use her car."

"How do you figure that?"

"She's got Lia stashed somewhere. This had to be an impulse. No way is Bucky stupid enough to be seen with Lia right before she disappears. So something happened today, that made Bucky break pattern. There were only a few hours when she could have acted.

"Bucky's a planner, and Bucky didn't have time to plan anything. So she stashed Lia, and now she has to go back and get her. Wherever she put Lia, it's temporary. I have to believe that."

"Where do you think she stashed Lia?"

"You tell me. You've known them longer than anyone. Wherever it is, it can't be out of the city. She'd have been caught in rush hour traffic, and she would not have been home when I called her. I'm thinking she took Lia's car to her little hidey-hole, dumped it in Clifton, then took a bus back up to Northside. The seventeen passes right through.

"Wherever she went, it can't be more than thirty minutes away. Where do you think she could have gone?"

"You mean like a storage space?" Jim asked

"Like that, though I hope not. There's thousands of those in the city."

"Anna's got keys to the Lieberman Foundation. That's downtown."

"They have staff on weekends?"

"There's a security guard at a desk in the lobby."

"That's out."

They lapsed into silence again. A car engine started in the distance.

"Anywhere else Anna or Marie might have keys? She have any friends out of town right now?"

"Last friend we had that went away was Roger."

"Shit," Peter said.

"I have a question."

"What is it?"

"I've been waiting for Anna to pull out of that garage for what, seven hours now?"

"And?"

"How do we know the car is in the garage?"

"Dammit, you'd think a highly decorated police detective would think of that. Will you stay on the phone and go look?"

Peter heard Jim exiting the car, winced at the slamming of the car door. Amateurs. As he waited, he tapped nervously on the steering wheel and silently castigated himself for making a rookie mistake. Not a rookie mistake. An amateur mistake. A mistake a ten year-old would make.

"I've got to go around to the side. No windows in the garage door . . . Hoo boy. Nothing in here but bare concrete and a lawn mower.

"Damn," Peter said. "I'm hanging up. I'm going to call Anna again.

This time Anna did not pick up.

Chapter 54

Sunday, October 7

Lia was thoroughly chilled by the time she heard a faint scuffling on the other side of the door. The sound sent a jolt of panic through her. She stood up and stepped back behind the door, the little pen knife in one hand.

The door opened slightly. Lia waited, holding her breath while the opening widened. When she spotted the tip of one shoe, she rammed into the door with her shoulder, slamming Anna's head against the door frame.

Lia heard Anna scream. She did not hear the clatter of a dropped gun. Anna shoved against the door. Lia rammed it against Anna again. Suddenly, the door fell shut as Anna apparently gave up struggling against it. Lia leaned against the door, panting. A shot blew through the door, into Lia's thigh. Lia grunted against the pain and limped around behind the elevator room as the door flew open.

She could hear Anna's ragged breathing.

"How long do you want to do this, Lia?" Anna called out. "I've got all night. And I've got an alibi, since Jim is busy watching my house. Nobody is going to find us here."

Lia remained silent.

"Dammit, answer me when I talk to you! Why did you have to ruin everything?"

"I don't know what you're talking about," Lia called back. "What did I ever do to you? I was your friend, and you shot Luthor."

"I did you a favor. All he ever did was suck you dry, and all you ever did was whine about how you wished he would go away. I set you free! Oh, but you couldn't appreciate that. You had to sit around whining about how he was dead."

"So, what did I ruin, Anna? What did I do that was so bad you had to kill people?"

"I had everything just the way I wanted it. Then you had to introduce Catherine to everybody, and nothing was the same after that. Every freaking morning I had to listen to her pathetic little rich lady problems and watch while she dragged Jim away from us.

"After that, you brought that whacko, Bailey, to the park. Now it's Renee and her ridiculous Stepford dog. Jim and I weren't enough for you. You had to drag in the whole freaking world."

"You did all this because I ruined your morning coffee?"

"Oh, don't be so outraged. I just do things other people want to do. You wanted Luthor gone, and I got rid of him for you."

"I wanted him out of my life. I didn't want him dead."

"Why do you even care? You didn't love him. Look at me! My life was perfect. You had to find my computer, and now I have to kill you. Do you think I wanted this?"

"What computer? What are you talking about?"

"Don't lie to me! I caught you looking behind that painting. I know you saw the netbook I hid back there."

"I wasn't looking behind the painting, and I never found a computer. Are you telling me you're doing all this because you thought I saw something?"

"I don't want to do this to you Lia, but I can't let you live, not now. I've got the gun, and I'm guarding the door. There's no other way off this roof. If you get back in the building, you're still locked in. I've already shot you once. You might as well give up."

"Why can't I remember anything? How did you get me here?"

Anna's laugh was mean and nasty. "That was easy. I put Rhohypnol in your water. You always hydrate after you're done drinking. I waited by your car and offered to drive you home because you'd had too much to drink. You were feeling woozy by then. I offered you some mini-cheesecakes so you could get something on your stomach. They also had Rhohypnol in them and you gobbled them right down. After that, you were a little lamb. I barely managed to get you here before you passed out."

"I don't get it. Why did you push so hard for me to date Peter? How could you want a cop so close to you?"

"Like you could ever stick with a relationship? Jim and I are the only people you ever kept in your life. Now, let me finish this so I can go back and offer Jim some coffee, since he's been sitting outside my house all night. Then I can help him look for you."

"You keep talking about you and Jim. I've got news for you. He's been computer-dating. I don't think it's going to be just Jim for much longer. Killing me is not going to give you your mornings back."

"Killing you will keep me out of jail."

"Peter already suspects you. We knew Bailey was set up. And Jim knows, too."

"They can't prove it. Nobody will find you up here. I'll have plenty of time to get rid of you before they work on this building. I'm going to drop you off that overlook on Renee's property. That will fix her self-satisfied wagon. Nobody will be able to connect me to anything."

"They'll know. Peter loves me. He won't stop."

"Oh, Peter loves you, does he? And have you returned the sentiment? . . . Thought not. Come on out, and I'll finish it with a bullet to the head, quick and painless. Or shall we continue discussing uncomfortable truths? . . . Cat got your tongue? . . . Oh, wait, you don't like cats."

Lia compressed the wound in her thigh with her hands. It hurt terribly. Blood was soaking into her jeans and running down her leg. She could still walk, for now, but she was feeling dizzy and she'd need medical care before long. She'd have to make a move.

~ ~ ~

Anna heard a noise behind the elevator shack. She edged to her right, around the corner of the little room. Something barreled into her lower back and tossed her forward. Her grip lost, the gun soared, spinning end over end in a lazy arc past the lip of the roof as she slammed face down into the tar paper.

~ ~ ~

Lia fell on top of Anna, pounding her wherever she could reach with her fists. Anna whipped over onto her back and grabbed Lia's neck with both hands. They rolled until Lia was under her, Anna still choking her. Lia clawed at Anna's hands but couldn't get any leverage. She attempted to buck Anna off, but the woman was too heavy.

Anna's eyes focused on Lia's face. She had an avid, animal expression of satisfaction as her thumbs pressed into Lia's throat. Her face grew more intent as black spots began to

261

explode in front of Lia's eyes. Anna's bared teeth became a manic, gleeful grin as she drove her thumbs in further. This was the last thing Lia saw as her hands clawed the roof and her world dimmed to one pinpoint.

Lia felt something under her fingers. It was small and metallic, the little knife she'd tossed over the shack to distract Anna. She whipped up her hand and stabbed the pocket knife blindly. The knife found something soft to penetrate, then stuck, pulling out of Lia's hand. Anna screamed and reared back. Lia planted the foot of her good leg into Anna's stomach and shoved with all her might. Anna fell back, turning as she fell, then lay still.

Chapter 55

Sunday, October 7

Lia sat up and leaned against the wall, eyeing Anna while she waited for her heart-rate to slow. Anna lay with her face against the tar paper. The only movement was the pool of blood forming around her face. The only sounds were the pounding of her heart and her own harsh breathing.

After a while, she stood up and limped over to Anna, nudged a hand with her foot. No movement. She picked up the lax hand and felt at the wrist for a pulse. Nothing. She rolled Anna over. The impact of Anna's face on the roof had driven the knife through Anna's eye into her brain. The other eye stared at nothing.

Lia turned away and vomited in dry heaves, convulsing on her hands and knees as what little remained in her stomach mixed with the pool of blood. She dropped over onto her side as the convulsions turned into sobs and she fell into a daze.

She lay on the roof, gradually becoming aware that she could not remain there. No one knew where she was. A hint of dawn touched the horizon. If she figured correctly, this was Sunday and the likelihood of flagging a passerby was zip.

She'd have to climb back down the ladder and drop through the hatch while trying not to make her wound worse. Then what? Stumble along until she found a house and a phone? Scare the residents half to death? If they called the police on her, she imagined they would take her somewhere to get stitched up, and that would be fine with her.

It was gruesome, digging through Anna's pockets. When she found Anna's keyring, she realized that Anna had probably driven over. She could take Anna's car. If she figured right, District Five was about a mile away. She checked Anna's other pockets, and found a single key with a tag that read "Ellis St." She found no phone.

Her trip down the elevator shaft was painful. She lowered her good leg first, then her other leg, then bore her weight on her arms as she lowered her good leg to the next step. She reached the top of the elevator and discovered a step ladder inside the car, explaining how Anna had made it to the roof. She silently gave thanks and continued her journey. When she made it to the bottom of the ladder, she wanted to kiss the rusty floor.

She was resting on the outside stoop when four police cruisers pulled up. Peter jumped out of the first car before it was fully stopped.

"You're . . . late . . . Dourson," she gasped past the burning in her throat, "I . . . could . . . use . . . a ride." Then she fainted.

Chapter 56

Monday, October 8

Lia sat in a nest of pillows on the couch and stared at the mosaic design she was attempting to refine for Renee. It wasn't going well. She closed her drawing pad and set it down, rubbing her temples. Maybe it was too soon for her to get back to work, but she didn't know what else to do with herself. She had to do something to get her mind off the ache in her thigh and the events that caused it.

Honey and Chewy looked up at the sound of Peter's car. Viola scrabbled out from under the couch. All eight eyes faced Peter when he walked in the door.

"Honey, I'm home," he intoned.

"You're very early Are all the criminals in Cincinnati taking a holiday?"

"Roller called me into the office. Reamed me a good one for going off the reservation and involving citizens. Then he sent me home and said not to come back for a week. I'm supposed to be looking after your welfare."

"Are you now?"

"Yep. I guess he's got a soft spot for vigilante artists. So what do you need?" He sat down on the couch by her feet, laying a hand on her good leg.

"I can't stop thinking about everything that happened. I need serious distraction."

"And how are we to accomplish that? Would you like to watch movies? Play Scrabble?"

"Let's see," she said, tapping her lip. She looked at him sideways. "You could always play Nubian slave to my Egyptian princess."

"Lady," he said gravely as he bowed his head, "your wish is my command."

"In that case," She pointed imperiously to the door, "Slave, fetch me pizza!"

"Somebody needs to talk to Dewey's about delivering," Peter said as he walked back in the door. "Keeping a pizza warm in an open chariot is a pain in the ass."

"Thy language is crude, Slave."

"I beg your pardon, Princess. I should have said it was painful in the hind-most end."

"That should not be possible. I did not ask for a pizza with jalapeno peppers, and you, Slave, have not been given permission to eat it."

"I was being metaphorical, my princess. One thousand apologies. Thy pizza is adorned with olives and garlic, as you commanded. Wouldst thou liketh thy pizza on thy couch? Wouldst thou care for dishes and silver? What is thy command?"

"You are a good and loyal slave. You may share half my pizza or have one of my kisses instead."

"My princess, one of thy kisses is worth my paltry life, a thousand times. It would be a gift beyond anything I can imagine. But if I share your pizza, it will give me strength to serve you more. And if my lips should touch where thy lips have touched, I should die a happy man."

"A meritorious answer, Loyal One. Carry me to my bower, and feed me with thine own hands. I need not dishes or silver. I shall reward you with pizza and a kiss. But keep the hounds at bay, they do endeavor to abscond with my dinner."

The dogs, salivating, followed Peter into the kitchen. He stashed the pizza on top of the refrigerator, then picked up Lia and carried her out of the living room.

"How beautiful are your feet in sandals, O noble daughter," Peter said as they made their way to the bedroom. "Your rounded thighs are like jewels, the work of a master hand."

"How knowest you this poetry?"

"As a young boy, I crept into the room where they kept the holy of holies, and read the sacred books. These words were burned forever in my heart, waiting for you."

"You must speak it to me, Slave."

Peter set her down on the bed. "Then I must show you as well." He lifted the hem of her t-shirt.

"Thou wishes my garments away?"

"Yes, Princess, if I am to show you properly." Lia lifted her arms and he removed her shirt. "Your navel," he continued, "is a rounded bowl that never lacks mixed wine." He leaned over and kissed her belly button, then placed his hands on either side of it. "Your belly is a heap of wheat, encircled with lilies."

"Though takest liberties, Slave. Still, I wish that you tell me more. But, my repast grows cold. How will you solve this dilemma?"

"Shall I recite poetry while I feed you, Princess?"

"You are ingenious as well as meritorious. Proceed."

Peter brought the pizza in and set it down on the bed. He opened the box and removed a slice, holding it up to Lia's lips.

"I shall take a bite, Slave, but you must take one also, a bite for every one of mine. Time enough for poetry later, and you must have strength."

When they finished the pizza, Peter lured the dogs out of the room with the crusts and shut the door. He leaned over Lia and kissed the top of each breast. "Your breasts are like two fawns, twins of a gazelle, that graze among the lilies . . ."

Chapter 57

Thursday, October 11, 7:00 a.m.

"Peter, I don't know if I'm ready for this." Lia sat in Peter's SUV, looking at all the cars in the parking lot. Jim was here, and Nadine, Terry, Marie, Jose, and a number of semi-regulars she hadn't seen for a while. She wondered if they all showed up to get the gossip.

"Relax. Asia will be here soon, and you two can go talk while I take the dogs and run interference with everybody. They care about you. It's not fair to shut them out."

"They're going to hate me for killing Anna."

"I don't think so. Everyone knows what happened by now. I made sure of it."

"You always going to have my back, Kentucky Boy?"

"I hope so. If you'll let me." He kissed her forehead and pulled her into a tight hug. Honey barked to get out and Chewy reared up against the back seat and butted Lia's arm with his nose. Viola whined.

"Hey, can't a guy make a little time here, you bunch of punks?"

Lia snorted. "I think the rule is 'pee first, cuddle later.' Go on and take them. I'll be okay until Asia shows up."

She watched as Peter trotted the dogs up the curving drive. He was always taking care of her, as if she were breakable. She felt breakable these days. She wondered if she let herself feel that way because she knew he'd be there for her.

Asia pulled up next to Peter's Blazer. As she exited the sporty little Kia, Lia noticed that her usual grand edifice of hair had been replaced by spiraling corn-rows.

"What's with the hair?"

"If I'm going to make time for you every morning for the next week, something has to go. It's a sacrifice, but I can live with it."

Asia placed a comforting hand on Lia's shoulder as they turned towards the park. "Let's go find a quiet spot, then you can tell me what's going on."

Lia leaned on her crutch and limped up the drive. "I can't go far."

"Whatever you want to do." They settled on a table at the front of the small dog park, which was empty.

It took a while for Lia to pour out her story. Asia sat beside her on their table, shaking her head and giving her "you-poor-child" looks. "I wish you had trusted me enough to let me know what was happening," she said.

"I wasn't sure where the law began and ended with your duty to report. I didn't want create a conflict for you. Anyway, we had enough to talk about without all that."

"Oh?"

"That, and I halfway wasn't believing it. I didn't believe it, not until I woke up in that building. I treated the whole thing like it was an annoying game."

"But the important thing is you did believe it, and you took care of yourself."

"If that's what you want to call killing a friend."

Asia caught her eye and held it. "She wasn't your friend. She may have said things that friends say, and done things that friends do, but it was all make-believe to her. She was all about keeping control of her little world. And if one of her dolls misbehaved, she smashed it. Do you get that?"

Lia shrugged.

"From what you've told me, she enjoyed smashing her dolls. You may have been her favorite doll, she may have left you all her money, but in the end you were just as disposable as everyone else. Real people with real feelings don't deliberately harm others."

"I hurt her. I stabbed her and she died."

"You weren't hurting the Anna you knew. You were protecting yourself from the monster inside her. From everything you've told me about her journal, you didn't have a choice. She was not going to stop until she killed you."

"I didn't want to kill her. It just happened. I only wanted to stop her."

"Of course you only wanted to stop her. That's because you have compassion, a compassion that she was probably drawn to but didn't understand. It sounds like she wanted you to be her little pet, that she wanted to own you. That's not love, no matter how pretty it looks from the outside."

"But why didn't I see it? I knew her for years."

"Lia, this isn't like Luthor. You may not have known exactly what Luthor was up to, but on some level, you knew it wasn't working. He did kick off your intuition. Why you kept him around is an entirely different matter.

"Someone like Anna is called a psychopath. It's someone who doesn't have feelings. They're very detached, dead inside, and much of their life is putting on an act so everyone will think they're normal. Since they lack normal emotions, it's easy for them to do things that sicken normal people. It's also easy for them to deceive people. They can even fool lie detectors. It wasn't just you who was fooled. I bet everyone around her was fooled. It's important for you not to blame yourself for missing it."

"I still feel like I should have known."

"I'm hoping you'll learn to forgive yourself for not being perfect.

I'm hoping all this will go away."

"There's a lot that may never go away."

Lia looked down at the bandage on her leg as she talked. "I know that. It's not fair that Anna could change my life like that."

"No, it's not. But you can find some good in this."

Lia looked at her sharply. "What good could there possibly be in killing someone?"

"You've faced something very few people ever have to face. You've faced it twice, in fact. When you first came to see me, you said you froze when Bailey put that gun to your head. This time, you were able to assess your situation and act effectively."

Lia shrugged. "When I woke up, she wasn't there. I had time to think about it. It might have been different if she'd been there when I woke up."

"What's important is what did happen. I'm hoping that you'll have greater confidence in yourself from now on." Asia smiled. "The important thing is, you were not a victim."

"I feel like a victim, like life tossed me into the Vita-Mix and pressed the puree button."

"You've had a lot happen over the past several months. Not all of it has been bad, but change still causes stress. You've been in and out of crisis mode for an extended period of time. Hopefully, this situation will settle down and you can start to make decisions based on everything you've learned in the past six months. Maybe we can start our next session by listing what some of those things are."

"Great." Lia stuck her tongue out. "More work."

"Enough for today. You have some friends over on the other side. Isn't it time you gave them a chance to be there for you?"

~ ~ ~

Peter met Lia and Asia at the corral. All three dogs were lined up at the gate, waiting for her. Asia handed Lia off to Peter, who wrapped an arm around her. As she limped along beside Peter, Lia felt that electric tingle of shame, that feeling she got in dreams when she was naked and everyone was looking at her. Heads turned. No one waved. The dogs, sensing something out of the ordinary, stayed close.

She'd felt this exposed once before. She'd visited a prison for an art project, and had to cross the yard. A quarter-mile of athletic fields and more than a thousand male convicts dressed in dark blue. All stood silent, all activity stopped. All staring at her as she made her slow progress, a thousand heads turning in unison until she and her escort reached their destination on the far side of the prison campus.

"Jim and the others are in the back. Just ignore everyone else."

Lia kept her head up, defiantly. "Screw them," she said.

"Atta girl."

Jim, Marie, Terry and Nadine were at their usual table. Terry was showing off his cast-free leg, pallid white and fragile from the shin down. Nadine was the first to speak. "Come sit over here, Lia. You should rest that leg." She scooted over on the table top, making room.

Lia boosted herself up. Peter sat next to her.

"How's the leg?" Jim asked.

"I think this is where I say 'it's only a flesh wound,' and slug down some bourbon."

"Now, Lia, you know alcohol isn't allowed in the park," Nadine joked weakly.

Lia cracked half a smile. "I don't know what to say to you all."

"We're just really glad you're okay," Marie said. "You don't need to say anything. Jim and Peter filled us in."

"And if any of those Looky Lous pop off at ya, I'll just taser 'em," Jose offered.

"Thanks, Jose," Lia sniffed. "This is so awkward."

Terry scuffed his shoe. "You may have saved my life. Peter says she sabotaged my ladder. She might have come back to finish the job."

"We're really sorry, Lia," Nadine said.

"Why are you sorry?" Lia asked, genuinely perplexed.

"We all liked her," Nadine said. "We never dreamed she had it in her to kill people. How many years has she been coming up here? There was never a hint of anything wrong."

Kita planted her forepaws on the bench and licked Lia's face, leaving a long streamer dangling off Lia's chin.

"Ick," Lia said, and everyone laughed.

Lia was suddenly struck by how her crowd had shrunk in the past six months. Luthor, Catherine, Roger, Anna, gone. Bailey sidelined, and Terry an infrequent visitor for now. She blinked back tears. She'd lost people, but she'd also gained. There was Peter, Asia and Renee, and Bailey would be back before long.

"We have to celebrate," she said.

Everyone looked at her.

"We're all alive. Bailey is coming back home as soon as she can convince the state she's not a danger to herself and others. Anna can't ever hurt anyone again. We need a party."

"What a wonderful idea," Nadine said. "How do you want to celebrate?"

"Something crazy. I feel the need to do something outrageous."

"Karaoke," Marie offered.

"Are you nuts?" Jim asked.

"Exactly," Marie said.

"You won't get me up there," Peter said.

"Singing badly in front of strangers is liberating," Marie said.

"Karaoke is an outstanding idea," Terry said. Where can we do this?"

"The Painted Fish has Karaoke on Wednesdays," Lia said. "And the sushi is half-price."

"Karaoke and half-price sushi?" Terry enthused, "What more could anyone want? When are we going to stage this debacle?"

"When Bailey gets out. But everyone has to sing. Except Bailey," Lia said.

"You don't want me to sing," Jim said. "I'm tone-deaf."

"Even better," Marie said.

"How does that help anyone?" Jim asked.

"We're doing it for Bailey," Marie said. "When she comes home, she's going to feel really embarrassed about everything that's happened. She's spent three months in a mental institution. Coming back to normal life is going to be strange. So we make fools of ourselves to make her feel better. She won't feel so weird."

"I'm supposed to make an ass out of myself so Bailey won't feel like an ass?" Jim asked.

"Exactly!" Marie said.

~ ~ ~

Lia sat next to Peter on the back stoop, watching the dogs. Her bandaged leg was carefully extended.

"You know," Peter said, "once probate clears on Anna's estate, you'll no longer be a starving artist."

"I don't want that money. I can't stand the thought of it. I still can't believe she left everything to me in her will."

"You're still going to have to deal with it."

She sighed. "I know. I suppose I'll give it away."

"There go my dreams of being a kept man."

Lia elbowed him. "I could never humiliate you like that. Just think what it would be like, having to ask for money every time you wanted to buy a new Ferrari."

"You're right. I could never live with myself. Doing nothing all day long except thinking of ways to make you happy. That would be terrible. Much better to see it go to a home for paraplegic finger-painters."

"Oh, stop it. I know who I want to give it to, but I don't know if they'll take it."

"Who's that?"

"According to the journal on her netbook, Anna had a lot of victims. Terry's going to need medical treatment for years to deal with his head injury. I could get him a speech therapist."

Peter's eyebrows shot up. "A speech therapist? For Terry?"

"Speech therapists do more than help people learn how to talk again. They also help people with brain injuries learn how to function with their disability. It may not look like it, but I think Terry's having a really hard time."

"Huh."

"And Bailey's got to be in bad shape after losing all her income for three months. She's probably lost a lot of her customers for good. From everything you've said about Anna's journal, there are probably children who lost parents. If we can identify them, I could help them with their education, or with starting a business or something.

"As it is, any one of those people could sue the estate for wrongful death and tie everything up for years. If I let them know up front I'm sharing the money, we can settle it all faster. I guess I should talk to a lawyer about a foundation."

Peter twined a lock of Lia's hair around his finger and tugged. "You're a victim, too."

"Maybe I'll take enough to pay for my therapy."

He wrapped his arms around her. "You're a good person. I don't know if I can live up to all this goodness."

"Tell you what. You keep being your bad self and I'll just make a project out of fixing you up."

"Does that mean I have to eat kelp noodles?"

"Absolutely. Or be punished."

He considered this. "Will you wear Marie's boots when you do that?"

"Maybe. Peter, I need to get serious for a minute."

"What's on your mind?"

"I love you, I really do."

"Good." He kissed her.

"But . . ."

He leaned back and looked at her. "But?"

"I really need my space back. I'm not ready for a twenty-four/seven relationship."

Peter sighed. "At least I won't feel guilty about my Pop Tarts anymore. Do I get a going away present?"

"You're not going that far, Kentucky Boy. Look, this isn't about you, it's about me."

"That sounds like a break up line."

"I've been figuring out some things about myself. My mother used to be totally dependent on the men in her life, and when she didn't have one, she focused all her energy on getting one. I didn't have a mother for much of my childhood, not one that paid attention to me. And the men never made her happy. She did better when she was alone but she never realized it.

So I think I'm phobic about being dependent on a relationship. And I think you're the type of guy who wants that kind of dependence. I don't want to lose you, but I still need to work some things out."

Peter pulled her into his lap. "I'm sorry if I've crowded you. I didn't mean to, but I didn't know any other way to protect you. I like that you aren't needy. But I do have 'serve and protect' in the blood. If there's a danger to someone I care about, I'll be there. You can still change your own tires. It won't threaten my manhood.

"I don't know where this is going. I see so many bad things, I want to grab onto the good things in my life. I don't know what's right for us, but I'd like there to be an 'us.' It makes my job easier, knowing you're around. I bet, if we try real hard, we can figure out something that works for both of us. But we don't have to figure it out today."

"You hardly ever talk about your work."

"I guess I just want to leave it all behind when I'm with you."

"That's not fair to me, Peter."

"What do you mean?"

"If you want me to share the good, I need to share the bad, too. Otherwise, I'm like a kid with a lollypop who doesn't know the rent is past due."

"Huh."

"Just think about it. If I can change my own tires, I can handle hearing about your day."

"Guess I never thought of it that way. So when do you want me to leave?"

"Not just yet. 'Person of Interest' is coming on in a bit. We can watch Jim Caviezel in poorly choreographed fight scenes and I can pretend that's what you do all day."

Chapter 58

Monday, October 22

Lia sat in the lounge and watched the door to the psych unit apprehensively. She told herself there was no reason to worry. Still, the remains of her breakfast smoothie roiled in her gut. She should have added some ginger. That would have fixed it.

Bailey was being discharged. This had been confirmed. Still, until Bailey was out, out of the unit, out of the building, she wouldn't believe it. The longer the exit process took, the more anxious she became, as if someone would realize it had all been a mistake. She twisted her hands, unconsciously mimicking her agitated stomach.

Finally the door opened and a slight, black man escorted Bailey out. She had only a second to register how much thinner Bailey was, how frail she looked, how much longer her hair was, before she was up off the chair and hugging her as hard as she could.

Their cheeks met, tears mingling. Lia rubbed Bailey's back. Bailey sobbed, "I'm so, so sorry. The gun went off by accident. I never would have shot you, never."

"Shhhh. It's all right. You didn't know what you were doing. It's not your fault. I've missed you so much."

"I thought you'd never speak to me again."

"That's past. We're going to fix you up." She guided Bailey into the elevator and pressed the button for the lobby. Bailey rubbed her eyes and shoved her overgrown bangs out of her face.

"We've got to take care of your hair," Lia said. "You're getting it cut tomorrow."

"I can't get an appointment that soon."

"It's already taken care of."

The elevator doors opened on the ground floor.

"I've got a surprise for you," Lia said.

"I'm already stressing, just about going home. I really can't handle anything else today." Then Bailey looked beyond the glass entry, where Jim stood with Kita on a leash. She burst into tears again and fumbled her way through the doors. Kita jumped up on her, bathing Bailey's face with her rough tongue, leaving behind a long streamer of drool.

Bailey dropped down and hugged her, rubbing her cheek against the silky muzzle. "Thank you for keeping her," she told Jim. "And for everything else you've done."

Jim nodded. "I'll just leave you ladies to your reunion." He walked back out to his car and left.

"He's a good person," Bailey said. "If he hadn't listened to Frank, I would still be in there, in there or in jail. And you would still hate me."

"I'd like to think that if Frank had come to me, I would have listened, but I honestly don't know. The important thing is, Jim did listen, and we were able to help. Now let's get you home." She steered Bailey towards her old Volvo. Kita jumped into the back and stuck her head between the front seats, where Bailey could continue to pet her.

"Goddess, Lia. I'm going home to such a mess. I'll be lucky if the utilities haven't been shut off."

"Relax. Jim's been mowing the lawn. I went through your bills and made sure the utilities were paid. I also cleaned out the fridge and bought you some groceries. I'm sorry to say we weren't able to save the potted plants on the back porch, they were toast by the time Jim and Peter went to your place to get your meds."

"Lia! You can't afford to pay my bills. I won't be able to pay you back for ages. I don't know if I have any customers left after I abandoned them in the middle of summer."

"It's going to be okay. My current project pays very well. And I think Renee's going to need some landscaping to go with it."

"She may not want me after everything I did."

Lia pulled out of the parking lot and headed towards Westwood. "Renee loves good gossip. If you promise to give her a few juicy deets to scandalize her country club friends with, she'll love you forever. I suspect, after all the publicity, more than a few of your old clients will take you back just to get the inside story."

"Great. I should take out an ad, 'Gardener for hire. Lurid tales of life in the looney bin included.' Or maybe I should just wear a t-shirt, 'I went to the nut house and all they gave me was this lousy shirt.'"

"Hey, after everything we've been through, we gotta find something to laugh about."

"You're allowed to say that because you had to face her. Anyone else says that to me and I'm decking them."

"Tell you what. I'll hold them so you can get a good shot."

Chapter 59

Wednesday, October 24

Lia held the door to The Painted Fish open for Bailey. Bailey balked in the middle of the doorway and turned. "You really don't have to take me to a place this nice. We could just get a salad at Melt."

Lia gave her a stern look. "That is not an option. Come on, this will be fun. Besides, sushi is half-price tonight."

Bailey gave a half-hearted shrug. "If you insist."

"I do. We're eating on the patio," Lia said as they walked between the linen covered tables.

"Will it be warm enough?"

"If it's not, it will be," Lia said cryptically. She nodded at Nick as they passed the sushi bar. She opened the door to the back, revealing a narrow path between a long bar and a fence. The space beyond the bar opened to a graveled yard with glass tables surrounded by bamboo fencing. Tiki torches lit a stage. A man and two women were setting up sound equipment. Immediately in front of the stage was a long table full of familiar faces. Nick and two waitresses came out with a trio of large sushi boats and set them down on the table.

"You didn't."

"I did."

"I can't face them. Not yet." Bailey pulled back.

"You can't chicken out. They want to see you. You're our guest of honor."

"I don't believe you," Bailey said, as she allowed herself to be led to the front table.

"You can get even later."

The group spotted them and began to cheer and wave. Bailey covered her face with her free hand and shook her head. Lia led her over to two empty chairs in the middle of the table. Peter rose on one side. Terry rose on the other.

"Ah, my lady, welcome!" Terry said. "You have graced us with your glorious presence. We live to serve. What is your potation of choice?"

"What did he say?" Bailey whispered to Lia.

"What do you want to drink?" Lia whispered back.

"Umm, tea is fine, thanks." She turned back to Lia, whispering, "You know I can't drink on these meds."

"Terry can't drink either. It's okay."

Marie called out from the other side of the table, "When you didn't come to the park, we knew we'd have to ambush you."

"Gee, thanks," Bailey said.

"Don't you worry about a thing," Nadine said. "We're taking care of it."

"Including the entertainment," Jose winked.

"What's he talking about?" Bailey asked.

"Don't you know? It's Karaoke night," Charlie said.

"Karaoke? Seriously?" Bailey asked, horrified.

"Just remember," Jim said, "when it gets painful, this was all Marie's idea."

Jim led off the singing with his old fraternity song, "My Buddy." He sang without music since the song was written in the twenties and was not in the Karaoke machine. "My Buddy," he crooned, "I think about you every day. . ."

"Sounds a little gay," Bailey whispered.

"The composer wrote it about his dead brother," Lia whispered back.

Charlie got up on stage and announced, "I'd like to dedicate this next song to my favorite flag burner. It's called 'Dang Me.'" A country tune started up. Charlie sang about how they ought to hang him from the highest tree.

Lia shook her head. When Charlie came back to the table, Nadine berated him for his poor taste.

He interrupted her scold. "Screw 'em if they can't take a joke, right, Lia?"

It was Terry's turn. He stood up and said, "Nadine, I'm doing "Whisky Lullaby", but they said it was a duet. I told them you'd do it with me."

"I don't know that song," Nadine protested.

"Doesn't matter," Terry said. "It's a country song. Just follow my lead."

Nadine surrendered and went with him. Terry started the song, with exuberance exceeded only by his atonality. He joyfully belted out the chorus. Nadine had nothing sensible to follow, but gamely struggled through to the end. Everyone stood up and cheered when they were done.

"Why are we clapping," Bailey asked. "Because they were gutsy enough to do that or because it's over?"

"Just go with it," Lia said.

Jose bounced around on stage and wailed "Honky Tonk Women." The crowd roared.

"This is terrible," Bailey said.

"That's really the point," Lia said.

"And now, Peter," the DJ announced.

"That's my cue."

Lia goggled as Peter headed for the stage. "He said he wouldn't sing," she hissed at Bailey.

"Maybe he won't sing," Bailey whispered back. "So far, nobody else has."

Then Peter took the microphone. He cleared his throat. Big band music started, an old tune, "And the Angels Sing." A few bars in, Peter began singing. He crooned in a beautiful, clear tenor about angels singing when they met. Lia sat, frozen, a deer in headlights. He beckoned to her. She shook her head. He continued singing as he gave her a long, level look and beckoned again. The rest of the table made shooing motions with their hands.

She rose, and went around the table and up on stage to meet him. He took her hand and sang into her eyes about adoring her face. He swayed and she swayed with him, her heart melting into a soft, gooey, mesmerized puddle at his feet. He finished, then he dipped her and gave her a lingering, mind-blowing kiss.

Lia became aware of whoops and cheers as Peter raised her back up. She looked out over the audience as her face turned strawberry red. She stumbled as he led her off stage. He caught her and helped her down off the platform.

"I told you I didn't like this sort of thing."

"I can see that by the way you ran out the door."

The crowd was still whooping.

"Aw, give 'im a break, Lia," Jose yelled.

She caught Peter winking to Jose and huffed, "I thought you couldn't sing."

"I never said I couldn't sing. I said Marie wouldn't get me up there. And she didn't. Nadine did." He pulled out her chair. She sat down with a thump.

"You sang Barry Manilow to me. I can't believe you sang Barry Manilow to me. I hate Barry Manilow."

"That wasn't Barry Manilow. That was Benny Goodman. It's not my fault they don't have the original version."

"It's still got Manilow cooties." He'd done something amazing and sweet, and here she was carping about it. She wanted to cry, and didn't know why.

She sat, stunned, as two girls sang "What about Love," only cracking a little on the high notes. The words worked their way through her daze. She asked herself, What about it? Don't I want to be loved? Bailey smirked and gave her "there, there" pats on her shoulder.

She felt caught in a moment of clarity that expanded as the girls sang on. This was the moment when she needed to make a choice. She'd told Peter she loved him, but she still held part of herself in reserve. For what? All he'd ever tried to do was love her. She understood that if she couldn't let Peter all the way in now, she might never be able to let anyone in.

"Move your chair back."

"Hmm?"

"Move your chair back. I want to sit in your lap."

She sat sideways between his arms. "Angels?" she asked his left ear.

"A couple imps, too. But they mostly blow razzberries. Sometimes they yell, 'Just look at that sorry fool.'"

"Want me to beat them up for you?"

"I'm touched. No woman has ever volunteered to beat up a baby demon for me before. It's very romantic."

"I will, you know."

"That's okay. I like being a fool."

"Me, too."

"Does that mean you're a fool, too?"

"I'm a fool for you, Peter Dourson. So we can blow razzberries right back at those baby demons together."

"We'll do that." He wrapped his arms around Lia as she sighed.

"And now, for the last song of the night," the DJ announced.

Marie touched Lia's arm. "That's us." She pulled Lia up out of her chair towards the stage.

"Oh, right. You're going to have to take the lead."

"No problem."

The DJ handed them mikes. Marie said, "We're singing the Monty Python song, 'Always look on the Bright Side of Life.' This song is meant to be sung by a crowd, so please join us."

The music started. Marie sang about things in life being bad and making her mad. Lia added her voice. Marie started waving to the audience. By the time they got to the chorus, half the crowd had joined in. Marie started beckoning people to come up on stage. A big guy with a corporate hair cut and an amazing array of tattoos on his left leg chimed in with a very convincing British accent. His very tall girlfriend followed. One by one, Terry, Jose, Charlie, Nadine, they all went up on stage. More people from the crowd joined in from their seats.

Peter smiled at Bailey and nodded his head towards the stage, questioning. She gave a self-deprecating shrug and stood up. They climbed onto the platform and were immediately enfolded into the group. Lia put her arm around Bailey and held up the microphone. Bailey read along with the monitor and sang in a tremulous voice about forgetting her sin. She smiled as tears streamed down her face.

Epilogue

Monday, November 19

"You sure about this?" Lia asked as Bailey stowed her luggage in the back of her cab top.

Bailey smiled. "As sure as I've ever been about anything. I've always wanted to meet Trees in person. I've been talking to him every day since I got out. The season's over, so I don't have to worry about work. And, thanks to Renee, I'll be okay for a while financially.

"He risked a lot to help me out. You've got your detective. Maybe there's somebody for me, too. We can be a pair of hackers. I can hack weeds while he hacks data-bases."

"Will you be coming back?"

"If I decide to stay, I'll have to sell the house. You'll see me again." She moved around to the passenger side of her truck and opened the door. "In, Kita." The large hound loped up and in. Bailey turned and hugged Lia. "Stay out of trouble," she said, giving Lia one last squeeze. Then she climbed into the driver's side of the truck and turned on the ignition.

They waved to each other as Bailey pulled out of the drive. Lia watched as the truck drove away, getting smaller and smaller until it turned a corner and disappeared. She wiped a tear and sniffed. "Not hardly likely," she said.

The Kibble Song

Who wants to eat?
Who wants to be my puppy?
Come find your seat
Lie down and get your suppy
It's such a treat
To make my babies happy
You're so elite
Cause I don't serve no yuppies

A lady knows
That when she eats her kibble
Her manners show
She does not gulp, but nibble
Viola glows
with delicate refinement
Such canine poise
She must be heaven-sent!

Honey is sweet
and she has got my number
Though I admit
she is a kibble fumbler
Upon the floor
Her dinner is all scattered
She'll eat that, too
It does not matter

My Chewy thrills
When I shake his kibble
He can't sit still
His body quakes and trembles
Though I deny
His ultimate fulfillment
Until he calms
His hyper temperament

Peter's my guy
And He likes to sleep in now
And when he does
He fixes his own chow
Pop Tarts it is
Or something equally nasty
I can't believe
What he thinks is tasty

Author's Notes

This series is based in Cincinnati, and one of the fun parts of writing this book is using places I know. All the businesses mentioned in the book exist.

Skyline Chili is a Cincinnati institution. Cincinnati chili is unlike chili anywhere else in the country. It is served over spaghetti and is rumored to have cocoa in the recipe. In Cincinnati, a Three Way is chili served on spaghetti with shredded cheese on top.

Nick Andersen and the Painted Fish served my all-time favorite sushi until he closed his doors this past summer. I'm heartbroken and hoping he'll have another restaurant going before long.

Lisa Story is real. She and Sitwell's are a Clifton fixture, serving coffee and supporting local art.

Red River Gorge is my favorite spot for hiking and camping. I've spent many hours on Swift Creek Camp Trail. Alas, there is no convenient overlook as described in the book, and no fork in the trail that takes you back to the parking lot. These features were invented to serve the story.

Marie, Jose, Charlie, Jim, Bailey and Terry are all based on my dog park friends. Roger is based on a dog park friend along with numerous alcoholics I knew when working in the field of addictions recovery. John Morgan is a real person. He has, in fact, performed Mac miracles for me. He is not a hacker. Any illegal activities performed by John in this book are strictly the product of my imagination. Viola, Chewy, Kita, Fleece, Napa, Jackson, Oggie, Sophie, Luke, Henry, Maddie, Lacy and Nita are real.

In the book, Lia hikes with her dogs off leash in the forest. This behavior is neither legal, nor do I condone it. Lia, like most people, is not perfect.

The Kavorker exists. A neighbor of mine stumbled across it the same way Marie did.

Alcoholism is a very serious disease. While Alcoholics Anonymous has helped countless alcoholics learn to manage their illness, manipulating someone into attending AA is likely to have poor results.

About the Author

Carol Ann Newsome is a writer and painter who lives in Cincinnati with two former street urchins named Shadda and Chewy. She and her tribe can be found every morning at the Mount Airy Dog Park.

Books by C. A. Newsome

A Shot in the Bark
Drool Baby
Maximum Security
Sneak Thief
Muddy Mouth (October 2015)

Carol loves to hear from readers. You can contact her at carolannnewsome@netzero.net . Join Carol's mailing list at CANewsome.com if you would like to be notified about future releases in the Lia Anderson Dog Park Mysteries series.

CPSIA information can be obtained
at www.ICGtesting.com
Printed in the USA
LVOW13s0338270217
525513LV00007B/174/P